little black dress
· IT'S A GIRL THING ·

Dear Little Black Dress Reader,

Thanks for picking up this Little Black Dress book, one of the great new titles from our series of fun, page-turning romance novels. Lucky you — you're about to have a fantastic romantic read that we know you won't be able to put down!

Why don't you make your Little Black Dress experience even better by logging on to

www.littleblackdressbooks.com

where you can:

- ▾ Enter our **monthly competitions** to win **gorgeous** prizes
- ▾ Get **hot-off-the-press** news about our latest titles
- ▾ Read **exclusive** preview chapters both from your **favourite** authors and from brilliant new writing talent
- ▾ Buy **up-and-coming** books online
- ▾ Sign up for an essential slice of romance via our **fortnightly email** newsletter

We love nothing more than to curl up and indulge in an addictive romance, and so we're delighted to welcome you into the Little Bla

With love from,

The *little black*

D1315352

Five interesting things about A. M. Goldsher:

1. If you laid all of A. M. Goldsher's CDs on the ground in one single row, it would run from the Tower of London to somewhere around Windsor Castle.

2. Favorite food: sushi. Favorite dessert: Sushi. Favorite snack: sushi. Favorite position: sushi.

3. According to the author's mother, A. M. began reading aloud at the age of two. First book? *Valley of the Dolls*.

4. Goldsher hasn't paid for a haircut since 1995.

5. A former sportswriter, the author has seen far too many professional basketball players wearing not nearly enough clothes.

By A. M. Goldsher

The True Naomi Story
Reality Check
Today's Special

Today's Special

A. M. Goldsher

little
black
dress

First published in 2008 by
LITTLE BLACK DRESS
An imprint of HEADLINE PUBLISHING GROUP

A LITTLE BLACK DRESS paperback

1

ISBN 978 0 7553 3996 9

Typeset in Transit511BT by Avon DataSet Ltd,
Bidford-on-Avon, Warwickshire

Printed and bound in Great Britain by
Clays Ltd, St Ives plc

Headline's policy is to use papers that are natural, renewable and
recyclable products and made from wood grown in sustainable forests.
The logging and manufacturing processes are expected to conform to the
environmental regulations of the country of origin.

HEADLINE PUBLISHING GROUP
An Hachette Livre UK Company
338 Euston Road
London NW1 3BH

www.littleblackdressbooks.com
www.headline.co.uk
www.hachettelivre.co.uk

Welcome to Anna's Life

A nna falls to her knees and raises her hands to the heavens above. 'Must . . . have . . . pizza,' she gasps. 'Must . . . have . . . it . . . immediately.'

Byron rolls his eyes. 'Baby, I've said it before and I'm sure I'll say it again – your diet is appalling.' Byron's right. As is the case with an astounding percentage of well-educated chi-chi chefs, Anna eats like a seven-year-old. Cap'n Crunch Peanut Butter Crunch for breakfast, microwave mac 'n' cheese (or more Cap'n Crunch) for lunch, greasy order-out (or more Cap'n Crunch) for those inevitable late-night dinners.

Adding up her pseudo-meals and the blips and blops of beef tenderloin, and flourless chocolate cake, and veal scaloppini she has to taste each night at her restaurant, Anna ends up taking in over 2,500 calories a day, seventy-eight per cent of which are empty, and thirty-one per cent of which have the potential to rot her pretty white teeth.

Regardless of her caloric intake, Anna believes that the

only reason she stays thin (or thinnish) right now is because she's on her feet approximately 5.2 million hours a week. She's certain that when she retires from the restaurant business, she'll have to trash her cute, underutilized size-six wardrobe and replace the whole kit and caboodle with many, many selections from the Lane Bryant catalog. Not that she'll miss her current clothes that much, anyhow. She rarely wears any of her going-out outfits: the BCBG tops, the Dolce & Gabanna bottoms, the De la Renta dresses, and the Chanel suits hardly ever see the light of day. And really, why should they? To Anna, wearing going-out outfits without actually going out is kind of silly. But it's the principle of the thing.

Anna gets up off her knees, kicks her beloved red Crocs across the room, missing her gluttonous brown and white cat Stinks by mere inches, and says, 'Fine, you're right, Byron, you're always right, I'm a lousy eater.' She pseudo-sexily peels off her black pinstripe chef's pants, spanks herself on the tush, then jokingly adds, 'But I'm still cute. Right?' Of course she's joking: Anna *never* feels cute after work. For that matter, Anna hasn't felt cute since culinary school.

The irony is that Anna *is* cute. Very cute. Her deep-set brown eyes: cute. Her full, naturally upturned mouth that makes her look like she's smiling even when she's in a lousy mood: cute. The tiny square-ish birthmark on her chin: cute. The fact she doesn't realize how cute she is makes her even cuter.

Byron also strips down to his underwear – off with the black, silky Armani pullover; off with the sleek, black

Kenneth Cole slacks – only without the sexiness or the spank. Tall, whippet-lean, and casually suave, Byron doesn't really have to try and be sexy – it comes naturally. 'But you're not even trying a little bit to stay healthy,' he complains. 'You don't take vitamins, and the only time you eat vegetables is when you're testing something for "doneness," and outside of all the cheese you nibble on at work, you get approximately zero protein.'

Anna unbuttons her solid black chef's jacket – not the least bit sexily this time – and throws it at her live-in boyfriend. 'Why do we always have this discussion on a Saturday night at two in the morning? I mean, it's not like I'm completely fried from overseeing two hundred and seventy-five meals tonight or anything.'

'Two hundred and ninety-seven,' Byron corrects. 'It was *hopping*.' He rubs his thumb and index finger together in the international hand motion for 'money, money, money' and smiles. 'August is my favorite month.'

'Whatever. Why can't we talk about my eating habits when I'm not, you know, dying of hunger and exhaustion and sweaty armpits?'

'Because Saturday night is *always* pizza night. What better time to talk about it? Let's straighten you up.' He walks across the room, puts a hand on Anna's hip, and kisses her neck. 'And I'm only doing it because I care.'

'Fine. Starting next week, *Tuesday* night is pizza night, so we'll talk about it Tuesday. But that's starting next week.' She rummages through her purse for a minute or three – her purse is huge, a disaster area filled with cooking magazines, and index cards with handwritten recipes, and Advil, and tampons, and a pair of gloves that have been there since three winters ago, and several kitchen sinks, and a dinosaur skull carbon dated approximately 108 million years ago – and pulls out her cell phone. 'What do you want on your half?'

'The more appropriate question is, what do *you* want on *my* half? Because we all know you'll probably eat your half and part of my half.'

Anna nods. 'True.' And the wheels start turning: she sees little sausages floating across the Chicago skyline. She sees fields and fields of pepperoni. She sees tomato plants, spinach plants, and zucchini plants, dancing in lockstep. The wheels turn some more. And some more. And some more.

Byron falls to his knees and raises his hands to the heavens above. 'Must . . . have . . . decision,' he gasps. 'Must . . . have . . . it . . . immediately.'

Anna says, 'Don't rush me. These things take time.'

Byron stands up and sighs tiredly. 'I'd better pee. This could take a while.' He pads down the foyer and into the half-bathroom across the hall from the guest bedroom.

Anna continues to consider her options. And continues. And continues. And continues. Finally, a mere six years, three months, four days and one hour later, she calls, 'Double cheese and extra sausage.'

She hears the toilet flush. Byron, wiping his freshly washed hands on his boxers, re-enters the living room and says, 'Double cheese and extra sausage would be lovely.' He gives her a not unappreciative once-over. 'Baby, I enjoy looking at your legs as much as the next guy, but I really don't want that next guy looking at your legs, so maybe you could put on some pants before the delivery man gets here.' Having shed her chef's gear, Anna is wearing only a blue striped Victoria's Secret Pout thong – her one worktime nod toward womanliness – and a tight black ribbed tank top that comes to a stop just above her outie belly button. Anna exaggeratedly purses her lips. 'Jealous?' she teases. She has the number for Art of Pizza, her favorite pizza joint, programmed into her cell's speed dial; she pushes '5,' and then 'send.' Knowing that fourteen inches of greasy, drippy, cheesy, sausagey goodness is on its way comforts Anna greatly.

Order complete, she closes her cell and drops it on to a pile of blankets on the floor – her and Byron's apartment is as carelessly messy as Tart's kitchen is anally neat – plops on to the couch, grabs the television remote, and surfs over to Channel 70.

Byron groans. '*FoodTube?!* Again with the FoodTube. I thought you were over it.'

'I've been seeing it behind your back,' she says, immediately engrossed in a five-year-old rerun of *The Golden Chefs*, a campily overdubbed cooking contest show from France.

'Wonderful,' Byron says. 'And just when I thought it was safe to turn on the TV again.' He plunks down next to her and puts his hand on her bare thigh. She rests her head on his shoulder, and looks around the apartment, inwardly grimacing at the pile of food magazines on the beaten-up, wooden coffee table, wishing that either she or Byron could spruce up what could be a lovely living space. An Afghan rug covering the scuffed hardwood floor in the living room would be nice. A couple of framed prints in the dining room wouldn't hurt. And if somebody put away the random CDs, books, and DVDs that are strewn everywhere, well, that wouldn't be a bad thing either. But let's be honest here: neither Anna nor Byron has the time. Or the energy. Or the inclination. Or, most damningly, the shelf space.

Twenty-some-odd minutes later, the doorbell snaps Anna out of her TV-induced trance. (Anna and Byron's flat is located in Lakeview, a mellow, centrally located section of Chicago where you can almost always get food delivered in twenty or so minutes, even in the dead of night.) She springs off the couch and buzzes in the delivery man, who, moments later, bangs on their door. Before she can receive the Art of Pizza delivery guy, Byron snaps out of his own stupor and yells, 'Anna! Jesus Christ! *Pants!*'

She looks at Byron, then at the door, then at her bare legs, then at her chef's pants all the way on the other side of the room – chef's pants that Stinks is utilizing as a temporary crash pad. Right then, her stomach rumbles big-time, so she shrugs and mumbles, 'Screw it.' In a half-hearted show of modesty, she tugs her tank top down as far as it can be tugged – which is more or less (less, really) even with her thong's waistband – then flings the door open and inhales the cheesy, sausagey aroma.

The delivery man inhales the vision of Anna's smooth, pale legs, then stammers, 'Fif-fif-fif-fifteen fif-if-if-if-ty.'

Anna gives the dumbstruck delivery man a twenty,

slams the door shut, flings the pizza box on to the ancient coffee table, runs into the kitchen and grabs a bottle of beer from the fridge, runs back into the living room and crashes down next to Byron, rips open the box, and gobbles up half a slice before Byron even touches the food. Like many chefs, when she's not in a restaurant environment, Anna's table manners – or, in this case, sofa manners – are all but non-existent.

Three-quarters of the way into her second slice, Anna, mouth overflowing with cheese, sausage, etc., points at the television screen and asks, 'Why don't you get us on FoodTube?'

Byron theatrically covers his eyes. 'Close your mouth when you're chewing. And what's the point? We don't need FoodTube. We don't need the publicity. We're packed every night. Movie stars up the bazoo.' (Johnny Depp, in town filming a movie, came by Tart the week before, and Kate Winslet, in town because Chicago is awesome, the week before that.) 'FoodTube is unnecessary.'

'I thought you love publicity.'

'Not publicity. *Visibility*. There's a difference.'

'Yeah, well, there's also a difference between being a nice boyfriend and a condescending wiener.'

Byron says, 'I'm not being condescending.' (Yes he is. Very much so. Not purposely, though. It's just Byron being Byron.)

'Whatever,' Anna grunts. 'How could getting us on FoodTube be bad? I mean, we're not *always* going to be packed every night, forever and ever. It'd be a good notch on our belt.' Then, because she knows Byron is loathe to spend a dime, well, *anything*, she adds, 'And it won't cost you a cent.'

Byron uncovers his eyes and rests his hand on the back of Anna's neck. 'Baby, as long as you keep doing what you're doing in that kitchen, I don't see any reason why we *wouldn't* be packed every night, forever and ever.'

Anna picks up her third – and possibly her final, but possibly not – pizza slice. 'But it's not only about the restaurant,' she points out. 'It's about me. Like what if I decide I want to write a cookbook? It'd look a lot better to a publisher if my biography says something like, "Chef Anna Rowan has made approximately two thousand appearances on FoodTube."'

'Saying "Anna Rowan is the finest under-thirty-years-old chef in Chicago" should be more than enough for any publisher,' Byron says. He takes a napkin from the coffee table and wipes the pizza grease from hands, and mouth, and arms, and legs, and back, and left earlobe. 'Can we please not get double cheese next time? I can feel the pimples forming on my forehead as we speak.'

'Don't change the subject. Forget about a cookbook for a second. Let's say I want to, I dunno, audition for FoodTube myself. There's no reason I can't have my own show.' She points at the screen. 'I mean, look at this lame-o loser chump. He's on a bunch of different shows, and he can't really cook. And he's not even that good-looking.'

This 'lame-o loser chump' is California-based chef Jordan DeWitt. Aside from running four unbelievably successful Asian fusion[1] restaurants in Los Angeles, Jordan hosts three of the more popular FoodTube programs: *DeWitt Goes DeWild*, a purposely low-rent-looking travelogue on how to throw a low-rent party; *Eastern Rebellion*, an in-studio show that features Jordan's quite excellent tips on Asian cuisine; and the show Anna and Byron are presently watching (sort of), *Sunday Sneak Attack*.

Byron asks. 'If you think he's such a lame-o loser chump, why do you even want to be associated with a network that gives a guy like him so much face-time?'

She says, 'Well, I'm not going to lie, *Sunday Sneak Attack* is pretty fun.' Anna's right – it *is* fun, which is why it's FoodTube's highest-rated program. The show's premise is brilliant in its low-budget, *cinéma-vérité* simplicity: on any given Sunday, Jordan and one of his sous chefs[2] – accompanied by a two-man camera crew and an unbiased *LA Times* food critic who serves as the judge – arrive unannounced at a random restaurant and challenge the head chef and sous chef to a two-on-two cook-off. DeWitt always arrives near the beginning of dinner service, but so as not to piss off the chef or the restaurant's brain trust, after the challenge is issued, he struts around the dining room and tells the patrons that if

[1] Asian fusion: A melding of Asian cuisine with any other cuisine the chef likes, which has been known to lead to such unfortunate dishes as sashimi fajitas and pad Thai Parmesan.

[2] Sous chef: Depending on your interpretation, it's either the head chef's right-hand man or woman, or the head chef's indentured slave.

they're willing to wait around for the end of the contest to finish their meal, dinner is on him. DeWitt's an honest-to-goodness celebrity – he's on Leno, and Conan and *The Today Show* so often that his FoodTube cohorts joke that he should buy stock in NBC – so most diners take him up on it.

Since Jordan has the element of surprise on his side, he lets his opponent pick the so-called 'Attack Cuisine', which sometimes leads to some hilarious missteps, as Jordan isn't at all that strong when it comes to either Mexican or Italian foods. In a nutshell, he's afraid of cheese. Most professional chefs are FoodTube junkies, and are thus well aware that Jordan can't make a decent carne chimichanga or a solid eggplant Parmesan if you held a Wusthoff[3] serrated knife to his boy parts, so if they feel like opening a can of whup-ass on Mr DeWitt, they'll choose a dish whose primary or secondary ingredient is of the dairy variety. Some chefs, on the other hand, want to beat down the flamboyant chef-you-love-to-hate at his own game, so they'll pick something from in or around the East, which might mean a lobster and crab pad Thai, or hamachi don, or Szechuan pheasant, or even a simple filet mignon stir fry. But much to the surprise of those viewers who think of him primarily as 'that showboat spaz from that FoodTube par-tay show' (or at least that's what *LA*

[3] Wusthoff: Chi-chi knife manufacturer. If a professional chef sees you putting one of theirs in the dishwasher, they will immediately remove it, hold it up by your carotid artery, and whisper, 'Knives. Don't. Go. There. Always. Wash. Them. By. Hand.'

City Paper once called him), Jordan is truly a fine Asian chef, one of the fifteen or twenty best in the country, so more often than not, the chef who chooses to do battle with DeWitt on a Chinese, or Japanese, or Thai, or Vietnamese playing field gets their lychee nuts handed to them on a silver platter.

Byron says, 'You want to be on FoodTube?' Anna nods. 'Really?' She nods again. 'Really really really?' Another nod. 'Okay. Fine. I'll make some calls.'

Anna claps her hands and bops up and down on the sofa, her brown pigtails bouncing in rhythm. 'If I didn't have two pounds of cheese sloshing around my stomach, I'd screw you blind.'

Byron pats his flat, lightly haired belly. 'If I didn't have one pound of cheese sloshing around *my* stomach, I'd let you.'

Half an hour later, they're asleep on the couch, Anna's head on Byron's lap, Jordan DeWitt's valley boy accent floating from the flickering television.

SIMPLE FILET MIGNON STIR FRY

Ingredients

Grapeseed or canola oil

1 lb of filet mignon, trimmed, and cut into 1 inch cubes

2 garlic cloves, minced

1 tablespoon of fresh ginger, grated

2 tablespoons of soy sauce

1 package of sizzling rice cakes

5 stalks of green asparagus, bias-cut into 1 inch lengths

1 small red or green bell pepper, cut into 1 inch dice

1 small white onion, diced

Kosher salt and freshly ground black pepper

Method

1. Prepare a fryer or stockpot filled ⅓ full with oil and heat to 400°F.

2. In a large bowl, combine beef, garlic, ginger and soy. Stir to coat thoroughly and marinate for 30–60 minutes.

3. When oil is hot, gently place rice cakes into oil and fry until puffed, about 30 seconds, turning halfway through cooking. Remove to a paper-towel-lined plate.

4. Heat a large sauté pan lightly coated with oil over high heat. Add marinated beef and stir-fry briefly, just until meat is seared on all sides, about 2 minutes. (You will be cooking the meat a second time.) Remove beef to a dish.

5. Lightly coat the same pan with oil over high heat. Add asparagus and cook for about 30 seconds, then add pepper and onion and stir-fry for about 1 minute. Check flavor and season with salt and pepper, if necessary. Add beef and stir-fry for about 2 minutes more, until vegetables are tender-crisp and beef is cooked but still medium-rare in center.

6. To serve, arrange sizzling rice cakes on platter and top with filet mignon stir-fry.

SIMPLE CAP'N CRUNCH
PEANUT BUTTER CRUNCH

Ingredients
1 box of Cap'n Crunch Peanut Butter Crunch
½ gallon of milk
1 enormous bowl

Method
1. Pour entire contents of cereal box into bowl.
2. Pour milk into bowl.
3. Serve cold.

Welcome to Tart

'**G**aaaah reservation?'

That's how Jeannie welcomes you to Tart, the stellar restaurant in the Lincoln Park section of Chicago, owned by Byron Smith, and head cheffed by Anna Rowan. Jeannie says 'Gaaaah.' Not 'Do you have,' not even 'Gotta.' It's 'Gaaaah.' Some have said it sounds like she's choking; as a matter of fact, during her four-year tenure at the well-reviewed contemporary Italian- and French-tinged American bistro, seven gentlemen have offered to perform the Heimlich maneuver on her. She graciously refused the first six. The seventh – he of the eggplant-purple Hedi Slimane suit, the raspberry-red Bentley Azure convertible, and the milk-chocolate-chip brown eyes – took her back to his tricked-out penthouse condo on the fanciest-schmanciest block of Michigan Avenue (which is saying something, because Michigan Avenue as a whole is seriously fancy-schmancy) and performed the Heimlich, along with several other maneuvers that Jeannie didn't even know existed. And Jeannie knows lots and lots of maneuvers.

If you do indeed gaaaah reservation – and if it's a week-end, you'd better, because Tart is a piping-hot restaurant, even five-plus years after the first plateful of steak frites[4] left its kitchen – Jeannie will reach into the slot inside her podium, grab a handful of menus – two times out of five, she'll actually grab the correct number – and walk you to your table. Most of Tart's heterosexual male customers have vivid erotic dreams about that little stroll because, as Nora the bartender and bar manager puts it, not unkindly, Jeannie has 'a killer-diller ass.' Truth be told, Jeannie also has killer-diller legs, and killer-diller hair, and a killer-diller chest, and, well, a killer-diller *everything*.

The Tart girls love Jeannie because she's utterly sweet and utterly guileless. The Tart boys love her because she's utterly sweet, and utterly guileless, and utterly crushable. But every Tart staffer dies a little death when they see her name on the schedule next to theirs, because Jeannie is unquestionably the worst hostess in Chicago, and quite possibly the worst hostess in the Midwest, and just maybe the worst hostess in the entire Northern Hemisphere. But to Byron, sweetness, guilelessness, and crushableness trumps competence, so here Jeannie is, four years after she was hired, still seating all the big parties in the same section, still overbooking on weekends, and still forgetting to tip out. Not to mention the 'Gaaaah' issue.

[4] Steak frites: Fancy-schmancy French fries.

Anyhow, almost immediately after Jeannie drops you off at your table, one of Tart's battalion of food runners appears bearing a tall, skinny, ice-cold glass of bottled water – Anna refuses to serve her customers water from the tap, which irks Byron and his bottom-line, bargain-basement sensibilities – and a basket of various toasty warm breads, courtesy of Chicago's finest, most exclusive bakery, a bakery so exclusive that it can't even be named here. Like everybody else who has enjoyed any one of this bakery's pieces of heaven – the ciabatta, the brioche, the dill sourdough, and the country white, praise you, dear Lord, that country white – Anna worships the secret bakery's bread, but a small part of her wishes they'd dumb it down a bit. You see, most Tart patrons shove down four or five pieces before they even order their entrée, so far too often, when the server ceremoniously places Anna's miniature work of culinary art before them, they're too stuffed to start their meal while it's still hot; a good number of the meals don't get finished at all. It breaks Anna's heart to throw away two-thirds of a plate of seared halibut in truffle vinaigrette that the slender gentleman at table twelve can't finish because he's scarfed down an entire rosemary-buttermilk baguette.

An appropriate amount of time later, your server will glide over to your table – unless it's Corrine or Keith, both of whom seem to prefer clomping to gliding – clad from head to toe in black, all black, all the time. The Tart wait staff are allowed to wear anything they like, so long as it's a member in good standing of the ebony family. And anything means *anything*: a black baby-doll Tart T-shirt with a black short skirt and black clunky ankle boots? No problem. An untucked black button-down number and a pair of black jeans topped off with a solid black bandanna? Bring it on. A black tux jacket with black mid-calf shorts and a black *Clockwork Orange*-like fedora? Nobody's gone that far yet, but they probably could if they were so inclined. Mr Smith wants his servers to be comfy and happy, because the happier they are, the better they'll serve, and the better they serve, the better their tips will be, and the better their tips are, the more likely it is they'll uncomplainingly buy their Grey Goose from the bar rather than beg Tart's beloved, award-winning, Amazonian dreadlocked bartender Nora for a freebie. Mr Smith finds begging to be unbecoming, plus, as already noted, he's a bottom-line guy, thus he's not a fan of the freebie.

If you follow your server into the kitchen after they take your order, you'll be astounded at how immaculate Anna's kitchen is. Sure, seventy-five per cent of the time there's some *mise en place*[5] run-off strewn on the floor (waterlogged sea salt marbles, peppercorn shrapnel, onion trapezoids, etc.). It can't be helped. No matter how much of a knife god (or goddess) you may be, stuff *will* fly off your cutting board. The remaining twenty-five per cent of the time, however, that floor is clean to the point that if you were so inclined, you could literally eat off most of it,

[5] *Mise en place*: French phrase loosely translated as 'setting in place' or 'all the junk a cook needs at his station to make all the junk on the menu.'

which is more than you can say about Tru, or Avenues, or Alinea, or any of the other stud restaurants in Chicago. Anna's kitchen is even neater than Charlie Trotter's, which, she's been told, pisses off the obsessively compulsive Mr Trotter no end.

Tart's cookplace is so immaculate because, unlike every other head chef in the Western world, at least twice an hour, regardless of how slammed the kitchen is, Anna leaves her station and cleans up all the miniature messes all by her lonesome. Her line cooks watch her wipe up a one-inch puddle of chicken broth off the stove at the height of the dinner rush, and collectively think, *What an anal retentive freak*. Miguel will take a huge guzzle of bottled water and whine, 'We're in the weeds[6] here, Chef. I'll pick up that microscopic fucking piece of chicken fat in a minute.' Anna Two will tuck a rogue lock of black hair under her bandana and simper, 'Cheffffff, I promise I'll throw out that sprig of mint after you fire my filllllletttttt.' Wanker will belch and say what everybody's really thinking: 'Dude, you're an anal retentive freak.' But the line cooks don't tease Anna too much about it, because she treats them better than any other chef they've worked for. Plus deep down, they admire the fact that the kitchen is neater than any of their apartments.

Billy, however, is a different story.

Like the line cooks, Anna's sous chef Billy Jorgenson

[6] In the weeds: Way behind. No, way way behind. No, way way way way way way behind.

believes his boss to be overly anal retentive, but unlike the cool, understanding line crew, Billy Jorgenson is a scumbag fart face (his words), and messes with her at every opportunity. One of the tall, burly, tattooed, multi-pierced, shaved-headed, self-proclaimed scumbag fart face's great joys in life is to purposely – and purposefully – drop a tiny piece of mango (or something equally slimy) on to the floor. None of the core Tart employees – the tenured servers and line cooks, Jeannie, Mr Smith – have ever taken a mango-induced tumble because they know Billy's MO, so they generally avoid getting within three feet of him. But if you're unfamiliar with Billy's somewhat sadistic sense of 'humor' – and humor is in quotation marks, because despite his unshakable belief in his comedic skills, Billy Jorgenson is *so* not funny – it's best to tread lightly when walking past the sauté station in Anna Rowan's kitchen. (Billy's second favorite trick is to scoop up a few ounces of crème brûlée and catapult it across the room. His favorite target, of course, is Anna. His second favorite target, Anna Two. Billy clearly has issues with women. Or at least women named Anna.)

If you were scoring by maturity and social skills, Billy Jorgenson is right – he *is* a scumbag fart face – but he's also one of the best sous chefs in the city. When it comes to cooking, he's egoless, he always follows his chef's game plan, and his dishes come out perfectly and, more importantly, identically each time. Also, he's a stellar teacher who instills the right combination of fear and awe in his line cooks, and when called upon – and when sober – and when in just the right mood – can and will lead his troops successfully into battle. (Anna gets nervous when she leaves him in charge, but little does she know that he tones down his scumbag fart face-ed-ness when she's not around.) Sure, at this point in his culinary career, Billy can't write a recipe to save his life, but that's just at this point. Right now, he's a craftsman, content to replicate, and replicate, and replicate some more. But to re-re-reiterate, most of the time he's a scumbag fart face, which is why, at Anna's behest, Mr Smith has fired, then rehired him four times in the last three years.

Not only does Anna's kitchen look good, but it sounds good. Anna is a big believer in the power of music, so she put together thirty-one ten-hour iPod playlists, thirty-one because she doesn't want to repeat any one list within a given month. Much to the often vocalized chagrin of the punk-rock-loving line cooks, the only thing Anna's lists have in common is that they're chill: chill female vocalists (i.e. Norah Jones), chill jazz saxophonists (i.e. Stan Getz), chill chick singer/songwriters (i.e. Joni Mitchell), chill classic rock (i.e. the Eagles). It makes for a chill kitchen, which helps make for good food.

But the most obvious reason Tart churns out yummy plate after yummy plate is simple: Anna Rowan is a fucking brilliant chef.

CHILEAN SEA BASS
WITH TRUFFLE VINAIGRETTE

Ingredients

For Fish

1 small whole Chilean sea bass, scaled and gutted (1–1¼ lb)
1 medium black truffle, sliced thin
1 tablespoon of sea salt
1 pinch of fresh, ground pepper
1 tablespoon of white truffle oil
1 small bunch of fresh rosemary
1 small bunch of fresh oregano
1 whole, roasted yellow tomato
½ cup saffron basmati rice
1 Japanese eggplant

For Vinaigrette

3 tablespoons extra virgin olive oil
1 tablespoon Champagne vinegar
1 small shallot, roughly chopped

Method for Fish

1. Preheat oven to 400°F.
2. Remove head from fish, clean and pat dry.

3. Cut 6–7 small incisions in thickest part of fish.
4. Stuff incisions with truffle slices and fresh, whole oregano leaves.
5. Generously season fish with salt and pepper inside and out.
6. Rub fish with white truffle oil.
7. Fill fish cavity with rosemary and oregano.
8. Roast fish in oven for 10–12 minutes, or until done (should be flaky and delicate).
9. Drizzle truffle vinaigrette around fish on plate.
10. Re-garnish with fresh oregano leaves for color.
11. Serve with whole roasted tomato with saffron rice and roasted Japanese eggplant.

For Vinaigrette

Purée olive oil, 3 slices of black truffle, shallot and vinegar in blender. Add salt and pepper to taste.

Slammed and Crushed

Tuesdays tend to be the mellowest night for Tart's kitchen, and tonight, a brisk late-October evening, is no exception. Orders come in mellowly, orders go out mellowly, Miguel isn't telling Wanker to commit impossible and/or illegal sexual acts upon himself, and there's only a minimum of culinary flotsam and jetsam on the floor by Billy's station. But the staff are aware that this mellowness can be fleeting – after all, we're talking about the kitchen of a popular restaurant, and it's empirically impossible for a popular restaurant's kitchen to be mellow for an entire evening. Everybody's doing their best to enjoy the calm, because as usual, there's a storm a-brewing.

It's name? Hurricane Jeannie. (Okay, referring to Jeannie as a hurricane might be overstating her chaos-creating abilities. Let's say she's more of a severe thunderstorm, or maybe an F-1 tornado.)

For reasons clear only to herself, Jeannie seats two

parties of eight in Keith's section within five minutes of each other. Her seemingly simple miscalculation causes a domino effect of annoyance among the wait staff:

Jenna, she of the black pageboy bob, the widely set ice-blue eyes, the impossibly tiny waist, and the saucy grin, is annoyed because she's only served four parties this shift, none of whom were particularly generous with the gratuity, and she needs some fat tips so she can buy her metrosexualized husband a big gift certificate to the Body Shop for his birthday.

Corrine, she of the unruly brown mop, the saucer brown eyes, the disproportionately large chest, and the abs of steel is annoyed because she's only served two parties, so she wants nothing more than for Byron to cut her so she can go home and see if anybody responded to her new GayMatchmaker.com profile. But she knows that Mr Smith's philosophy of 'one big party leads to more big parties' means she ain't going nowhere.

Keith is annoyed because, well, how many big-ass tables can one dude handle at a time?

The kitchen isn't annoyed just yet. But give it a few minutes.

Much to Keith's chagrin, both of his big parties are either ignoring or are unaware of the unwritten foodie rule that when you go to a fine restaurant, you keep your dish alteration requests to a bare minimum. You trust the chef will do right by you, so unless it's a dire circumstance, you don't change a thing. Sure, if you're not a pork eater, it's fair to ask that they make the halibut cheeks without the soprasetta,[7] but in the majority of places, once you start telling your server to have the chef put the sauce on the side, or asking if you can sub out some apple sauce for the broccoli, you're asking for trouble. But Anna is a big believer in customer rights – 'They're paying, so if they want to screw up their meal, that's their prerogative,' she shrugs – so she instructs the wait staff to say yes to any and all alterations. And no disdainful nose-scrunching allowed, even if the diner requests their steak well done, or asks if the kitchen can go very light on the butter.

Keith's two big parties are substituters to the nth degree: the skinny gentleman wants everything as spicy as possible, the chunky lady wants to keep any trace of tarragon away from her plate, and the fourteen-year-old FoodTube fanatic wants to know if she can have her steak tartare only a *little bit* tartare. Keith yesses his customers, then speedwalks to the kitchen so he doesn't forget both his tables' convoluted orders. Immediately after Keith's arrival, *boom*, the kitchen's mellow is harshed. Anna et al are slammed.[8]

Billy roars, 'Hey dumbass, spread the shit out! You couldn't wait five extra minutes to take table three's order? They've got all that awesome fucking bread, for fuck's sake. They won't die of starvation.'

Keith glares at a fixed point over Billy's left shoulder, sarcastically mumbles, 'Sorry,' and for approximately the

[7] Soprasetta: A tasty, salty pork product that isn't seen on nearly enough menus. Too little causes cravings. Too much causes heart attacks.
[8] Slammed: Overwhelmed. Overworked. Hosed.

three thousandth time, visualizes himself hacking off Billy's left arm with Miguel's tricked-out meat cleaver.

'Lay off him, Billy,' Anna says. 'He's doing fine.' She favors Keith with a warm, white smile. 'You're doing fine.'

Keith simultaneously flushes, grins and gulps. 'Thanks, Chef,'[9] he says, then he spins on his heel and heads back to the floor, confirming there aren't any visible armpit stains on his tightish black T-shirt.

Billy says, 'Anna, why do you lead that kid on?' He's chopping shallots at a hundred and three miles per hour. Shallot shrapnel covers the floor, his apron, the ceiling, the BMW across the street.

Anna puts the finishing touches on a lovely crab-stuffed duck breast, then grabs a towel and wipes a stray piece of shallot from Billy's forehead. 'What're you talking about?' Anna asks. 'Who am I leading on? What kid?'

Billy plucks a shallot shard from his cutting board and flicks it at Anna's stomach. 'Jesus, Anna, just tell him, "Keithy-boy, there's no chance. Give it up. I will never touch your pee-pee, never, ever, ever. You're a decent, good-looking kid, so go and slip it to Jeannie or something."' He shakes his head sadly. 'He honestly believes he has a shot with you.'

'He doesn't like me That Way, and even if he does, he knows I'm living with his boss. This conversation is over.'

---

[9] It's proper protocol to address your head chef as 'Chef.' Only scumbag fart faces don't.

(By the way, when you think of somebody in That Way, it should be capitalized.)

Billy sings, 'Keith and Anna, sitting in a tree, D-O-I-N-K-I-N-G—'

'Shut up,' Anna growls.

'—first comes tongue—'

'Shut up.'

'—then sweat like rain—'

'Get back to work!'

'—then comes Anna coming like a train—'

'Billy, if you don't shut the fuck . . . oh. Keith. Hey.' The waiter stands in the doorway, again flushing and gulping, but no longer grinning. Anna senses his mortification, and for approximately the three thousandth time, she visualizes herself hacking off Billy's right arm with Miguel's tricked-out meat cleaver. 'What do you need?'

Keith, unsuccessfully trying not to picture Anna coming like a train, looks at Wanker, who's manning the salad station. 'Wank, could you put the dressing on the side for the frisée?'[10] Then he gives Billy a death look and clomps back to the dining room.

Anna gets right up in Billy's personal space. He has eight inches on her, but he shrinks away from the comparatively diminutive chef. 'That's it. Go. Go home. You're done for the night. Call me on my cell tomorrow before noon. You might still have a job. I'm not sure yet.'

[10] Frisée: Pretentious salad greens.

'We're slammed, Anna.' He gestures to the line cooks. 'You guys can't handle this without me.'

Maintaining eye contact with Billy, Anna yells, 'Miguel, take sauté! Anna Two, take grill two! Wanker, help Anna Two whenever you have a free second! Billy, fuck off!'

Anna can be scary when she needs to be, so Billy fucks off . . . but not before waltzing behind the bar and stealing a shot of Jack. On his way out, he flicks Keith on his ear. But Keith barely notices, because he's thinking about Anna. As usual.

You see, Keith Cole has a crush on a woman he believes to be the cutest chef in America. A huge crush. A bottomless crush. A secret crush. Well, sort of secret. Okay, it's not even the least bit secret – Keith just likes to *think* it is. Of course, that's just Keith being his sometimes delusional self.

This lack of crush secrecy stems from Keith's inability to keep a single thought unsaid. He's a serial confider, which is why he has the following conversation at least three times a month with a co-worker, or a friend, or even a casual acquaintance:

KEITH: Hey [co-worker or friend or casual acquaintance], I have to tell you a secret, but you have to promise not to tell a soul.

CO-WORKER OR FRIEND OR CASUAL ACQUAINTANCE: I promise.

KEITH: Seriously. Not a word.

CO-WORKER OR FRIEND OR CASUAL ACQUAINTANCE: Okay, I promise.

KEITH: I'm telling you this in complete confidence. If you tell anybody, you are in so much trouble. I'm not kidding. I'll never speak to you again if you tell.

CO-WORKER OR FRIEND OR CASUAL ACQUAINTANCE: Jesus, I *promise* Keith. *Enough*. Spill already.

Keith then spills. Big time. Happily, even, because what's more fun than talking about somebody you love and lust after? He tells the co-worker, or the friend, or the casual acquaintance that he wants to spend the rest of his life with Chef Anna Rowan because her dozens of freckles are so damn adorable, and her bandanna-covered pigtails are sexy and sassy, and she's so neat and tidy both as a person and a cook, and even though he's never seen her in form-fitting clothes, he's pretty certain she has a 'devastating bod,' and she's kind of funny but has the potential to be funnier, and she's way smarter than he is and he digs smart chicks because they challenge him, and she's seven years older than he is and he digs older chicks, because, well, because older chicks are his *thing*.

Jeannie's heard this rap at least ten times. So has Nora. And so have Corrine, and Eileen, and Jenna, and Kirsten, and Billy, and all the line cooks, and all the runners, and all the dishwashers, and all the valets, and all the English-speaking people who live or work in the Chicago metropolitan area. But even if he hadn't told the entire city about his not-so-secret secret crush in great detail, the moony-eyed, sexually hungry looks he sends Anna's way make it pretty obvious to anybody who knows even the tiniest bit about romance that Keith is smitten.

Who are the only two Tarters that don't know about the crush? You guessed it. Ms Rowan and Mr Smith.

Byron is unaware of Keith's Anna-lust because he deals with his floor staff on only the most superficial level. Like he knows nothing about the eternally strapped Nora's rule about only dating guys who are in at least the thirty-three per cent tax bracket, or about Corrine's newly discovered bisexuality, or the fact that Eileen lives at home so she can save money to move to Los Angeles and give it a shot as an actress, or about Jenna's marriage of semi-convenience with that smelly guy from Cuba, or about Kirsten's attempt to save money so she can open up a bookstore in that empty retail space three blocks east of the restaurant. As far as Byron is concerned, all he needs to know about the staff is that they show up to work on time, and do their jobs well, and don't steal.

It's not that Byron is a cold fish (although after almost five years together, Anna knows that he can tend toward chilliness); it's that the service industry is a revolving door. The second a Corrine or a Jenna leaves for greener pastures – or, as is often the case, similarly colored but more interesting pastures – they're basically off Byron's radar and vice versa. What's the point of becoming buddy-buddy with somebody if there's a more than likely probability that in two, or four, or six months they'll be out of your life? Taking all that into account, how could he possibly know that one of his waiters is head-over-heels with his girl?

Anna doesn't know about the crush because she doesn't think about it, and she figures that if she doesn't think about it, it doesn't exist. Which, strictly speaking, means she *does* know about it. But she *doesn't* know about it. But she *does* know about it. But she *doesn't* know about it.

And so on.

When Anna's non-thoughts about Keith become real thoughts, they're mostly about his physicality. He's a cutie, and she can't figure out why somebody that attractive would A) not have a girlfriend, and B) be interested in the likes of her. She likes his brown faux-hawk hairdo, although what with all the product he uses, it's undoubtedly difficult (and sticky) to run one's hand through it. He has some meat on his bones, and in this case, meat doesn't mean muscle – meat means beef. See, Keith can eat. Anna appreciates a man with an appetite. It's a chef thing.

Anna never thinks her non-thoughts about Keith's personality, or sense of humor, or brains, because she knows so little about them. Like Byron, her relationship with the wait staff is strictly professional. Unlike Byron, Anna feels bad about the distance, and would like to get to know her crew a little bit better, to have a beer or four with them once in a while, to find out exactly what makes them tick and let them know exactly what makes her tock.

But that'll probably never happen, because her schedule and myriad of responsibilities simply won't allow for it. If she doesn't even have the time or energy to make love to Byron nearly as much as she'd like, how can she justify staying at the restaurant until 2.30 a.m., pouring down shots with a bunch of people who, unlike her, can sleep until noon.

Thirty minutes after Keith dumped his orders on the kitchen, things have calmed considerably. The remainder of the evening is manageable and even enjoyable. It's times like this – times when she can give equal and loving attention to each dish that leaves the kitchen, times when she can admire how talented her line cooks are, times when she can gaze around the kitchen and think, *This is mine* – that Anna silently thanks her mother for suggesting culinary school.

Anna glances at Billy's station, and cringes at the memory of the way her obnoxious sous chef attacked her good-natured, triangle-haired server, so right at the end of service, she tracks Keith down at the bar. She sneaks up behind him, puts her hand on his shoulder and says, 'Billy's a jerk. Don't sweat him. I promise it won't happen again.'

When he realizes who it is that's touching him, Keith spits Stoli & soda at Nora. Nora, bless her heart, dabs the drink from her face and tactfully slithers away. Once he gets his coughing fit under control, Keith says, 'So you're letting him back.'

Anna shrugs. 'Sorry. I need him. He's damn good. And you know it.'

Keith slams the rest of his drink. 'Don't worry about me, Chef. I'm a big boy.'

She looks at his teddy-bear tummy and thinks affectionately, *Big boy, indeed.* Then she realizes it's probably a really, really bad idea to think of him affectionately. But she still wants to make him feel better, so she says, 'Please, Keith, call me Anna.'

He stares deeply into her eyes for a long moment. Anna wants to look away, but she's enjoying the connection. She'd forgotten how warm and fuzzy hard-core eye contact can be. Byron never tried to connect with her like that . . . at least not that she can remember.

Keith gulps, and says, 'Really? Cool. Awesome. Thanks, *Anna.*'

The unadulterated happiness in his voice – as well as the residual effects of the disconcertingly intimate, almost sexy staring contest – at once flatters and freaks Anna out, so she mumbles a good night, and jogs back to the kitchen to regain her composure. And to hide.

Keith watches Anna sprint away, thinking, *She told me to call her Anna. Mr Smith and me are the only dudes in the place who get to call her Anna. It's a sign. She likes me. She likes me. She really, really likes me.*

Anna glances back over her shoulder. Keith doesn't look like a teddy bear any more. Now he looks like a puppy dog. A cute, floppy dog. A distinctly pettable puppy dog. Anna thinks, *That was probably a bad idea.*

WILD ALASKAN HALIBUT CHEEKS WRAPPED IN SOPRASETTA

Ingredients
1 wild Alaskan halibut cheek filet (approximately ¼ lb)
Pinch of salt
Pinch of pepper
¼ tablespoon of chopped rosemary
¼ teaspoon of chopped thyme
2 strips of soprasetta
2 thin wood skewers

Method
1. Sprinkle filet with salt and pepper.
2. Mix rosemary and thyme and spread on plate. Dredge the filet.
3. Cut strips of soprasetta into four even pieces. Wrap each piece around halibut, overlapping pieces by 1 inch. Put skewers through halibut so it holds the soprasetta in place.
4. Heat a large non-stick skillet over medium high heat. When the pan is hot, sauté each side of the halibut for 2½ minutes.
5. Increase heat to high. Sauté on each side for 1 more minute.
6. Place halibut on serving plates. Carefully pull out the skewers. Serve as hot as possible.

Preparing For Battle

'Knife bag, check. Two sweatshirts, check. Two sweaters, check. Two pairs of cords, check. Hat and gloves, check and check. Two pairs of longjohns, check. Two pairs of houndstooth chef's pants, check. Clothes for normal people who don't live in the goddamn Arctic Circle, check, check, check, check, and check.'

Like many native Californians, Jordan DeWitt despises visiting any city where there's even the slightest chance the temperature will drop below fifty-three degrees, which is why he kvetches at the FoodTube research department whenever they plan a *Sunday Sneak Attack* anyplace north of ninety-three degrees longitude. Unfortunately for Jordan, there are thousands of phenomenal *Attack*-worthy restaurants in the upper two-thirds of the United States, so, much to his chagrin, he ends up spending a combined total of one month out of each year in some random Northern US city, huddled up in his puffy black North Face jacket, shivering like a kitten, even on the most beautiful and temperate of autumn or spring days. Little surprise, then, that Jordan has mixed feelings about Chicago and its wonky climate. Truth be told, he'd avoid the entire state of Illinois altogether if it weren't for Chicago's stellar food scene.

See, Chicagoans like their food, and Chicago restaurateurs are all about accommodation, so there are a vast array of big eateries for big eaters to choose from, the majority of which offer up big servings. For a guy like Jordan – an eternally hungry, adventurous soul who'll eat virtually anything you put in front of him, from venison to antelope, from green beans to lizard's tails, from cheeseburgers to monkey brains – a city like Chicago is sheer nirvana.

Despite what your typical New York- or Los Angeles-based foodie believes, the Windy City is arguably one of the two most culinarily innovative metropolises in the country. There are several chefs in the area who are deep into molecular gastronomy,[11] so the adventurous eater has a chance to sample such goofball dishes as beet balloons filled with nutmeg-scented oxygen, or pumpkin pie ice-cream tempura served on a cinnamon stick, or a fingernail-sized sausage pizza served on the head of a pin. (Our Chef Anna knows her molecular gastronomy up and down, but as a member of the less-is-more school, she finds the whole concept kind of silly. She'd rather sear up

[11] Molecular gastronomy: A scientific discipline involving the study of physical and chemical processes that occur in cooking. Or, in layman's terms, cooking weirdo food with weirdo lab equipment.

a hot-out-of-the-ocean sushi-grade tuna steak with oregano oil, and serve it with a mixed baby greens salad, and a spinach and ricotta risotto, then call it a night.) In terms of food for the masses, Chicago is also loaded. We're talking gloriously doughy deep dish pizza (like at Anna's favorite place, Art of Pizza), and overstuffed Italian beef sandwiches, and ostentatious hot dogs, and all the sweet and savory pad Thai you can shake a chopstick at.

This is why FoodTube sends poor shivering Jordan DeWitt to the Windy City two or three times a year. This is why Jordan DeWitt is one of only a dozen or so Los Angelinos who own a dozen or so pairs of thermal undies.

Jordan considers Chicago to be a safe place weather-wise only between April and September, and his producers do their best to schedule his Windy City trips in that six-month span. But sometimes the dates don't jibe, so right now, on this balmy LA Thursday in late October, we find the handsome, burly, shaved-headed, ice-blue-eyed, charmingly arrogant celebrity chef in the master bedroom of his Los Feliz bungalow, throwing far too many winter clothes into his suitcase for what he believes will be a less-than-balmy trip to the Midwest. And he's throwing fast and hard, because a car will be arriving at his house to take him to LAX in thirty, no, make that twenty-nine minutes.

As he's deciding which chef's coat to pack – it's a tough call, because the white looks great with his tan, but he (mistakenly) believes that the black one intimidates his opponents – he considers the *Sneak Attack* three days hence.

The restaurant: Tart. The contestant: Chef Anna Rowan.

He's never been to Tart, but he's heard whispers about Anna for a couple of years now, if only because she's the youngest three-star female executive chef in the country. There's this thirty-two-year-old ace woman cookie[12] heading up the kitchen at this Japanese restaurant in Greenwich Village that Jordan loves, and he himself hired a thirty-year-old female type to helm the kitchen at his soon-to-be-opened place in Las Vegas. But this Anna person is only twenty-eight, and according to everybody he's spoken to, she has some serious game.

And based on the photos he's seen of Anna (thank you very much, Google image search), she's also seriously cute. She isn't necessarily Jordan's type – he tends to gravitate toward the stereotypical tall, willowy California girl – but he finds himself attracted nonetheless. Maybe her supposed kitchen skills make her seem hotter. Maybe it's because he's finally ready to move forward from Nadia. Maybe it's because . . .

Jordan's ironically obnoxious cell phone ringtone ('The Final Countdown' by Europe . . . yikes) blows away all thoughts of Anna and Nadia. 'Hello?'

'J-Money.'

'M-Class.' It's his producer, Michelle Fields.

'You finished packing?'

---

[12] Cookie: In this case, an affectionate term for a cook. In other cases, a round thing made with sweet stuff.

'Almost.'

'Well, get your ass in gear, buddy.' Michelle has worked with Jordan for almost four years, and is well aware that her boss moves slowly when getting ready to fly to a cold-weather city. 'Got your fur-lined ski boots?' she asks.

'Funny, funny.' He thinks, *Fur-lined ski boots sound kind of nice, actually.* 'Hey, tell me more about this Anna Rowan.'

Michelle sighs. 'Didn't you read the clip packet I sent you?'

Jordan throws the black chef's jacket into his suitcase, then slams it shut. 'What clip packet?'

'Jordan, I messengered them over to the restaurant last week.'

'Who signed for them?'

'Hold on a sec. Let me find the receipt.' He listens to her ruffle through some papers. 'I can't make out the signature. Jerry Sideburns? Jerky Swordfish?'

'Very funny. You know who it is. It's Johnny.' That's Johnny as in Johnny Samuels, Jordan's sous chef, he of the indecipherable doctor-like handwriting and the surgeon-like knife skills. 'I'll call him and tell him to bring the stuff with him.'

'You can't call him. He's already on a plane on his way to Chicago. He likes to get where he needs to be early. Unlike yourself. Finish packing.'

'I *am* finished packing.'

'Sure you are.'

'I *am*.' Michelle pushes his buttons harder and more expertly than anybody in the history of button pushing.

But unlike Nadia, it's all about teasing. The ex was all about emasculating.

'Whatever.' She chuckles. 'I'll bring the clips with me. You can read about Chef Rowan on the plane.'

Which is exactly what he does. When it comes to their stars' traveling comfort, FoodTube is a free-spending entity – odd, because most of the rest of the time, they're cheapskates – so Michelle and Jordan are seated in first class. As Jordan sips his Maker's Mark, he slowly slogs his way through the dossier Michelle diligently assembled. He learns that Anna is a Chicago native who graduated high school in three years (it takes most people four), then blew off college and went straight to culinary school; she earned her Bachelor of Arts degree in Culinary Arts from Kendall College in two years (which also takes most people four). After graduation, she interned for six months under Thomas Keller at the French Laundry in Napa Valley, California, then six more months at Gordon Ramsay's place in New York City. She then fell off the map for almost two years, during which time Jordan correctly assumed she developed her cooking style, solidified her food philosophy, and wrote hundreds of recipes. When Anna resurfaced, it was with a Chicago food-industry wunderkind/trust-fund guy named Byron Smith, and a sweet little restaurant in the city's most yuppie-heavy section of town in tow. A few years and a whole heap of laudatory magazine and newspaper features later, here we are.

Impressed and a tiny bit jealous with Anna's seemingly smooth life path, Jordan stares thoughtfully at his bourbon. Anna's high-tone, fast-track background is practically the diametric opposite of his own. He didn't finish high school early; for that matter he didn't finish high school at all, dropping out after his junior year. He didn't go to culinary school. How could he? He was too busy slaving away on a line at one dive restaurant or another. He had to. Jordan was the only DeWitt who had enough wherewithal, brains, drive and skill to support the family.

After six years of bopping from kitchen to kitchen, Jordan turned himself into a true cooking craftsman. Give the guy a recipe, and he'd execute it, more often than not even better than the chef who wrote it in the first place. But the tedium of preparing somebody else's recipes night after night finally got to him, so he put word out that he would be interested in a head chef position at any restaurant, regardless of cuisine or salary. Cuisine didn't matter because Jordan enjoyed doing it all, so long as it didn't involve using too much cheese. Salary didn't matter, because his parents had passed away two years before, and his two brothers and one sister moved out of the state soon thereafter, so all he had to worry about financially was making his rent. As somebody who grew up impoverished, material goods weren't a priority.

Jordan's first head chef gig was at Greenery, a failing Thai/Japanese joint in a strip mall[13] in Glendale. He

---

[13] Many of Los Angeles's fine restaurants are situated in strip malls. Why? Contact the LA Mayor's office. Maybe they'll know. Because we have no idea.

started work on a Monday, and by Thursday, he'd canned and replaced the entire line, brought in both a new sous chef and sushi chef, streamlined the menu, overseen a redecoration of the front of the house,[14] and convinced (read: threatened) the owner into putting some real money into advertising. Six months later, Greenery was humming – stellar reviews, long lines, a feature on FoodTube – and Jordan was a commodity, something that some chefs aspire to, and something that other chefs shun. Some people don't like being thought of as commodities, because it simply is cold. Jordan has no problem with it.

After his FoodTube appearance, Mario Batali asked Jordan to fill the recently vacated chef de cuisine[15] position at Osteria Mozza, which, after serious consideration, he turned down, primarily because there was too much cheese involved. He was recruited by four other restaurants in a two-week period, and was *this close* to accepting a gig at an up-and-coming American contemporary place in the Valley, but he turned it down because the location sucked, plus the big money investors came a-calling. One year and change later, Jordan was the executive chef at Rayong Eniwa, another Thai/Japanese place, but a far hipper and far more expensive Thai/Japanese place than Greenery. Then came FoodTube and

[14] Front of the house: Where people eat, and servers serve, and hostesses host.
[15] Chef de cuisine: The dude who gets paid slightly less than the executive chef, and slightly more than the sous chef, and usually works harder than either of them.

DeWitt Goes DeWild, then *Eastern Rebellion*, then *Sunday Sneak Attack*, then his thirty-fifth birthday, then an ugly, ongoing separation from a former-FoodTube-employee-slash-psycho-hose-beast named Nadia.

Michelle elbows Jordan in the ribs. 'So what do you think? You going to beat her?'

Jordan sits up with a start. 'What? Beat who?' He was thinking about Nadia, who, if he was a violent person, he probably *would* beat. And nobody who'd ever met Nadia would object.

Michelle rolls her eyes. 'Chef Rowan, space boy.'

'Oh. I'm not sure. She seems pretty sharp across the board.' He picks up Michelle's dossier, opens it to one of the pages he's dog-eared, and points to a review from a Chicago alternative newspaper. 'Says here that part of the reason Tart works so well is because she mixes and matches and nails it all: Italian, American, French. But it doesn't say anything about her doing Asian.'

Michelle says, 'I spoke with one of her professors at Kendall the other day, and he said she's a really sweet girl in everyday life, but when she's cooking, she gets kind of high strung, but in a good way, if that makes sense. He also said that she's hyper-competitive, even though she'd never admit it. I'm thinking that her choice of cuisine will depend on what her definition of competitive-ness is. If she wants a better chance to win, she'll go Italian. If she wants more of a challenge, she'll go Asian. If she wants a level playing field, she'll go, I dunno, Indian or something.'

'If she's super-competitive, I sense a Parmesan

budino[16] in our immediate future.' He chuckles, but it's a nervous chuckle, because he doesn't want to be forced to prepare a Parmesan budino, or a four-cheese veal lasagna, or a white pizza with caramelized onions, or any of that ooey-gooey Italian crap.

Because Jordan DeWitt likes to win.

Jordan's *Sunday Sneak Attack* persona is a combination of joviality, know-it-all-ness, and arrogance, tempered by a bit of self-deprecation, all of which masks his unshakable desire to crush his opposing chef into culinary submission. The show has been on the air for three seasons, and Jordan's record is forty-one wins versus fourteen losses. (He feels like he was jobbed twice during the first season, which, much to Michelle's chagrin, he still whines about whenever he loses a battle he thinks he should've won.)

Jordan asks, 'Hey, can you put together synopses of all the women chefs I've lost to?'

Michelle says, 'Why? You scared of girls all of a sudden?'

Jordan thinks, *Maybe a little bit*, then says, 'I want to do some profiling. Maybe I can find a way to get inside her head. Or maybe at least figure out how to keep her from getting inside of mine.' He thinks, *Then again, keeping out of my head might be a problem, because this Anna Rowan is a serious cutie. Not my type, but still super-cute.*

---

[16] Parmesan budino: An Italian savory cheese custard that can clog a healthy artery in six seconds flat.

The stewardess's voice over the loudspeaker interrupts his reverie: 'We'll be landing in about ten minutes, so we ask that you put up your tray tables and return your seats to the upright position. We hope you enjoy your stay in Chicago, where the temperature is currently forty-nine degrees, headed down tonight to a low of thirty-seven.'

Jordan sighs, then shivers, then pulls his balled-up North Face down jacket from under the seat, then says, 'Thirty-seven degrees? Christ, how the hell do people live here?'

SEARED TUNA WITH OREGANO-INFUSED OIL

Ingredients

1 small bunch of fresh oregano
Large pinch of sea salt
1 tablespoon of fresh lemon juice
¾ cup of extra virgin olive oil
1 sushi grade tuna steak (approximately ½ lb)
Fresh ground pepper

Method

1. Pound oregano and salt into a paste using pestle and mortar.
2. Add lemon juice and olive oil. Stir for 1 minute.
3. Season tuna with salt and pepper, then pat with ⅓ of the oregano mixture.
4. Pour ⅓ of oregano mixture into non-stick skillet. Heat at medium high.
5. Sear tuna one minute per side.
6. Drizzle with remainder of oregano mixture. Serve immediately.

Sunday Steak Attack

It's Sunday, and Stinks is sick, and Anna's exhausted from last night's 250-plus covers,[17] and she's freaking out because she hasn't yet hired a new sous chef to replace Billy the scumbag fart face whom she fired the day after she hired him back because he tore off Anna Two's bandanna and mushed a small handful of garlic mashed potatoes into her pretty black hair, so Anna One has to work brunch and dinner, and her vet's office is closed because it's frigging Sunday, and the cat just puked again, this time on her and Byron's lovely new maroon and gold duvet cover, and she hasn't come up with any specials for tonight, and she should've been at the restaurant two hours ago, and Byron's taking one of his bubble baths which, as usual, is taking forever, which sucks because she hasn't even showered yet, so she still smells like last

[17] Cover: A customer. Heaven forbid those restaurant folks just say 'customer,' right?

night's special, which was a grilled deconstructed beef tenderloin Wellington with wild mushroom sauce, and let's face it, nobody wants to smell like a grilled deconstructed beef tenderloin Wellington with wild mushroom sauce.

But first things first. The kitty.

She calls the seven-days-a-week, twenty-four-hours-a-day emergency animal hospital and tells the receptionist Stinks's symptoms: he's sluggish, he's not eating – a rarity for the twenty-pound bruiser – and, as noted, he's barfing. The receptionist tells Anna to bring the cat in, and if she hurries up, they'll be able to see the doctor immediately because there aren't any other dogs, or cats, or ocelots in the waiting room. The hospital is thankfully only a quick cab ride away, so Anna says she'll be there in ten minutes.

She hangs up, then pokes her head into the bathroom and says, 'Byron, I'm out. I'm not sure when I'll get to the restaurant. Call Billy. Get him in, stat.'

Byron groans, wipes the bubbles from his face, then says, 'You're kidding. What's this, the seventh time you've hired him back?'

'Sixth. I have to get Stinks to the hospital, and I don't know how long it's going to take there, and there is no way I will leave Wanker or Miguel in charge of dinner. I love those kids, but it'll never happen. Call Billy. Tell him if he gets to the restaurant by three, he can write the specials. He'll like that.'

Byron pulls the plug from the drain – the plumbing in their apartment building is antiquated, so the escaping water sounds like a jet engine – and climbs out of the tub. 'I'll take your cat to the hospital. Go to work. Have a glass of wine . . .'

'Wine? Honey, I think this situation calls for a shot. Or three.'

'. . . or have three shots, take some deep breaths, and relax. Stinks'll be fine.'

She opens the bathroom door all the way and leans against the jamb. 'Really? You'll take him?' She's surprised, because Byron isn't exactly the President of the Stinks Rowan Fan Club, mostly because the cat has a habit of jumping on the bed and asking his stepdaddy for breakfast at six-thirty a.m., each and every day, without fail.

Byron grabs a towel, speed dries himself off, kisses Anna on the cheek, then says, 'Really. I'll take him. I'll call you when I get a diagnosis.'

'Thanks, sweetie.' She runs back into the bedroom, plops on to the bed and gives Stinks a quick nuzzle. 'Stepdaddy's going to take you to the doctor,' she tells the cat. 'Mommy'll see you at home later. I love you, you fat, smelly furball. Feel better.' She runs back into the bathroom – almost crashing into Byron, who's on his cell, cajoling-slash-threatening Billy into coming back to work – then she strips and jumps into the shower. As she rinses the conditioner from her hair, she considers her boyfriend.

They met a few months after Anna finished her internships with Thomas Keller and Gordon Ramsay. Her parents had given her a few thousand dollars as a graduation gift, which she decided to use for research,

research that entailed eating at pretty much every quality restaurant in Chicago. Byron was the maître d' and sommelier at one of those supposed quality places, a place in the trendy area of Bucktown called Bistro Molleux. The food wasn't all that terrific – Anna thought of it as Franco American 101 – but she became a regular at the bar partly because it was walking distance from her apartment, partly because the wine list blew her away, and partly because the bartenders were cool. But she was there two or three times a week mostly because she made it her mission to jump Byron's bones, which, when she remembers those pre-Tart days, is kind of funny, because she's not a bone-jumping kind of girl. At least until the fifth date. Okay, maybe the fourth.

To this day, they still debate over who picked up whom. Anna claims that Byron plied her with fancy and expensive wines. Byron claims that his fancy and expensive wines weren't about plying, but rather about sharing and teaching. He also claims that she wooed him with intimate, vaguely inappropriate full-body-contact goodbye hugs whenever they bid one another farewell. She doesn't deny the full-body-hug part, but claims that one night – the night that they hooked up, as it so happened – Byron accidentally-on-purpose breathed in her left ear just the way she liked it. Which is why she discreetly and lightly kissed him on the neck, just the way *he* liked it. Which is why she waited around until the restaurant closed, then dragged him back to his place, where she completed her bone-jumping mission.

Their relationship took about eight months to gain a

solid foothold, because Byron worked constantly at Molleux, and Anna cooked constantly in the patently unprofessional kitchen in her patently tiny apartment. They were lucky if they saw each other away from Byron's restaurant more than one night a week. Their typical date was going to Byron's apartment after Molleux closed, blabbing until three-ish in the morning, having insane sex until four-ish in the morning, crashing until nine-ish in the morning, then sleepwalking through the remainder of their respective days. Still, they were happy to sacrifice sleep for those stolen moments.

On one of their rare afternoons together – during one of their now-rarer hand-holding destinationless walks – Byron asked Anna where she saw herself in ten years.

She shrugged. 'I'm not a planner. I don't know what I'm doing next week, let alone next decade.'

Byron said, 'Okay, let me put it this way: where do you *want* to be in ten years?'

'What's the difference between seeing and wanting?'

'Reality versus fantasy. If you could be doing anything, what would it be?'

'Anything? Hmmm . . .'

'Okay, forget ten years. Let's say five. No, let's say one.'

'Okay, one year I can imagine. One year is easy. One year from now, I'd love to be a head chef somewhere.'

'Like at your own restaurant?'

'God, no. I want nothing to do with ownership. I've read about too many chefs flaming out after they try to run a place and cook good food at the same time. I just want my own kitchen.'

Byron nodded. 'You know I love your food.'

'Yeah, you've mentioned that.'

'When I tell you that, I'm not just giving you lip service.'

'I like it when you give me lip service.'

'C'mon, Anna, I'm being serious here.'

'Sorry.' She brought his hand up to her mouth and kissed his knuckles. 'Thank you. You're sweet.'

'And you're talented. Let's go back to my place. I have to show you something.'

'Are you showing me lip service?'

'No. Something better.'

'Better than lip service? Can't wait.'

When they got to his apartment, Byron went straight into his office. Anna thought he was coming back with some lingerie, or some earrings, or some perfume. She wasn't even close. He had his laptop. He pointed to the kitchen table and said, 'Sit.' After they got settled, he opened up his computer and started bashing the hell out of the touch pad.

Anna said, 'Lighten up there, handsome. Don't hurt yourself.' He didn't say anything; it was all *bash, bash, bash*. 'I feel like I'm at a high-powered yuppie business meeting,' Anna said.

'You are.' He shoved the computer at her. 'Check this out.'

It was an unbelievably elaborate thirty-four-page business plan for a multi-culti restaurant, full of optimistic financial projections, and architectural and design concepts, and detailed demographic breakdowns. Anna had taken only one business course at Kendall – given her choice, she wouldn't have taken any, but it was a requirement – and despite sleepwalking through the class, she had retained enough to understand ninety-five per cent of what she was reading now. She also understood that it was an awesome business plan. She wanted in.

After she read the entire document twice, she said, 'I guess this is the point where the visionary boyfriend says to the chef girlfriend, "I did it all for you. You are going to be my chef." '

Byron said, 'I did it all for you. You are going to be my chef.'

'Really?'

He said, 'No. I've been working on this on and off for about three years. I have enough seed money set aside, but I was waiting for the right chef to come along before I got serious. And here you are.' He stood up, walked behind her, rubbed her shoulders, kissed her underneath her ear, then whispered, 'It's time for you to get serious, Chef Rowan.'

Anna had never mapped out a career path, opting for a more whatever-is-meant-to-happen-will-happen sort of approach; Byron's business plan had meant-to-happen written all over it. But she was self-aware and realistic enough to accept that in terms of both her cooking and her maturity level, she wasn't quite there yet. (Cooking-wise, watching Thomas Keller in the French Laundry's kitchen every night for six months would make anybody think they weren't there yet – or wonder if they'd ever get there at all.) Sure, she could jump into a kitchen that very day, write a competent menu, whip a line more-or-less into shape, and crank out decent food night after night, but she knew that wouldn't be enough to make any kind of mark in a big, cosmopolitan, restaurant-laden, food-obsessed city. St Louis, maybe, but not Chicago. And she wanted Chicago, or New York, or Los Angeles ... but mostly Chicago. Chicago's home, and the whole hometown-girl-makes-good appealed to her quietly competitive nature.

But Byron had no idea that Anna's personal business plan was so deliberate and logical – away from the kitchen, she had a charmingly ditzy demeanor that sometimes masked her seriousness of purpose – that she wouldn't make a move till it was the right situation and the right time. How could he possibly know? Out of the kitchen, she masked her intensity with goofiness, which is why he looked surprised when Anna said, 'I'm not ready yet. Almost. But not quite. And I'm not going to become a head chef just to become a head chef. I want to come out strong.'

'Hunh. I thought you'd jump on this.'

'I am jumping,' she said, 'but I'm jumping slowly.'

He nodded. 'That's cool. It'll take at least a year to make this happen anyhow. Will you be ready in a year? You said you would.'

She chuckled. 'Yeah, I did say that, didn't I?'

'Yeah, you did. Now if I rent you some professional kitchen space, can you solidify your cooking style, and come up with a food philosophy, and write a bunch of recipes, and be ready to roll in twelve to eighteen months?'

'Of course.' Anna's calm, matter-of-fact response masked her sense of pee-in-your-pants excitement. She never guessed the right situation and the right time would fall into her lap.

'Great.' Then, almost as if it was an afterthought, he asked, 'Now if I rent us an apartment, would you move into it?'

'Sure,' she said, so wrapped up in imagining her restaurant that she barely processed the question. Whenever things got rocky between the two of them – which happened every four or so months – she sometimes wondered whether he'd planned the timing that way, whether he'd manipulated her into cohabitation.

But five years later, she still loves Byron and Byron still loves her, but it's debatable as to whether they're still *in* love on a 24/7 basis. Anna's reason for the love/in love conundrum is simple: the majority of their time together is spent at the restaurant, and the Tart Byron Smith is way less fun than the regular old Byron Smith.

The regular old Byron Smith is thoughtful and free-spending, so two dozen roses or some fancy birthday jewelry isn't uncommon. The Tart Byron Smith is a bottom-line cheapskate, loathe to buy even the most regular of regular patrons a bottle of wine to celebrate a fortieth birthday. The regular old Byron Smith likes to take those long, destinationless walks – although if there's a Dairy Queen at the end of the jaunt, well, that's as good a destination as any. The Tart Byron Smith sits in front of his laptop all day, moving only when he has to scowl at a server or chastise Jeannie. The regular old Byron Smith is a kisser, a snuggler, and a hand-holder. The Tart Byron Smith is a closed-off haphophobe.[18]

Even though his dual personae drive Anna nuts, she generally overlooks it, because restaurant Anna and Anna Anna aren't exactly one and the same either, the main difference being that restaurant Anna is competent and confident, whereas Anna Anna is a bit of a spaz. You want proof? Okay, here goes:

Anna gets out of the shower and towels herself off and, distracted by the thought of poor Stinks getting poked and prodded by a stranger, puts on a plain white T-shirt, which she immediately removes, because she has forgotten to use her deodorant. So she rolls on some Ban, then does one of her infamous slapdash make-up jobs, which she ruins when she puts her T-shirt back on. After a quick sniff, she realizes she's wearing her T-shirt from last night – the overwhelming scent of grilled deconstructed beef tenderloin Wellington with wild mushroom sauce is a dead giveaway – so she has to again take off her T-shirt, again put on more deodorant, put on yet another T-shirt, then re-redo her make-up. Post-shower missions finally complete, she throws on her crisp white chef's jacket and black chef's pants (both of which are squeaky clean and smelling nice . . . yay!), then, unable to find her red Crocs, she engages in a fruitless search for any pair of matching clogs, so she ends up with one white Croc and one black one. She fashions her hair into a quick bun, wraps a white

[18] Haphophobe: A pretentiously multi-syllabic way of describing somebody who's afraid of being touched.

bandanna over the whole mess, checks herself out in the mirror, and thinks, *Lovely. Black and white and black and white. I'm a walking yin/yang symbol.*

On her way to the train station, Anna takes in the gorgeous fall day, enjoying her home's big city/small town/mix-and-match vibe. She likes the fact that on any given street, you can find ancient trees and brand-new high-end restaurants, green grass and funky boutiques, flocks of birds and flocks of trucks. She's always thought that Chicago has a bad rap, weather-wise. Sure, there are times when the hot and cold extremes are ridiculous to the point of comedic, but a sunny, sweet-smelling autumn day like this almost makes up for all the bad stuff. Anna firmly believes that anybody who feels differently is nutsy-cuckoo in the head, and should be summarily boiled in oil. Not olive oil, though. Olive oil is too good for somebody like that. The best they deserve is generic, store-brand vegetable oil.

When she arrives at Tart, she's mildly cheered by the line snaking down the block. Chicago is a brunch city – actually, Chicago, which is statistically one of the most overweight areas in the United States, is also a breakfast, lunch, dinner and midnight snack city, but for the sake of this discussion, we'll say it's brunch city – and Tart offers one of the best. Banana granola buttermilk pancakes with coconut cocoa whipped cream, veggie pizza frittata (pepperoni optional), fried oatmeal squares with cinnamon-apple syrup, eggs Benedict with truffle hollandaise sauce, fresh orange juice, fresh watermelon juice, fresh pear juice, fresh carrot juice, fresh *everything* juice. The late mornings and early afternoons on Saturdays and Sundays are always packed, thus the kitchen is always insanely busy, but since she completely trusts Billy and her line cooks to handle breakfast foods, she's rarely seen at Tart during brunchtime.

As she's about to enter the restaurant, her cell vibrates. Byron. 'What's the deal?' she asks.

'He's fine. He has a bit of the flu. I didn't know cats could get the flu. They rehydrated him and gave him some kitty antacid. We have to give him antibiotics for the next ten days. They also want you to switch his food. The stuff you're feeding him now is too greasy, or fatty, or something. We're on our way home. I'll be at the restaurant right after I drop him off. Billy will be in at three.'

She didn't hear a single word he said after 'He's fine.' Anna lets loose with a little wordless scream, then yells to the waiting patrons, 'Stinks is okay! Do you hear me? *Stinks is okay!* Peach juice on the house!' The crowd offers up some confused applause. She gets back on the phone and says to Byron, 'So what was wrong with him?'

Byron sighs, seemingly put out that Anna had stopped listening to him. 'He has the flu.'

Anna says, 'I didn't know cats could get the flu.'

Byron sighs again, then again explains, 'They generally can't. Apparently, Stinks is special.'

She tells one of the couples in line, 'You hear that? Stinks is special. *Stinks is special!*'

The male half of the couple says, 'I've always felt that way.' He looks at her mismatched Crocs. 'Nice shoes.'

Anna giggles, gives him a gentle punch on the bicep,

and says, 'You're silly.' Then she tells Byron, 'I'm buying everybody peach juice.'

'Must you? Peaches are out of season. They're expensive.'

'Yes, I must. See you in a few. Give my fuzzball a kiss.'

'No.'

'Asshole. Love you.'

'Love you too.'

Anna hangs up and floats through the door. She's met by Jeannie, who, concentrating intensely on the reservation book, says, 'There's a thirty-minute wait. What's your name, miss?'

'Anna Rowan.'

Jeannie smiles, 'That's funny. Our chef is named . . . oh . . . hi, Chef.'

Anna grabs Jeannie by the cheeks and says, 'You look beautiful today, Jeannie. Absolutely gorgeous.' She musses Jeannie's hair, then zigzags her way through the restaurant and gives high-fives to Corrine, Jenna, and Keith. Then she bursts into the kitchen and yells, 'Stinks is okay!'

Miguel, who happens to be the Vice President of the Stinks Rowan Fan Club, casually flips three banana granola pancakes at once, then asks, 'What's wrong with my big buddy, Chef?'

'He has the flu.'

Anna Two says, 'I didn't know kitties could get the flu.'

Anna grins and says, 'I know, right? But the vet says Stinks is special.' Then she looks at Wanker's station and her smile evaporates. 'Wank, you're a slob.' She wanders over and picks up a stray piece of eggshell that had fallen on the floor, a pinky toenail-sized piece of shell indiscernible to all but the most anal retentive neat freaks.

The rest of the afternoon is a pancake-filled barrage, and by the time dinner service rolls around, Anna is pooped. They do 5,207,253 brunch covers – okay, it was more like 175, but it sure feels like 5,207,253 – and there are twenty reservations on the book for tonight, one of which is a party of ten, and as much as she'd like to go home, get into her jammies, play with Stinks, crawl into bed, and fall asleep to FoodTube, Anna's afraid to leave the kitchen, because the newly returned Billy is a tad stoned. Billy being stoned isn't tragic in itself, but it's his first day back, and why take a chance leaving him alone?

Anna loathes substance abusers in her kitchen – over the years, she's canned eighteen line cooks for showing up to work drunk or high; on one memorable occasion, she threatened to bash a saucier over his head with a wooden cutting board after she caught him doing coke in the walk-in[19] – but she tolerates Billy's periodic altered states. You see, he tends to be both more productive and easier to work with when he's inebriated. When Billy's had too much vodka, his concentration and focus is at its highest level, similar to that of a drunk driver who wants to make sure he doesn't get pulled over. When he's smoked too much pot, his food is consistently lovely as he's exceptionally relaxed and creative; on the downside, the presentation and speed of delivery tend to suffer. Anna

---

[19] Walk-in: A big-ass refrigerator used for food storage, as well as post-dinner-service make-out sessions by adventurous servers.

would have axed Billy for good if he used hard stuff, but that will never be a problem – he wouldn't touch cocaine or heroin, as he's perfectly content getting wrecked on booze and/or grass. (By the way, unbeknownst to anybody else in the kitchen, Billy buys most of his weed from Miguel, who, ironically enough, doesn't smoke, or even drink. But please don't say anything about Miguel's criminal activities to anybody – he has family back in Mexico to support, and we don't either want Anna or the cops finding out about his moonlighting.)

Tonight, Billy's moving exceptionally slowly, and what with the impending full house, Anna sacrifices her night at home for the good of the restaurant. She can wait a few hours to see Stinks. She loves the big guy, but, well, he's a cat, and cats are independent entities who usually take pretty good care of themselves. Restaurants aren't.

Meanwhile, there are some strange goings-on in the front of the house:

Keith, who Jenna all but seduced into working a double,[20] is exhausted and not performing at his usual high level. He hasn't made any tragic mistakes – he forgot to put in substitutions on a couple of orders – that could happen to anybody – but he's spaced out big time. He's bumped into runners on six occasions, blanked on reciting the specials three times, and knocked a glass of chardonnay on to Nora's pink pastel T-shirt. Nora, also on her second shift, understands and forgives him.

---

[20] A double: Two consecutive shifts. They suck.

Another odd thing: Nora is mixing some terrible drinks; shocking, because she's one of the ten best bartenders in the city, at least according to *TimeOut Chicago*. So why are her vodka and tonics so weak and her Martinis so wet tonight? Well, it's not because she's pooped. You see that guy sitting in the stool closest to the window, all by himself, peeking at his watch every thirty seconds? His name is Jim Shackleford, and Nora had a mad crush on him in high school. He didn't know she existed back then, and he doesn't know she exists right now, and she's afraid to reintroduce herself, and is thus so distracted that she's reverted to the stingy style of bartending she was forced to master at the Jazz Showcase, a downtown club where the cheap-o owner insisted that all Old Fashioneds consist of tap water, store-brand sugar, food coloring, and three drops of gin. Okay, Nora's drinks aren't turning out *that* badly, but they're far more watery and sloppy than usual.

Stranger yet is the sight of Mr Smith wandering through the front of the house, asking each table if they're enjoying their meals, making wine recommendations, taking orders (!), making jokes (!!), comping desserts (!!!), and generally being a pleasant dude. The staff are shocked. They've never seen this sort of behavior from their owner. They're all certain something is very wrong. They fear for their jobs. Some fear for their lives.

Into the midst of this oddness walks our special guest. Ladies and gentlemen, straight from FoodTube, please welcome the cook you love to hate and hate to love, straight from the City of Angels, none other than Chef Jordan DeWitt.

Jordan bulls through the front door, followed closely by his sous chef Johnny Samuels (who looks to Keith remarkably like Billy Jorgenson), his assistant Michelle Fields (who looks to Keith remarkably like a young, but less gothy Winona Ryder – and Keith, it should be noted, digs Winona Ryder), *LA Times* food critic/official *Sunday Sneak Attack* judge Eric McLanahan (who, aside from a mischievous glint in his gray eyes, looks remarkably like a cynical journalist from a 1950s film noir), and a pair of rather large individuals with high-end video cameras perched on their shoulders. Jeannie peers at the FoodTube logo on the sides of cameras, then at Jordan, then again at the cameras, then at the reservation book, then again at Jordan, then scratches her head and asks, 'Gaaaah reservation?'

'I don't,' Jordan says. He spins around, points to the cameramen, and says, 'Roll camera and follow me, gentlemen.' He strides purposely past Jeannie, past the bar, stops in the middle of the dining room and yells, '*I'm looking for Chef Anna Rowan! Chef Rowan, this is Jordan DeWitt, and you are being attacked!*'

Byron, who, unbeknownst to Anna, arranged the attack, jogs into the kitchen. 'Anna. Billy. Front of the house. Now.'

Anna, who's practically buried in a pile of tenderloin, says, 'Byron, I'm deconstructing a beef Wellington. Fuck off.' Like many chefs, when Anna's in the weeds, she develops a severe case of potty mouth.

Byron says, 'I thought the Wellington was last night's special.'

'Somebody who was here last night ordered it off-menu.'[21]

'How long till it's done?'

'Couple of minutes. Why?'

'Finish it and get out there.'

'*Why?*'

'*Just finish it and get the hell out there.* And you're meeting a VIP, so try and make yourself presentable.'

The line cooks are stunned. They've all suffered Mr Smith's wrath at one point or another, but they've never seen him bark at Anna. But Anna is unfazed. She's gone toe-to-toe with her boyfriend dozens of times, and is prepared to do it again. She also intends to pay him back by not having sex with him until Wednesday, or till he starts literally begging for it, or till she herself gets super-horny, whichever comes first.

After she puts the finishing touches on the Wellington, takes off her apron, removes her bandanna, stomps out of the kitchen, undoes her ponytail and shakes out the tangles (which Keith somehow sees in slow motion), then puts on a big fake smile and makes her way on to the floor, she's blinded by what seems to be a thousand-watt bulb. She puts her hand over her eyes and says, 'What the hell is going on?'

Jordan again says, 'Chef Rowan, I'm Jordan DeWitt and you are being attacked.'

---

[21] Ordering off-menu: When a customer wants something not on the menu. A word of advice: chefs aren't enamored with the off-menu process, so unless you're a well-tipping multi-zillionaire or a super-hot celebrity type, you're best off choosing from what's offered.

Over the shock of being blindsided by spotlights, Anna surveys the scene: Jordan and Johnny in their matching black chef's jackets; one camera a foot from her face and one pointing at her over Jordan's right shoulder; Michelle jotting down notes on to a legal pad; Eric jotting down notes into a tiny notebook; Byron simultaneously grinning and sweating.

She stares at Jordan for a full minute, then says, 'You're shitting me.'

Michelle, who, for budgetary reasons, was appointed the *Sunday Sneak Attack* de facto director in the middle of last season, yells to the cameramen, '*Cut!*' She turns to Anna and sweetly asks, 'Chef Rowan, FoodTube is basic cable, so if it's cool with you, could we have you come out of the kitchen again and greet us without swearing? And maybe you could look a little bit happy to see us?'

Quickly getting into the spirit, Anna says, 'You bet.' She calls to Byron, 'Hey, how long have you known about this?'

'Remember in August when you told me you wanted your own FoodTube show?'

'Of course.'

'Remember I told you I'd make some calls?'

'I guess.'

'Well, I made some calls. And here we are.'

As she walks over to hug her boyfriend, she decides that she'll forgive him for yelling at her in front of her staff and sleep with him before Wednesday ... probably tonight, for that matter. Michelle gestures to the cameramen to start rolling again, so they capture on tape Anna kissing Byron, then saying, 'I can't believe you'd do that for me,' then Byron answering, 'I didn't, really. It was more for the restaurant,' then Anna saying, 'How romantic,' then Byron saying, 'This isn't romance. This is business,' then Anna asking, 'Can't the two intersect?' then Byron saying, 'Usually not in my world. You should realize that by now.'

Jordan blinks and says, 'Ooooooookay, and on that warm and fuzzy note, Chef Anna Rowan, will you and your sous chef take on me and Johnny here in a battle for culinary supremacy?'

Still in vulgar mode, she looks directly into the camera, grins devilishly, and says, 'Fuck yeah.'

Michelle sighs and says, 'Cut. Chef Rowan, can we take it from the top?'

Anna says, 'Of course we can. Give me a minute, though. I'd like to run to the washroom.' She jogs through the kitchen, and down some stairs into her basement office. She grabs some make-up from the top drawer of her desk, slapdashes on some lipstick and powder, unbuttons the top two buttons of her chef's jacket and readjusts her bra and tank top so she has some semblance of cleavage, then sprints back upstairs, runs past the line cooks, and bursts into the dining room.

She notices Jordan noticing her chest, but he seems unfazed – not that she was trying to faze him, but still. Jordan coolly repeats his challenge, then Anna sweetly says, 'Yes, Chef DeWitt, my sous chef and I would love to take you on.'

Jordan says, 'Excellent. What do you choose as your battle cuisine?'

Anna looks at Jordan and takes in his Hollywood tan, and his perfectly creased black chef's jacket (*Are those guys trying to intimidate me with that black?* she wonders) and his smarmy grin, and decides that, despite the fact that he's way cuter in person than on FoodTube, she wants to destroy him. She steps over to the California chef, sticks a finger in his face, and whispers, 'Italian. With lots and lots of cheese.' She looks into the camera again and says, 'Jordan DeWitt, I'm going to make you my bitch.'

Michelle sighs and says, 'Cut. Chef Rowan, can we try this once more? And don't forget: basic cable.'

VEGGIE PIZZA FRITTATA

Ingredients
4 eggs
¼ cup grated mozzarella cheese
⅛ cup grated Parmesan cheese
⅛ teaspoon oregano
⅛ teaspoon basil
⅛ teaspoon thyme
⅛ teaspoon salt
⅛ teaspoon pepper
1 tablespoon butter or margarine
½ teaspoon olive oil
½ cup sliced mushrooms
½ medium bell pepper, chopped
⅛ cup sliced olives
½ small onion, chopped
10–15 pieces of thinly sliced pepperoni (optional)

Method
1. Preheat oven to broil.
2. Beat together eggs, cheese and seasoning.
3. Cook butter and oil in large skillet over medium heat till butter is completely melted. Cook mushrooms, pepper, olives, and onion until tender.
4. Pour egg mixture over vegetables. Reduce heat to medium

low. Cover and cook for 9–11 minutes, until eggs set in center.

5. If using pepperoni, place slices on frittata, covering completely.

6. Place frittata in oven, approximately 5 inches from heat. Heat for 2 minutes.

7. Cut into wedges. Serve immediately.

Little Cheese

Though he's developed a healthy appreciation for a good meal, Keith isn't a hardcore foodie, so he never watches FoodTube – he's a sports/music video/movie/ ESPN/MTV/HBO kind of guy – thus he has no idea who the hell Jordan DeWitt is. But the way Anna perks up at his presence, and the excited manner in which most of the diners react to his dramatic entrance make it obvious that this Jordan dude is a Big Deal.

Having grown up in the LA show business community, Keith Cole isn't fazed (or even particularly impressed) by Big Deals. His parents are both television personalities – Dad is an anchorman on the local NBC affiliate, and Mom is a recognizable character actress who played some version of the goofy second or third banana on seemingly dozens of failed sitcoms – so he's encountered enough locally, nationally and internationally famous folks in his time to glean that 'talent' is most often a neurotic bunch who are just like you and me, except louder and more pampered. He isn't intimidated in the face of celebrity; he's bemused.

But Keith is a respectful young man, so he figures before he passes judgement on Jordan, the least he could do is find out who the guy is, and what the heck he's doing here. He sees Eileen leaning against the bar, unabashedly gawking at the scene unfolding in the dining room, clearly aware of what this whole thing is about. He sidles up to her and asks, 'What's the scoop with the cameras?'

'You don't know? It's *Jordan*.'

'Jordan who?'

'Jordan *DeWitt*. Duh. You work at a fancy and exciting restaurant like this and you don't watch FoodTube?' Keith shakes his head, then Eileen sighs and gives him a thumbnail sketch of Jordan, before filling him in on the ins and outs of *Sunday Sneak Attack* – a show concept that sounds a bit silly to him – then she says, 'I don't know who to root for.'

'What, you wouldn't root for Chef Ro— er, Anna?' He's still not used to referring to Anna by her first name, but he sure digs doing it.

'I like Jordan. He's way cute and he's pretty funny.' Eileen smirks. 'I know who *you're* rooting for.'

'Of course I'm rooting for Anna.'

'*Of course I'm rooting for Anna*,' she says in a not half-bad impersonation of Keith. 'Of course you are, because you *soooo* want her.'

He firmly squeezes her bicep, pulls her in close, and whispers into her ear, 'How the hell do you know that? Did Nora tell you?'

'No, you told me, dummy. In great detail. Remember? That night we went to that gross bar in Wicker Park?' She again affects Keith's voice: '*She's so hot. And her food is awesome. I don't understand what she sees in Mr Smith. I'm better-looking than him, aren't I? He's got more money than I have, and he's skinnier than I am, but whatever.*' Then, in her normal Eileen voice, she adds, 'It's kind of cute. But you've got no shot. Keep dreaming, babe.'

'I don't remember that conversation at all. I must've been trashed.'

'You totally were. But I already knew you wanted her anyhow. Everybody knows.' Just then, Corrine walks by. Eileen grabs the back of her collar to stop her and asks, 'Hey, did you know Keith looooooooves Chef Anna?'

Corrine says, 'Who *doesn't* know?'

Eileen points to one of the cameramen. 'That dude doesn't. I think I should go tell him.'

Corrine says, 'Yeah, I think so, too.'

Keith says, 'I think both of you can suck it.'

Eileen says, 'I already did. Twice. And that was *more* than enough.' Yes, Keith and Eileen hooked up about a year ago. It didn't stick. No hard feelings. Just periodically awkward ones.

Corrine asks, 'Wait, what's that supposed to mean, Eileen? Did you guys get together?'

Eileen cocks a thumb at Keith. 'What, he didn't tell you? He tells everybody everything.'

Keith says, 'You said you'd castrate me if I talked.'

'You don't have to chop off his junk, Eileen,' Corrine

says. 'He didn't say anything. I figured it out all by my lonesome. And frankly, the whole thing astounds me.' Corrine is likely shocked not because Keith and Eileen messed around – other than Jeannie, who doesn't like to shit where she hostesses, most everybody at Tart has messed around with one of their fellow servers at one point or another – but because the servers as a group are more gossipy than the *National Enquirer*, *People* and *Us* combined, and nobody ever hides anything. Especially, as we know, Keith. Until now. 'I've got to say, Keith, I'm proud of you for keeping a secret. Is this the first time, like, ever?'

Keith tries to walk away, but Eileen grabs his hand, holds it to her heart (it was her breast, really), and says, 'It destroys me to even think about my oh-so-brief time with Keith, let alone discuss it. You see, Corrine, Keith Cole hurt me. He hurt me badly. Hurt me like I've never been hurt before.'

Keith groans, 'Oh, for God's sake.'

'We didn't have sex,' Eileen continues. 'We didn't fuck. No, we made passionate love, the kind of love that builds mountains and realigns the planets.' (It's probably worth mentioning again that Eileen is a wannabe actress.) 'It only happened two times . . .'

'Six times,' Keith mumbles.

'Two times, six times, a million times, who's counting?'

'Clearly not you,' Keith says.

'But before we could get to number seven,' Eileen continues, 'Keith realized that his love for Chef Anna was greater than his love for *moi*, so he threw me to the wolves. I'm still glueing the broken pieces of my heart back together.'

Corrine fake sniffles, then wipes an imaginary tear from her cheek. 'That's the saddest story I've ever heard.'

Keith says, 'Eileen, you went back to your boyfriend. *You* blew *me* off.'

Eileen lets Keith's hand go. 'Yeah, there's that. But there was something about Keith's curved little thingie that—'

Much to Keith's relief, Eileen's description of his curved little thingie – which is only a tiny bit curved, thank you very much – is interrupted by Jordan DeWitt. 'Listen up, ladies and gentlemen,' the celeb chef yells. 'Everybody who's eating right now, I'm sorry to cut your meals short, so dinner's on me . . .'

Corrine says, 'Shit, we're going to get so hosed on tips.'

'. . . but in exchange,' Jordan continues, 'I ask that since you're getting free food, you throw your server a little bit of extra cabbage, if you know what I mean.'

Eileen yells, 'You rule, Jordan!'

Jordan spins around and gives Eileen a killer smile. 'Thank you, pretty lady. Very kind of you to say. You know, I've only been here for about six minutes, but you Tart people have been pretty damn nice to me. It really kills me that I'm going to have to smack your Chef Rowan around her very own kitchen.'

Anna says, 'You wish, pal. Our kitchen is ready for you. Bring in your goons.'

Jordan laughs, clearly pleased that Anna is into it. He tells Johnny, Eric, Michelle, and the cameramen, 'Goons, you heard the lady; to the kitchen. What say we open up a can of whoop-ass on Chef Rowan?'

Keith tells his fellow servers, 'I'm going in with them.'

Eileen asks, 'Why? You afraid your dreamgirl is going to get her butt kicked?'

'Hell no. She'll smoke him. But I think she'll need some moral support from a member of the home team.'

Eileen points to Byron, who's following Jordan and his goons into the kitchen. 'Looks like your buddy Mr Smith has beaten you to it.'

'So what? I'm going.'

Eileen says, 'Yeah, you should. What's the worst that can happen? They'll throw you out. So what? Go. Watch your girl.' She gives him a once over. 'You look cute tonight. They'll be happy to put you on television.' Despite being well into his second shift, Keith does indeed look good. His faux-hawk is in perfect triangular condition, his black button-down shirt is still crisp, and his almond-shaped and almond-colored eyes are sharp and alive.

Keith asks the girls, 'Seriously? I look okay?' They both nod. He stands up and sighs. 'All right. Here goes nothing.'

Keith navigates his way through the dining room, gently opens the kitchen door, tiptoes in, and positions himself behind some pot-and-pan-laden metal shelving. Naturally, his nemesis Billy spots him immediately. 'Hey, dumbass,' Billy yells, 'shouldn't you be in bed, curled up with your teddy bear?'

As Keith considers doubling up on his mixed martial

arts lessons – the better to destroy the sous chef with – Jordan looks at Keith and asks, 'Who's this now?'

Anna peers across the room. 'Keith, what're you doing in here?'

'I'm a huge fan of *Sunday Cookoff* . . .'

'You mean *Sunday Sneak Attack*,' Jordan says.

'Yeah, what he said. And I wanted to give you some moral support.'

Anna says, 'That's sweet. But I don't think Chef DeWitt likes having non-cooks around for this sort of thing.'

'Nah, it's all good,' Jordan says. 'Who am I to deny Chef Rowan her little rooting section—'

Michelle interrupts, 'As long as he signs a non-disclosure agreement to not tell anybody who wins.'

Jordan continues, '—because frankly, she'll need all the support she can get.'

'Dude,' Keith says, stepping out from behind the shelves, 'she's going to spank you so hard, it won't even be funny.'

Byron glares at the server and says, 'Keith, settle down.'

Anna beams. 'Keith, ignore him. Thank you. That was very sweet of you.'

Anna holds eye contact with Keith a few seconds longer than he expected, causing his stomach to do a little dipsy-doo. He says, 'You're welcome, *Anna*.' He puts emphasis on Anna's name, still relishing uttering it aloud.

Billy says, 'Shouldn't you be referring to her as Chef, dumbass?'

Anna tells Billy, 'Take a pill, fart face. He's our only cute male server, so he's allowed to call me Anna.'

Keith blushes, and experiences a second dipsy-doo, this one far more dipsier than the last.

Jordan looks into the camera and rolls his eyes, then bangs a spoon against a stainless-steel bowl. 'Okay, people. Enough blabbing. Let's get ready to rumble.'

And rumble is exactly what they do. As per the *Sunday Sneak Attack* rules, each two-person team prepares a five-course meal which consists of whatever ingredients they choose, so long as it adds up to an Italian dish. If they want to do a soup, a salad, a starter, an entrée and dessert, that's fine. If they want to do five desserts, that's fine too.

Despite having worked at Tart for a year and a half, Keith hasn't ever watched Anna work for any significant amount of time. His trips into the kitchen are, on average, fifty-two seconds long; he doesn't like to hang out, as he always gets the feeling that the line cookies don't appreciate his presence. (He's right. They don't. But it's nothing personal. During service, they don't appreciate *anybody's* presence.) For Keith, checking out Anna is a treat. Not only does he get to see how she cooks, but he gets to stare at her ass without fear of getting busted.

As the battle progresses, Keith finds himself focusing on Anna's cooking instead of her body. He's amazed, yet unsurprised at her competence, her confidence, and her pinpoint focus. She speaks forcefully, so forcefully that Billy is following her every command without comment or question. She barks out directions, she asks for ingredients, she tells Billy to hurry up – there's a ninety-minute time limit – and, seemingly out of nowhere, her five dishes begin to come to fruition.

Chef DeWitt, conversely, is a lunatic: he screams, he cajoles, he jokes, he talks trash, he plays with his utensils, he gooses his sous chef, he sneaks tastes of Anna's works-in-progress, and he speaks directly into the camera. Keith can see why Jordan is a star in the cooking world; his on-camera personality is magnetic. But Keith has known many, many people whose magnetic on-camera personalities mask some serious insecurity and attitude.

With ten minutes left before the bell, Anna spikes a spatula into the sink and yells, 'Done!'

Jordan looks up from the five-mushroom risotto he's plating and says, 'You're kidding.' He looks into the camera and screws up his face. 'Ladies and gentleman, if Chef Rowan is telling us the truth, if she's actually finished with all of her courses, your pal Jord-o is screwed.'

Anna walks over to the other camera, sticks her face directly into the lens, and says, 'Chef Rowan is telling you the truth. So yeah, Jord-o is most definitely screwed.' Keith has never before seen Anna this giddy and giggly. He thinks, *Beautiful face, amazing body, oodles of talent, and now a sense of humor. I must have her*. He glares at Byron. *Would blowing up Mr Smith's car be too extreme?*

Jordan slinks behind Anna, puts his hands on her shoulders, and says, 'If Chef Rowan says I'm screwed, well, then I'm screwed.' He turns to his sous chef, the whole time touching Anna. 'Johnny, we're screwed. Let's just quit now and go home. Chicago sucks anyhow. It's too damn cold.'

'We're fine, Chef,' Johnny groans. 'Shut the fuck up and finish plating.'

Michelle grimaces. 'Language, Johnny. Basic cable, remember? Basic fucking cable, you dickweed!'

Everybody in the kitchen cracks up. Anna skips over to Michelle, gently slaps her on the back, says, 'You go, girl! Fucking awesome!'

Jordan ducks. 'Take cover, ladies and gentlemen, there're F-bombs flying all over the place tonight.'

Johnny shakes his head. 'Great. Look what I fucking started.'

One of the cameraman says, 'Guys, our editor's going to be as angry as fuck, having to bleep all this shit out.'

Keith continues laughing, his attention fully drawn away from Anna for the first time in eighty-two minutes.

Byron remains silent.

Seemingly seconds later, Michelle yells, 'Time's up! Put down your utensils!'

It turns out that our pal Jord-o isn't screwed at all. He has easily completed all five dishes, and each looks lovely. His mushroom risotto sits in the middle of a large white square plate, surrounded by lightly sautéed, thinly sliced, strategically placed chanterelles, matsutakes, porcinis, criminis and champignons. Gooey with Parmesan, pecorino and fontina, his zuppa gallurese[22] is happily steaming away, begging to be slurped. His fettuccine with brown butter, sage and toasted pine nuts is chilling out,

---

[22] Zuppa gallurese: A soup made with bread and cheese. Sounds weird. It's not.

minding its own business, smelling divine. Johnny tells Anna that their chicken dish with the sausage and peppers is called Italian peasant chicken. And it takes all of Keith's restraint to keep from stealing a taste of the Tuscan beef stew that's parked next to a scoop of fried polenta cakes.

Anna surveys Jordan's dishes. 'Fettuccine *and* risotto *and* polenta? You've got a lot of starch going on there, Chef DeWitt.' She points at Eric. 'Are you trying to fatten our judge up?'

Eric grins. 'Yeah, DeWitt, what's the deal? You couldn't mix it up a bit? I think maybe I'll deduct five points right off the bat, teriyaki boy.'

Jordan scowls at Eric, then tells Anna, 'Your kitchen isn't particularly well stocked, Chef Rowan. There's only so much I can do with so little.'

Anna gestures to her five dishes. 'I seem to have done pretty okay. And surprise, surprise, I barely used any cheese.'

She's done more than pretty okay. The parsley soup with truffled chestnuts, the crostini with beef tartare and white truffle oil, the pappardelle with squash and spinach, the tilapia[23] in puttanesca sauce, and the pear, goat's cheese, honey and pistachio tartlets all look and smell heavenly. Keith isn't an expert – plus he's a bit biased – but he feels certain that Jordan is toast.

The judging takes seemingly forever, because Eric has to sample, and then comment on each dish. And it's not

[23] Tilapia: A mellow whitefish that, in the right hands, can be crazy yummy, but in the wrong hands, can be crazy dull.

the kind of thing where he can take a quick nibble and say, 'Mmm, tasty.' FoodTube viewers demand detail, so his samples are significantly sized, and his analysis is on the long-winded side. Plus he has ten dishes to deal with, and one can only eat so quickly.

In the interest of saving time, here are some of the highlights:

On Jordan's risotto: 'Texture-wise, it's almost perfect, but either you left it on the stove a minute too long, or you put in one too many scoops of broth. It's also a bit underseasoned, and could have stood some more Parmesan.' (As it so happens, Jordan didn't put in any Parmesan, but doesn't think it would be a good idea to mention that.) 'But the mushrooms blend was astounding. It was like a meta-mushroom.'

On Anna's tilapia: 'Like many flat fishes, it's often difficult to cook tilapia just right, but you managed to make it happen: it's done all the way through, but it's still moist. And I've had probably about three million puttanescas in my time, and this has to be in the top fifty, which is saying something, especially since I've grown to hate the stuff.'

On Jordan's peasant chicken: 'Jordan, you screwed the pooch on this one. This is baseball stadium food. This is airline food. Okay, it doesn't suck that badly, but it's a snooze, and you've done stuff like this before, and I know you can do better. Next time you're forced to go Italian, for the love of Mario Batali, try something different. And don't be afraid to use cheese.'

On Anna's tarts: 'Chef Rowan, in the spirit of today's

battle, all I can say is this shit is fucking amazing.' (Michelle winces and yells, 'Eric, I *so* hate you.') 'It's light but substantial. It's sweet and savory. It's crunchy and melty. A lovely capper to a lovely meal.'

Unable to help himself, Keith yells, 'You rule, Anna!'

Byron snaps, 'Keith, relax.'

Michelle says, 'Don't listen to him, Keith. As long as you don't mind being on TV, you can be as unrelaxed as you want. If Chef Rowan wins, why don't you go and give her a celebratory hug. And if she loses—'

'Which is exactly what's going to happen,' Jordan says.

'—you can give her a consoling hug.'

Byron says, 'I thought this was reality television. That's not particularly realistic. Especially since she's *my* girlfriend.'

'Uh oh,' Jordan chuckles. 'Catfight.'

Byron says, 'Listen, DeWitt, why don't you mind your own—'

'Guys, guys, guys,' Anna says, 'you can both hug me. The more hugs, the better.'

'Do I get to hug you?' Jordan asks.

'God, no. You're my sworn mortal enemy. Plus you dissed Chicago. No hug for you, Chef DeWitt.'

'Yeah, yeah, yeah,' Jordan says. 'I didn't want to hug you anyhow.'

Keith doesn't believe that for a second. How could somebody not want to hug Anna? Even covered with sweat and *mise en place*, she's the most huggable creature Keith has ever laid eyes on, even more huggable than that gorgeous redheaded violinist from his high school orchestra, whose name he can never remember – Laura, maybe? Lori? Lana? – but who he still has biannual graphic sex dreams about.

Michelle says, 'Okay, gang, this is all great television, but let's finish up here.' She points at Eric. 'Go.'

Eric looks at his notes. 'Both contestants delivered wonderful meals. Jordan, if it seems like I was being harder on you than I was on Anna, well, that's only because I was. She's cute. You're not. So there.'

Jordan sticks his face into camera number two and says, 'Ladies and gentlemen, next week, on a very special two-hour episode of *Sunday Sneak Attack*, judge Eric McLanahan will be hung by butcher's string over a boiling pot of tom yum.'[24]

'I have no problem with that,' Eric says. 'You make a really nice tom yum. It's certainly better than that Italian peasant crap I had to shove down.' He clears his throat, pauses for almost a full minute, then says, 'I offer a hearty *Sunday Sneak Attack* congratulations to tonight's winner . . . Chef Anna Rowan.'

Anna pumps her fist, whispers '*Yes*,' then gives Billy a high-five. 'Good work, buddy,' she tells her sous chef. 'You're back in my good graces, fart face. I'm totally taking tomorrow off. Can I trust you to run things here?'

'Yeah, man. For sure.' Billy snuck out back and smoked half a bowl right after Anna spiked her spatula, and is again stoned, thus is exceedingly agreeable.

---

[24] Tom yum: A spicy, sweet, and sour Thai soup that isn't nearly as yummy as its name would suggest.

Anna then walks up to Jordan, offers him her hand, and says, 'Thank you for the opportunity. It was a pleasure and an honor cooking beside you.'

Jordan smiles, takes Anna's hand and, rather than shaking it, he raises it to his lips and gently kisses her middle knuckle. 'Right back at you, Chef. I'm sure we'll meet again on some other FoodTube extravaganza.'

'You think so?'

'I know so.'

'Okay, fine, you can have a hug.' Anna grabs Jordan around his neck and gives him a distinctly non-sexual squeeze. (It still gives Keith a case of the envies.) Byron's deep in conversation with Eric, and doesn't really notice any of what's going on. She releases Jordan and calls to Keith, 'Hey, good luck charm, come over here and get some sugar.'

Keith gets plenty of sugar. His stomach goes goofy. It's a veritable festival of dipsy-doodles.

And Byron still doesn't notice.

PEAR, GOAT'S CHEESE, HONEY AND PISTACHIO TARTLETS

Ingredients
4 sheets thawed puff pastry
1 egg, beaten
6 oz soft, fresh goat's cheese
1 tablespoon fresh lemon juice
¼ teaspoon coarse kosher salt
3 medium Bartlett pears, quartered, cored, cut into
⅛ inch thick slices
3 tablespoons unsalted butter, melted
¾ cup dark honey
½ teaspoon of ground allspice
¼ cup ground pistachios

Method
1. Preheat oven to 375°F.
2. Line 2 rimmed baking sheets with parchment paper.
3. Roll out each puff pastry sheet on lightly floured surface to 11 inch square.
4. Using 5 inch diameter cookie cutter or bowl, cut out 4 rounds from each pastry sheet, forming 16 rounds total.
5. Divide 8 pastry rounds between prepared baking sheets; pierce rounds all over with fork.
6. Using 3½ inch diameter cookie cutter or bowl, cut out

smaller rounds from center of remaining 8 rounds (reserve 3½ inch rounds for another use), forming 8 5 inch diameter rings.

7. Brush outer 1 inch edges of 5 inch rounds on baking sheets with beaten egg; top each with 1 pastry ring. Freeze for at least 30 minutes.

8. Mix cheese, lemon juice and salt in bowl; spread mixture inside rings on frozen pastry rounds. Overlap pear slices atop cheese.

9. Mix butter and ¼ cup honey in small bowl; brush over pears. Sprinkle with allspice.

10. Bake till pears are tender and pastry is golden, about 35 minutes.

11. Place tartlets on plates. Drizzle remaining honey and sprinkle pistachios over each and serve warm or at room temperature.

The TV Star

On your first day of culinary school, before you even finish tying up your apron and buttoning up your chef's jacket, you're told that the moment you become a serious professional cook, you forfeit the right to celebrate any major holiday on the holiday itself. For instance, if you want to go to a New Year's Eve party on New Year's Eve, forget it, because you'll be stuck working the salad station in some insanely busy kitchen, so save your noisemakers and plastic tiaras until January 15. Thanksgiving on Thanksgiving? Are you kidding? Freeze the turkey and cranberry sauce till, like, June. And Christmas Eve? Dream on, cookie. Santa will be back at the North Pole before you'll even roll into bed.

Back in the day, Anna was a huge proponent of the Christmas season. The holidays meant essentially the same thing to her as it did to her fellow Christmas proponents: giving and receiving needless but welcome gifts, enjoying the company of the entire family (except for her gross, perv-o cousin Peter, who's been trying to feel her up ever since she developed anything worth feeling up), playing and watching football with her two brothers and her brothers' many friends (a couple of whom actually *had* felt her up – the friends, that is, not the brothers – but they'd been given access, so it was all good), and, most importantly, culinary excess. Part of the reason she fell in love with cooking in the first place was that she adored seeing how happy her family was before, during, and after a killer Christmas meal.

But that was back in the day. Now, for Anna, the month between Thanksgiving and New Year's Day means three things: working, sleeping for nine minutes a night, and working some more. It sounds like a drag, but could be worse. She just has to focus on the nice moments in the midst of the madness.

On paper, being open on Thanksgiving doesn't make much sense for a mid-to-high-end place like Tart, but ever since year one, in the interest of the bottom line, Byron insisted that the restaurant provide a feast fit for kings – or at least people who earn a king's salary. From the get-go, the Thanksgiving feast was a windfall for the restaurant, as there are few other restaurants in Chicago of Tart's caliber serving up fancy-schmancy turkey. (You don't want to know how much people pay to eat Anna's Thanksgiving food. Suffice it to say it costs an arm, a leg, and a drumstick.) For Anna, despite it being a logistical nightmare, the Tart Thanksgiving supper is usually a relatively enjoyable experience, primarily because all the customers are in such a relaxed, overstuffed, cheerful mood that she forgets it's a logistical nightmare until the night is over. Sure, she misses being with her family – her most enjoyable recent Thanksgiving was two years back, when her Mom, Dad and brothers celebrated at the restaurant – but she sucks it up and makes the best of it.

The night before Christmas can be pretty cool, too. Aside from fruitcake, Anna loves cooking (and eating) Christmas food, so it's no surprise that a *Chicago Tribune* food critic once wrote that Tart 'serves the finest holiday feast this side of my mother.' It's another super-expensive prix fix nine-course chef's tasting menu that features Anna's new spin on classic holiday favorites such as roast goose (nobody can figure out what the hell is in that mindblowing stuffing of hers; she refuses to divulge the recipe to anybody outside of her kitchen – even Byron – and has told her line cooks that if they utter the ingredients aloud, they'll be decapitated and fired, in that order), mashed potatoes (which she jazzes up with both truffles and truffle oil) and a dizzying international cheese plate that won't be described in detail here because reading about it would make you drool so profusely that you'd ruin several pages of the very book you're holding in your hands.

The weeks between the holidays are more problem-atic. It's a blurry, chaotic, far-from-jolly stretch, and the fact that Anna – our little anal retentive kitchen control freak – can't control the main problem drives her nuts. See, many of Anna's purveyors are unable to handle the holiday rush – to paraphrase Richard Nixon, mistakes are made – and it's not uncommon for her fish guy to deliver twenty pounds of halibut rather than ten pounds of tuna, or for the produce guy to show up with four boxes of severely smushed heirloom tomatoes. Anna has loudly, eloquently, and profanely bitched out these purveyors at one point or another, and they're all now a little frightened of her, so the problem is less prevalent than it was during Tart's first couple of holiday seasons, but it still happens too often, the result of which is that at least twice a week during December, Anna has to temporarily remove an item off the menu, which mortifies her. That sort of thing probably never happens to Thomas Keller, and definitely not to Gordon Ramsay.

This year, however, the purveyors haven't screwed up a single order, but that's not the sole reason the holidays feel warmer and more celebratory for the Tart-ers. Why is everybody so chill? Well, Byron, much to the shock of Anna et al, decided to close the restaurant on the Sunday evening before Christmas. Why? Well, that's the night Anna's episode of *Sunday Sneak Attack* is airing, and he thinks that a combination employees-only Christmas party/FoodTube viewing party/pizza party/free booze (but not the good stuff) party will be great for the staff's morale.

'When have you ever cared about the staff's morale?' Anna asks him. It's three a.m. on the Friday night – or a Saturday morning, depending on your point of view – the week before the Tart party. The dinner rush started at four and didn't slow down till midnight. Byron made them keep the kitchen open for an extra two hours. They're both having major trouble winding down.

Byron says, 'I'm just being a swell guy.' He pauses, then adds, 'Plus, if the party makes everybody more cheerful, they'll be more apt to not bitch about working doubles.'

'Don't you think it would make everybody more cheerful if you let them at the top-shelf booze?'

'The bar stuff is fine. As long as it's free, everybody'll be happy.'

'You think so, Mr Former Sommelier? You feel good about yourself offering our hard-working staff shitty vodka and crap wine?'

'Okay, fine, I'll bust out a few nice bottles. But I'm trying to keep my costs down on this thing here. We're losing a night's business, don't forget.'

'So this isn't *really* about being a swell guy,' Anna says. 'This is about . . . I don't know what. What's it about?'

'It's about productivity.'

'Productivity?'

'Yeah. Happy cooks and servers equals focused, uncomplaining cooks and servers, which, when you think about it, is better for both of us. If shutting down dinner service for one night makes for a perfect holiday season, I'm all for it. And if it makes me come across as a swell guy in the process, well, so much the better. Two birds, one stone, boom.'

'Byron, when's the last time you did something just to be nice?'

'*Sunday Sneak Attack.*'

'Excuse me?'

'What, that wasn't nice?'

'It was brilliant, but there's no way you would've done that of your own accord. If I hadn't have said anything the night we were watching DeWitt, it wouldn't have happened.'

'But you *did* say something. And it *did* happen. The end result is that it worked out for everybody.'

'Wait, what do you mean, *Worked out for everybody*?' Anna already knew the answer but she wanted to see if he'd admit it aloud.

'When this thing airs next week, it's going to be great for the restaurant.' Yep. Sure enough. He admitted it. Not great for *her*. Not great for *them*. Great for Tart.

'And that's what it's always all about for you,' she says, 'what's best for the restaurant. Restaurant first, people second.'

Aside from Stinks's snoring, the room is silent for a moment. Finally, Byron says, 'I *do* want this to be a great Christmas for you, and me, and Tart. And if I have to move some pieces around to make everything work, so be it.'

Anna turns on her side, her back to Byron. 'Ho, ho, ho, you manipulative, Machiavellian scrooge.'

When Byron tells the staff about the party, Jeannie pipes up with the suggestion that instead of giving each other gifts, they do a Secret Santa. Anna can get behind that. She'd rather buy one person an awesome, appropriate gift than do what she usually does, which is give everybody in the crew – both the front and the back of the house alike – either a nice bottle of wine or liqueur. Anna knows her alcohol is appreciated, but adding some semblance of a personal touch would be nice.

It's only recently that Anna is at all concerned about personal touching with her staff. She generally doesn't like to bring her non-Tart, day-to-day life into the restaurant – which frankly isn't a problem, because for the most part, her non-Tart, day-to-day life is relatively pathetic, comprised mostly of playing with Stinks, going out to the periodic brunch with Byron, zoning out in front of the television, reading six paragraphs of a book before promptly falling asleep, and spending minutes, if not hours, searching the apartment for whatever essential item (e.g. keys, wallet, bandanna, bra) she misplaced the night before – so nobody on the line has much to talk about with her other than work anyhow. Miguel is the only cookie she ever sees outside of the restaurant on a regular basis, but that only happens because A) he lives around the corner from her and Byron, so they bump into one another three or four times a week; and B) he likes to pop in and visit Stinks. And aside from Nora, with whom she has to discuss inventory, Anna has virtually no regular contact with the front of the house.

Nobody at the restaurant really knows Anna. And Anna really doesn't know anybody at the restaurant. Everybody at Tart will say nothing but nice things about Chef Anna – nobody will deny the girl is a total sweetie, except for maybe Billy, who sarcastically disses her only because he's a scumbag fart face – but she hasn't made herself into the most approachable person in the world. Ever since *Sunday Sneak Attack*, she's been in a far better mood, which has made the staff less hesitant to engage with her, and it turns out she likes being engaged with. Now that she's bonded with Tart-ians other than Miguel, Anna Two, Wanker and the rest of the line, she realizes she has some damn cool co-workers in the dining room. She gets a kick out of Eileen who, despite being quite the drama queen, has a goofy sense of humor, and can always get Anna laughing with some story about one of her many freakish actor friends, or a tale about a sexual encounter gone awry. Jenna is also hilarious, what with her vampy sex-bomb act contrasting with her beautiful, innocent, ivory-soap face. And Keith . . . ah . . . well . . . Keith . . .

After having had several honest-to-goodness conversations with him, Anna finally admits to herself that Keith is head over heels. (Ninety-nine per cent of women between the ages of twenty-one and thirty-five would have admitted that to themselves months before, but Anna has been known to periodically reside in the State of Denial.) She also admits that he's a truly nice person: he's unpretentiously intelligent, he's slyly funny, he's guileless, and, most importantly for Anna right now, he listens. No, let's amend that: he doesn't merely listen. He hangs on her every word. She can tell he tries to be at his best whenever he's around her, and effort counts. As things have been rocky with her and Byron for the last two months, she can't help but be flattered.

Okay, maybe rocky is an overstatement; disconnected is probably a more appropriate description. Ever since the *Sunday Sneak Attack* filming back in October, Byron's been kvetching about Anna, and Anna's been kvetching about Byron, and it often makes for a less-than-enjoyable home life. Some of their respective kvetches are completely reasonable. Others, not so much:

Byron's annoyed that when Anna's at home, she's distant, distracted and boring. (She's aware that distance, distraction and boringness have become prevalent in the Smith/Rowan household, but she can't do anything about it because the moment she leaves her adrenaline-fueled kitchen, she becomes bone tired. She truly wants to be perky at home, but most of the time, she is simply unable to make it happen, even with the aid of many, many espressos loaded with lots and lots of sugar.)

Anna's annoyed because Byron's upset she's not acting more grateful that he set up the FoodTube appearance. (That's not quite as legit of a complaint as the Anna-is-distant thing, because the truth of the matter is that she's been plenty grateful. She bought two Armani suits for him to wear to work, and two tons of Victoria's Secret lingerie for her to wear to bed. What does he want, for her to kiss his feet every morning?)

Byron's annoyed because he feels Anna is getting too big for her britches. (Okay, fine, maybe she's been a bit more confident since she whupped Jordan's butt, but as Anna has always tended to lack self-belief outside of the kitchen, most would agree that this is a good thing.)

Anna's annoyed because, well, because *Byron's* annoyed. (Legit, legit, legit. He has little right to be seriously annoyed, because when she's on her game, Anna Rowan is an exemplary girlfriend. But you can't be on your game all the time. Can you?)

Individually, these may seem like minor quibbles, but

if you add them all up, then factor in the huge number of high-pressure hours the couple spends together at work during the holiday season, well, all of a sudden a sexy guy with a sexy faux-hawk who worships the ground you walk on sounds pretty damn sweet. Not that she'd ever do anything with Keith. Aside from the obvious issue – she has a live-in boyfriend whom she loves and is even sometimes in love with – there are plenty of good reasons why Anna could never be with the waiter: he's too young, and, er, um, well, that's pretty much it. When she allows herself to think about it for real, Keith's age is the only hurdle.

All of which is why the night of the Tart *Sunday Sneak Attack* holiday extravaganza, Anna isn't as happy as one would expect, but to her credit, she's trying. She's working the room, making sure everybody has a drink and a full plate of pizza, generally being a perky party hostess. She even got all cuted up for the occasion; no baggy chef's coat or chef's pants, but rather a Christmassy red DKNY button-down blouse that she unbuttoned as much as she could without being slutty, and a pair of Lucky low-rider jeans. Her body looks great, but even a casual Anna-ologist would take one look at her face and recognize she's bumming. Not a lot. Just a tiny bum.

Byron used to be an Anna-ologist extraordinaire, but his attention has been wandering for weeks, if not months, so he had no clue she's not as happy as she should be – after all, she's about to make her national television debut, and he assumes she's ecstatic. Keith, on the other hand, just received his undergrad degree in Anna-ology, so fifteen minutes before the Rowan vs DeWitt battle is set to air, he sees Anna being subtly mopey, so he toodles over to the Chef and says, 'DeWitt's going to destroy you. I don't think I can bring myself to look.' The drinks are free, and Keith is almost-but-not-quite drunk.

Anna, who has a buzz of her own, takes a pull of her Guinness. 'Yeah, you're probably right. Maybe we should watch *The Simpsons*, or the football game, or CNN.' Keith cheered her up by just being Keith. Impressive.

Keith nods. 'Dudette, CNN sounds *awesome*. That is *so* Christmassy.' He turns to the bar and yells, 'Hey, Nora, screw FoodTube, Anna wants to watch CNN! Change the channel!' (A couple weeks back, Anna told everybody to call her Anna. The whole Chef thing was starting to feel elitist. Gordon Ramsay wouldn't roll that way – but she's not Gordon Ramsay.)

Shouting to be heard over the staff's protesting chorus of boos, Nora yells back, 'Fuck you, handsome, change it yourself!' She reaches under the bar, grabs the TV remote, and wings it at Keith, who deftly catches it, then gently tosses it to Anna Two, who tosses it to Billy, who tosses it to Jenna, who tosses it to Byron, who shakes his head, walks behind the bar, and puts it back in its rightful place.

Anna hears somebody mumble, 'Man, Smith can be a buzzkill.' At this moment, she can't help but agree.

Keith looks at his watch, and tells Anna, 'Three minutes until ignition.' He puts his arm around her shoulders in a comradely fashion – clearly wanting to touch her more intimately, but also clearly wanting to make it seem like touching her doesn't mean a thing to him – and asks, 'You excited to see yourself on the little screen?'

She guzzles down a significant percentage of her stout, daintily burps, smiles a cute little I-just-belched-aren't-I-funny smile, then says, 'Yeah. I kind of am.'

Keith nods and pats her on the back. 'I kind of am too. I hope you win.' Aside from Billy and Byron, Keith is the only staffer who knows the outcome, and Anna is oddly touched that he hasn't spilled the beans, because, as she now knows, Keith is a notorious bean spiller.

They gaze at each other wordlessly for a few seconds – yet another one of their staring contests – and she feels like Keith is going to touch her on the waist, or rub her forearm, and she kind of wants him to, but she knows her mind shouldn't head anywhere near that direction, so she starts to feel guilty and forces herself to think of something distracting, which, in this case, is the fact that Billy, for no particular reason, has taken off his pants and is traipsing around the restaurant wearing only a tight white T-shirt and loose red boxers covered with green Christmas trees and white snowmen.

Eileen wanders over and draws Anna and Keith into a group hug. 'I'm so psyched, Anna. I decided just now that I hope you beat Jordan.'

Anna laughs. 'Wait, you were going to root for him?'

Eileen says, 'What can I tell you? The guy's totally hot. I'd totally do him.'

Anna nods. 'He is kind of hot, I'll give you that.'

Keith mumbles, 'He's all right-looking. But he's really short.'

Eileen says, 'Keith, he's one inch shorter than you.'

Apropos of nothing, Keith points out, 'I'm also taller than Mr Smith.'

As if summoned, Byron appears. 'Somebody call?' He puts his hand on the small of Anna's back. Eileen and Keith disengage from their collective embrace.

Eileen says, 'Anna and I were talking about how hot Jordan DeWitt is.' Anna can't tell if she's drunk, or if this is the way she is all the time. (She's not drunk. This is the way she is all the time.) 'Anna says he's hot. Keith thinks he's too short. What do you think?'

Byron checks his watch and says, 'It's eight on the nose. I think we should watch the show.' He yells across the room, 'Nora, it's time! Turn it up!' Nora cranks up the volume, and the cheesy *Sunday Sneak Attack* theme music fills the restaurant.

Anna comes off brilliantly. The camera adores her, and the way the show was edited makes her seem at once hyper-professional and hyper-cool, which surprises her. She knows she's a good chef, but she always figured she looked like a big dork while she was cooking. Anna and Jordan have a natural rapport, and she finds herself fantasizing about doing television on a regular basis, maybe her own show, maybe teaming up with Jordan, maybe cameos here and there on FoodTube. The more she thinks about it, the more fun it sounds, and she wonders if Byron could figure out a way to make that happen. Or maybe if *she* could figure out a way to make it happen herself. If Byron managed to land Anna her own show, he'd probably want her left pinky toe as a thank-you gift.

She also wonders if she has it in her to be a so-called celebrity chef. Could she be away from the Tart kitchen for more than a few days without suffering withdrawal symptoms? Could she be happy in LA – and thus away from Chicago, in her mind the finest city in the country – for a significant amount of time? How would it affect her and Byron? And what about Stinks? *What about Stinks?!*

Her reverie is broken by a huge cheer. The verdict is announced, and everybody freaks out. Keith starts up a chant: 'Ann-*nuh*! Ann-*nuh*! Ann-*nuh*!' Corrine gives the victor a bear hug. Byron plans a little kiss on her cheek. Billy roars, 'Fuck Jordan DeWitt. We beat his bitch ass! We fucking *rock*!' It's bedlam, and Anna's dazed. Keith starts up another chant: 'Speech, speech, speech!'

Eileen grabs Anna from behind, lifts her up – who knew such a skinny chick could be so strong? – plops her on the bar, and says, 'Your people are summoning you, Chef.'

'Okay, um, first off, thanks to Little Billy Fart Face for not embarrassing me on national television . . .'

'I was stoned,' Billy says. 'Wait'll next time. I'm going to get plastered and embarrass the fuck out of you.'

'Thanks, Bill. Can't wait for that. Also, thanks to Keith for his moral support.'

Keith winks and grins at her. 'Anytime, Anna.'

'And finally, thanks to Mr Smith for making it all possible. Thank you, Byron, thank you, Byron, thank you, Byron, thank you, Byron, thank you, Byron.' She feels like five thank-you-Byrons is enough for the time being. Hopefully it'll keep him from sulking.

'You're welcome, baby,' he says. 'I love you, and I'm very proud of you.'

Byron isn't given to public declarations of love, so Anna is momentarily shocked into silence. Finally, she answers, 'I love you too.' Out of the corner of her eye, she sees Keith abruptly turn away. She likes the kid a whole bunch, and she certainly feels for him, but, well, what're you going to do? Maybe they're meant to be together in another lifetime. Or in another dimension. But in this life, and on this planet, she's stuck with Byron Smith. No, wait, not 'stuck with.' Just 'with.' Right?

Right.

Jeannie says, 'You guys are soooooo cute together. Okay, now it's time for everybody to open presents. God, I love presents! Mr Smith, I'm your Secret Santa! Wait'll you see what I got you!' The hostess sounds so giddy and giggly that Anna expects to see her jump up and down and clap her hands like a three-year-old.

Everybody groans. Nora says, 'Jeannie, this is called Secret Santa for a reason.'

Jeannie says, 'Yeah. And?'

'And who's Secret Santa are you?'

'Mr Smith's.'

'Is it a secret anymore?'

'No, but . . . Oh. My bad.'

'Yeah. Your bad.'

Keith says tersely, 'Nora, chill.'

'What's your problem?' Nora asks, taken aback by Keith's distinctly un-Keith-like tone.

He erases a drop of sweat on his forehead with his

index finger, and says, 'Stuff on my mind,' pauses, then repeats, 'Stuff on my mind.' He takes a deep, seemingly nervous breath, gently grabs Jeannie's arm, pulls her toward the kitchen, and says, 'Girl, let's you and me get those presents from the back and kick it Santa-style.'

Jeannie jumps up and down, claps her hands like a three-year-old, then yells, 'Yaaaaay' right into Keith's ear.

Keith winces theatrically and says, 'I've always thought the ability to hear was overrated.'

The next fifteen minutes are a montage of torn wrapping paper, ripped-open envelopes, oohs, ahhs, laughs, groans, and eye rolls. The gifts are uniformly clever and thoughtful, and for the most part, nobody can guess who their Secret Santa is.

But that doesn't mean *you* don't have to know who got what for whom:

Jeannie buys Byron a collection of Laurel & Hardy DVDs. She thinks he needs to laugh more. She's right. He does.

Nora, knowing Miguel is a soccer fanatic, buys him a Manchester United replica jersey.

Byron buys the make-up-obsessed Anna Two a shockingly generous gift certificate to a cosmetics place called Sephora. Anna Two, who's up to her ass in student loans and hasn't been able to afford anything other than bargain-basement lipstick and mascara for the last three years, breaks down in tears.

Eileen goes over the top and buys Keith a tube of hair gel, a Miles Davis CD, and an orange T-shirt adorned with a Reese's Peanut Butter Cup logo. It's possible she still digs him, but it's also possible she still feels guilty about blowing him off. She doesn't even know herself.

Anna also goes over the top and buys Wanker a gorgeous chef's coat with his name embroidered on the breast. And much to Wanker's secret delight, it doesn't say Wanker. It says Wayne. He professes to like being called Wanker, but he's twenty-seven, and deep down, he's over it. But he doesn't want to tell anybody, because he's worried they'll think he's not down with the crew. Anna personally thinks Wanker is a stupid nickname, and her thinking is that if he has 'Wayne' written on his chest for the world to see, people will finally stop referring to the poor guy as a masturbator.

Unlike Eileen, Byron and Anna, Billy seems to have gone *under* the top, buying Jenna a huge vibrating black dildo. When she unwraps it, she says, 'Gee, I wonder who my Secret Santa was?' She then marches up to Billy and clubs him on his ass with her new toy. But to Billy's credit, he taped an overly generous Barnes & Noble gift card on to the vibrator's seemingly endless shaft.

And yes, as you probably guessed, as fate would have it, Keith draws Anna. And Keith, being a desperate, lovestruck soul, breaks the time-honored, internationally recognized, punishable-by-death Secret Santa edict: he eliminates the Secret part from the equation. (Santa himself was big-time pissed with Keith's behavior. Cupid, on the other hand, was totally cool with it.)

The only pieces of jewelry Anna ever wears to the restaurant are the diamond stud earrings Byron bought for her on their first anniversary. It's not that she doesn't like jewelry – she loves it, actually – but she's always afraid that her pretty little amethyst ring or her super-cute onyx necklace will fall off and end up in somebody's pumpkin spice soup.

Keith notices her lack of jewelry, as he notices most everything about Anna, and figures she's at the very least due for some updated ear adornment. He doesn't have a lot of money – he does more or less okay at Tart, but like Anna Two, his student loans are killing him – and is resigned to the fact that at this point in his life he'll never be able to compete with Mr Smith on a financial level. But Keith believes he has better taste than his boss, and he is proven correct with the purchase of a pair of hand-crafted dangly earrings he found at a crafts place in Lincoln Park.

Anna adores her earrings. It's jewelry love at first sight. She'll wear them to work. She'll wear them to go out. (Not that she goes out, but whatever.) Not pegging Keith for the kind of guy to have nice taste in jewelry, she has no idea who her Secret Santa is.

Until she finds this handwritten note folded up into a tiny square at the bottom of the box:

Dear Anna,
Please destroy this note the moment you finish reading it. I don't want anybody to see it. Especially Mr Smith. As a matter of fact, you probably shouldn't read this till you're alone. So go some-where else. Definitely into the kitchen. Maybe into the walk-in or something.

After surreptitiously looking around the restaurant and determining that nobody's seen her reading the note, Anna follows Keith's instructions and goes into the kitchen. She's afraid to go into the walk-in, however, because there's a distinct possibility that two or more of her staffers are making out in there (she was right to be afraid; Kirsten and Miguel, both completely topless and practically bottomless, are going at it hardcore), so she heads out into the alley.

You know I have the biggest crush on you, don't you? I've tried to keep it secret, but I'm not really good at secrets, so I guess most everybody at the restaurant knows, and since most of them have big mouths (especially Eileen!), I'm sure you know too.

I know I have no shot with you. I'm not saying that in any kind of 'woe is me' sort of way. I'm not being self-deprecating. I know I'm a good guy, and I'm maybe a little bit cute, but you should be with a guy like Mr Smith. You're a class act, and he's polished, and loaded, and suave. Class acts and polished, loaded and suave guys go together like tenderloin and lavender. (I learned about tenderloin and lavender from you, one of the many things you've taught me without even knowing you've taught me stuff.)

I once saw some movie a long time ago where the leading man was nuts about the leading lady, and it was obvious they weren't meant to be together. He sent her some note like this one, and the last line went something like, 'It's enough for me to know that you know how I feel.' I like that line a lot.

Merry Christmas, and Happy New Year's, and X's and O's, Keith

P.S. – Now please, for both of our sakes, <u>destroy this note</u>!!!

Anna doesn't destroy the note. She folds it up small and tight, and sticks it in her back pocket. It feels as if it's burning a hole in her jeans.

TRUFFLE MASHED POTATOES

Ingredients

4 lb white potatoes, peeled, cut into 1 inch pieces

1 cup half and half (half cream and half whole milk)

¼ cup butter

¼ cup olive oil

1 tablespoon white truffle oil

Salt

Pepper

3 teaspoons finely chopped black truffles

Method

1. Cook potatoes in large pot of boiling salted water until very tender, about 20 minutes.

2. Drain and return potatoes to pot.

3. Stir over medium heat till excess moisture evaporates, about 1 minute. Remove from heat. Add half and half, butter, olive oil and truffle oil and mash until smooth.

4. Season to taste with salt and pepper.

5. Stir in ⅔ of chopped truffles; once plated, sprinkle remainder on top.

6. Serve hot.

ANNA'S CHRISTMAS
GOOSE STUFFING

She'll never tell, so don't even bother asking.

Meanwhile, back at the Foodtube
Studios in Los Angeles . . .

There's sticky eggplant-colored goop *everywhere*, and the spring rolls are ruined, and Jordan, who rarely gets even a *little* pissed about minor things like sticky goop, is *really* pissed. 'Fucking hoisin[25] bowl,' the chef roars as he tries to clean his blue T-shirt with several dish towels. The sauce isn't coming out. He doesn't feel like dealing with the wardrobe department right now – they hate that he doesn't wear an apron, and take every opportunity to chastise him about it when he ruins yet another outfit – so he hopes the camera won't pick up the dark stains on the dark shirt. Alas, it does.

'CUT!' A short, balding man with a kindly face and a

[25] Hoisin: An ooey gooey Chinese dipping sauce known in China as hǎixiānjiàng. Fifty bucks to the first person who can correctly pronounce 'hǎixiānjiàng.'

walrus mustache steps out from behind the cameras. 'JD, what's the problem?'

Jordan glares at Rory Stapleton and says, '*Two* problems, O Great Director of Mine. The first problem, obviously, is that my nice spring rolls are fucked because somebody wiped down the side of this bowl of hoisin with soap, and as you might've heard, soap makes glass slippery, and when the soap isn't rinsed all the way off, the glass will *remain* slippery, and slippery things have a tendency to, y'know, *slip*, which is why there's fucking hoisin all over the studio.'

'Seriously, you suck at sarcasm, JD.' Rory turns to the crew and says, 'Okay, take five, kids.' He notices Jordan's face is bright red, which won't look particularly good on the small screen. 'No, wait,' he tells the crew, 'take ten.' He then asks Jordan, 'What's the second problem, JD?'

Jordan says, 'That you keep calling me JD.'

Rory says, 'Right. Sorry, JD.' That elicits a teeny, tiny, itsy, bitsy, no-teeth smile/smirk from the chef. Rory continues, 'I'd put money on there being a third problem.'

'You would, would you?'

'Yeah. I bet you a dollar that you talked to Nadia at some point within the past forty-eight hours.' Rory has been the director for both *Eastern Rebellion* and *DeWitt Goes DeWild* since day one, and thus has watched the Jordan/Nadia tryst (with horror) from the beginning to the end. Actually, it hasn't ended yet. And as those who have had an ugly separation from their spouse probably know, on some level, it'll never end.

Jordan says, 'I owe you a dollar, Rory. You know me so well.'

'Unfortunately, I do. Let's do a walk-and-talk.' Rory puts his arm around Jordan's shoulders and guides his star off the set, toward the studio exit, and into the parking lot. It's a lovely Los Angeles late January day – four months after the Anna Rowan episode of *Attack* that everybody up at FoodTube still raves about – and you'd have to be in an extraordinarily foul mood not to appreciate it. Jordan doesn't appreciate it. 'So what happened?' Rory asks. 'Isn't she only supposed to speak to you through the lawyer?'

'Yep.'

'So why'd you answer your phone? I thought you were screening her calls.'

'She blocked her number.'

Rory scowls. 'I truly despise that girl. If my wife hadn't have made me eliminate the C-word from my vocabulary, I'd call her a C-word.' He slaps Jordan on the back of his head. 'And you, you idiot, what're you answering blocked numbers for anyhow? Nobody who has anything good to say will block their number.'

'Yeah, I usually don't, but I had a nice date with this writer from *Bon Appetit*[26] last week, and I thought it might be her.'

---

[26] *Bon Appetit*: A stellar food magazine whose February 2007 issue featured the best recipe for macaroni & cheese in the history of mankind. And the author isn't saying that in order to get a free subscription. He means it. Sincerely. Honestly. Okay, if you want to send a free subscription, go for it.

'*Bon Appetit*, eh? Was it a date, or was she interviewing you?'

Jordan shrugs. 'Little bit of both?'

'Are you asking me, or telling me?'

'Asking, I suppose.'

'If you have to ask, it was probably an interview.'

'Shit.' Jordan smiles. 'She was taking notes. That probably should've been a dead giveaway.'

Rory laughs, then shakes his head and sighs. 'One word, JD: celibacy.'

Jordan chuckles sadly. 'You'll never understand, Rory. You're married, and you have an amazing wife who doesn't let you say the C-word, and an amazing kid, and you'll never get divorced, and you'll never have to be *out there* again.'

'Hope you're right, man. Looks like being *out there* sucks . . .'

'It does.'

'. . . but it couldn't suck more than being with Nadia.'

Rory's right. The only thing that sucks more than being with Nadia is getting all four wisdom teeth pulled without Novocain, although some would argue that the dental surgery is slightly less painful and not nearly as traumatic. Plus tooth extraction takes far less time, which is also a mitigating factor.

Nadia was a production assistant on *DeWild*, and the attraction between her and Jordan was immediate and potent. (It took months of therapy for Jordan to accept the fact that said attraction was purely physical and sexual. Not that there's anything wrong with that – you just can't build a marriage, let alone a serious relationship, around that sort of thing.) Jordan, who'd never had a relationship last longer than three months, decided far too quickly that Nadia was The One, and he proceeded to arrange what little life he had outside of the restaurant around her. They were engaged six months later, and married four months after that.

The red flags were there from the beginning. Jordan's friends saw them. Everybody at FoodTube saw them. The multitude of waiters and waitresses whom Nadia abused and then stiffed on tips saw them. Blinded by lust and what he believed to be love, Jordan ignored them.

Here are some of Nadia's more noteworthy red flags: she would never admit that she was wrong about anything; her attitude about her rightness was such that she'd throw a heavy object against the nearest wall if you disagreed with her assertion that, say, the sky wasn't blue, but rather yellow with purple polka dots.

She also had no edit button, and her favorite adjective, noun and verb was 'fuckington,' which she'd drop anytime or anyplace, regardless of the situation: over some fries at an In 'n' Out Burger, or during the intermission of a performance of the Los Angeles Ballet, or on the set of *Rebellion* while standing right next to a cadre of FoodTube executives.

She also had a proclivity toward violence – sometimes during sex, sometimes not – and she had long, strong fingernails, which meant that for the majority of their time together, Jordan's back was covered with gouge tracks. (Those blood lines never fully healed until after the couple had been separated for three months. And one of them didn't heal at all; if you look closely, you can see a six-inch-long scar in between Jordan's shoulder blades.)

The then-budding TV personality was the only person in the continental United States who didn't recognize that Nadia wasn't wife material, and it took him catching her *in flagrante delicto* with one of his line cooks – in their own bed, for God's sake – for Jordan to finally realize that Nadia Walton might not be the best possible mother to his future children. Thus began one ugly fuckington of a divorce – a divorce that still hasn't been finalized and, if Nadia has anything to say about it, never will. (She's been stalling for one reason, and one reason only: to drive Jordan nuts. Seriously, folks, she's heinous.)

Jordan's first instinct after his separation was to find a nice, calm, mellow girl to help him take his mind off Nutbag Nadia, and regain his confidence. A good-looking and basically sweet man, it wasn't long before Jordan found that somebody . . . then he found somebody else . . . then somebody else . . . then somebody else . . . and so on, and so on, and so on. He makes it clear to the zillions of women he goes out with that he can't get serious because he isn't officially divorced, *and* he travels all the time, *and* he's at Rayong Eniwa when he's not shooting a show, *and* he's afraid to open up his heart because he's worried somebody will pour acid on it. Okay, he keeps that last one to himself.

Rory checks his watch. 'Are you cooled out now? Can we go back inside and finish up?'

Jordan says, 'Yeah. Let's do it. I'll nail everything in a single take so we can all get home, cool?'

'Very cool. Go get a new shirt and get your ass back on the set.'

'Wardrobe is going to be so pissed that I ruined another shirt.'

'So wear an apron.'

'I hate aprons. They make me look fat.'

'It's a cooking show. You're supposed to look fat.'

'So you're saying that I *do* look fat in an apron?'

'Relax, JD. You look beautiful.'

'Enough with the JD already.'

And so on.

After the latest episode of *Eastern Rebellion* is in the can, Jordan wanders up to Michelle's office and slumps down on to her sofa. Michelle examines her boss up and down, then down and up, then gives him a once-over, then a twice-over, then says, 'You talked to Nadia, didn't you?'

'Jesus, is it that obvious?'

'Jordan, I can read you like a book. All I need is one look in your eyes, and I know everything. I know when you got laid. I know when you had a good night at the restaurant. I know when you're hungry, or tired, or happy, or sad.'

Jordan has never viewed himself as an open book. He has always thought that he is mysterious and enigmatic. He sits up straight and says, 'Really?'

'No. Rory called and told me you talked to her. He also told me to remind you that you owe him a dollar. What the hell are you doing answering blocked phone calls? Did you think it was that girl from *Bon Appetit* or something?'

'You *do* know me well, don't you?'

'Nah, Rory told me that, too.'

'Christ, can't a guy have any secrets?'

'Not around here.' She sits next to him on the couch and pats his knee. (It should be noted that she's touching him in a completely non-flirtatious, non-sexual manner. Two years ago, they made out in Jordan's office after a booze-filled FoodTube holiday party. They were so embarrassed that they never spoke of it again, and any touching that goes on between the two of them now is of the brotherly or sisterly variety.) 'Seriously, we're concerned about you, J-Money. And not just because you're our meal ticket.'

'You're hilarious.'

'For real, we love you. I love you. I want you to be happy. And avoiding that shrew is a certain path to happiness.'

Jordan pats her hand. 'Thanks, M-Class. I love you too. I do. And I appreciate your and Rory's concern, even if I don't ever show it.'

'You show it. You just don't realize it.' She stands up. 'There's some stuff I want to talk to you about before you go to the restaurant.'

He shakes his head. 'Unh-unh. No restaurant. I'm taking the night off. Could you call my sous chef on his cell and tell him, I don't know, tell him that I'm in a meeting with the suits that's running way late. It'll sound better than me calling him and saying, "Yo, Johnny, I know it's a Friday, and I know we have a zillion reservations on the books, and I know you're overworked enough as it is, but could you cover for me because I'm feeling weak and vulnerable?" '

'Done.' She takes a thick folder from atop her desk. 'Okay, I don't think you're going to like this . . .'

Jordan groans. 'They finally greenlighted the American version of *The Golden Chefs*, and they want me to do it. I've been dreading this day.'

'The French producers are being douchebags with the licensing, so you're safe there. *The Golden Chefs: United States* is at least three years away. No, what happened was a couple of the pilots they were planning for March tested badly, so they need some extra shows from you.'

'Fucking hell. I thought after next week, we were done until April.' Jordan enjoyed his spring hiatus. Most people wouldn't consider six weeks off a true hiatus, especially when four of those weeks are boring old February. But most people aren't Jordan DeWitt.

'I know. I tried, Jordan. I tried to get them to show reruns. I also suggested we put together some "Best Of . . ." shows. A blooper show might've been fun, too.'

Jordan doesn't care to watch himself on TV, but he especially doesn't like to see himself from seasons past – especially before he dropped the twenty pounds of baby fat and started shaving his head – so he figures that nobody else does, either. 'It's cool, I'll do some new shows. How many do they want?'

'Seven *DeWilds*, seven *Sneak Attacks*. And they need four of the *Attacks* by the end of February.'

Jordan sits up ramrod straight. 'Are you kidding me? Four *Attack*s in six weeks? Pre-production for one episode takes at least three days, but it's usually more like a week. They know that. If they need fourteen shows on the quick, tell them I'll do fourteen *Rebellion*s. I'll have them done in a month, boom. Three weeks, even. It'll save them a ton of money, too.'

'They don't care about the budget. They saved a lot of money by nixing those pilots, and they want to give it to us.'

'Is that "us" as in you and me, or "us" as in DeWitt Productions?'

'The second one. As a matter of fact, they have an interesting idea for *Attack* that's actually pretty expensive.'

'*Interesting*? I despise that adjective. I'm afraid to ask.'

'Four episodes in a single city, in a single restaurant, with a single opponent. We'll be planted in one place for a month, and we can plan the *DeWild*s at our leisure during our downtime, and maybe even shoot a couple of "on-location" episodes while we're out there.'

He scratches his chin and nods slowly. 'Hmm. Hunh. *Hunh*. That's actually not a bad idea.' He knows it'll be hard for him to be away from the restaurant for so long, but on the plus side, it might be kind of nice to get out of the city for a while, and Johnny can certainly handle things for a few weeks. At the very least, there's no chance he'll run into Nadia on the street. 'Okay. Fine. Let's do it. What's the next step?'

Michelle opens the folder, pulls out a thick manila

envelope, and drops it on to Jordan's lap. 'Well, the next step has already been taken care of. Here's your itinerary and the dossier.'

'Wait, what do you mean "taken care of"?'

'They kind of already set everything up. You're leaving on Monday.'

He cups his ear. 'Excuse me?'

'Everything's in motion. Flights are booked. Hotel rooms are reserved. The venue is solidified. Read the damn itinerary.'

Jordan stands up, tosses the unopened envelope on to Michelle's desk, and starts pacing. Her office is about as big as your average walk-in fridge, so his pacing isn't particularly fulfilling. 'What if I'd said I didn't want to do this? What if I'd said no?'

'They made it clear that "no" wouldn't be an acceptable option.'

Normally Jordan would be righteously indignant about being ordered around – head chefs, whether they run a kitchen at a dumpy Mexican joint or a three-star French house of snoot, don't take kindly to taking orders – but between Nadia, the restaurant, and the thought of the extra filming, he's too tired to fight. He slumps back down on to the sofa and says, 'Okay, fine. Where do they want me?'

'Chicago.'

He pops up again and screeches, '*Chicago*?! In *February*?! Are they out of their fucking minds? Why don't they just send me to Antarctica, or the South Pole?'

Michelle takes the envelope from her desk and throws

it at Jordan's face, which he catches out of self-defense. 'It won't be so bad. You'll get to hang out with your girlfriend.'

'What do you mean, girlfriend?'

'Open the envelope.' Her phone rings. She looks at her watch. 'This is my five o'clock phoner with the suits. Can I tell them you're good to go on this?'

'Yeah, I'm in. What do you mean, girlfriend?'

'Open the goddamn envelope.'

He opens the goddamn envelope. He reads the itinerary, then the dossier.

He smiles.

CHICKEN AND LYCHEE SPRING ROLLS WITH HOISIN-CHILI SAUCE

Ingredients
For chicken:
2 teaspoons sesame oil
8 oz chicken-thigh meat, cut into ¼ inch strips
Salt
Pepper
½ red onion, chopped
2 oz canned lychees in syrup, drained, thinly sliced
6 oz mung bean sprouts
¼ cup chopped fresh basil
¼ cup chopped fresh mint
16 rice paper rounds
8 large whole iceberg lettuce leaves

For hoisin sauce:
4 tablespoons soy sauce
2 tablespoons peanut butter or black bean paste
1 tablespoon honey or molasses or brown sugar
2 teaspoons white vinegar
⅛ teaspoon garlic powder
20 drops Chinese hot sauce, habanero or jalepeño
⅛ teaspoon black pepper

Method

1. Heat sesame oil in large heavy skillet over medium-high heat.
2. Sprinkle chicken with salt and pepper. Add chicken and onion to skillet and sauté 3 minutes. Stir in lychees. Remove form heat. Cool, then stir in bean sprouts.
3. Toss basil and mint in small bowl to combine.
4. Dip 1 rice paper round into bowl of warm water until soft, about 10 seconds. Place on clean, moist kitchen towel to drain 1 minute. Repeat with another rice paper round. Place second round atop first round for double thickness.
5. Top with a lettuce leaf, then place ⅛ of chicken and bean sprout mixture near lower edge of round.
6. Sprinkle with ⅛ of herb mixture.
7. Fold in sides of round, then roll up, starting near filling. Repeat with remaining rounds, lettuce leaves, chicken and bean sprout mixture and herb mixture.
8. Slice each roll diagonally into 4 pieces, for a total of 32 pieces.
9. Mix together ingredients for the hoisin sauce till completely combined. Pour sauce into individual shallow bowls and place in center of each of 8 plates; surround with spring rolls and serve.

Kitchen Aid

'So let me get this straight. This all starts next Sunday, yes?'

'No, I told you, the Sunday after.'

'And you just found out about it today?'

'No, it got *solidified* today. It's been in the works for about two weeks.'

'And why you didn't tell me?'

'I didn't want to say anything till it got solidified.'

It's early Monday evening (or Tuesday morning, really), and Anna and Byron are discussing Jordan DeWitt's and FoodTube's impending invasion of Tart, and have been doing so for the past hour. The communication breakdown is profound.

'I don't think it's a good idea,' Anna says.

Byron drily says, 'You've made that abundantly clear.'

'No, apparently I haven't. I mean, come on, do you, of all people, want us to be closed for four Sundays in a row?'

'For the millionth time: *We. Don't. Need. To. Close.*'

'Explain to me again how we'll keep the customers happy without a working kitchen.'

Byron speaks slowly, enunciating each syllable as if he's addressing a disobedient child. 'The bar will remain open. We will serve gourmet pizzas, including my personal favorite, and your four cheese with caramelized onions and roasted garlic. We will do a finger-food buffet. Fifteen dollars, all you can eat, and all the soft drinks you can drink. Twenty-five dollars, all you can eat and all the alcohol you can drink. Domestic beer, house wine and well[27] only, of course.'

'An all-you-can-eat buffet,' she says flatly.

'Yes. For the millionth time, yes, an all-you-can-eat buffet. What's wrong with that?'

'Byron, for the millionth time, we're not a Holiday Inn. I won't have people eating food that's being kept warm with a Bunsen burner in my restaurant.'

'It's not really your restaurant, Anna.'

'Yeah, well, it's my kitchen. It's my reputation.'

Anna and Byron (and Stinks) are huddled up in bed, buried under approximately 153 blankets, the heating system in their apartment having gone on the fritz again. Despite the tension created by their circular discussion/ argument, Anna and Byron (and Stinks) are spooning. But that's the way things have been at Chez Rowan & Smith since Christmas: sex leads to cuddling, which generally coincides with a mild blowout.

[27] Well: Bar talk for lower-end liquor. 'Premium' is the good stuff. 'Call' is the okay stuff. 'Well' sucks.

'Of course we're not a Holiday Inn,' Byron says. 'We'll give the people good food. Those pizzas of yours are terrific.'

'Yeah, but they'll come out of the oven, like, four hours before they get served. How do you intend to reheat them? Microwaves? They'll be soggy and gross.'

'They won't be soggy or gross. And even if they are, it'll still be better than the crap you like to order in from Art of Pizza.'

'Art of Pizza *rules*. But a bad night at the pizza joint doesn't mean a damn thing to your average pizza cook. A bad night for me is a bad night for *us*. Think about that.'

'Listen, don't worry. I'll make it work. *We'll* make it work. I want you to do this. It'll be huge.'

Byron's right: it *will* be huge. Anna's episode of *Sunday Sneak Attack* has been rerun almost two dozen times since its initial Christmas airing. That's not unprecedented, as FoodTube is all about reruns; however, the reruns in this case aren't about filling time slots, but, rather fulfilling the requests of the masses. Michelle Fields told Byron that she's received more emails about Anna than any previous *Attack* contestant. Women viewers like Anna because she's cool, calm and funny under pressure. Male viewers like her because she's cool, calm and funny under pressure . . . and she's really sexy, even when she's wearing a bandanna and a shapeless chef's jacket. But according to Michelle, what blew away the FoodTube programming department was that the general consensus amongst viewers of all demographics is Anna's energy seems to have turned Jordan into the best Jordan he can be.

Byron reiterates all this to Anna, who, after hearing it

for the fourth time, seems to have finally taken it to heart. 'They really think I made DeWitt look better?' she asks.

'Yup.'

'And they think I'm cool and calm?'

'Mmm hmm.'

'And people think I'm sexy?'

'The guys do.'

'Do you?'

Byron smirks. 'Most of the time, I suppose.' He's joking, of course. At least Anna hopes he is. She wants him to think she's sexy *all* the time. She can't be sure he's kidding, though. With Byron these days, she's not sure about a lot of things.

'Hunh. How about that.' If Byron had told her about the reaction to her television work while she was in her kitchen at Tart, she would've thought, *Damn right I'm cool, and calm, and funny and cute*. But he told her while they were in their cold apartment, hiding in bed, far away from the restaurant, and right here, right now, it's hard for her to believe. Right here, right now, without pots, or pans, or knives, or a bunch of respectful line cooks to prop up her ego (no, not ego, let's be honest here, we're talking more about self-esteem), she's doesn't feel the least bit cool, she's definitely not calm, her funny bone is on vacation, and being cute is the last thing on her mind.

Anna concludes that the *Attack* thing with Chef DeWitt is going to happen, no matter how much she protests, so she may as well make the best of it. She tells Byron, 'Fine. You win. I'm going to take a hot shower. I'm freezing.' She takes a deep breath, counts, 'One . . . two

. . . *three*!', then springs out from under the covers, sprints to the bathroom, cranks the water temperature as high as it can go, and cowers in the corner of the tub, waiting for the hot water heater to kick in.

Okay, first things first, she thinks as the icicles melt away from her chin, *write a menu for this all-you-can-eat disaster. Maybe I'll make mushrooms stuffed with crabmeat, and maybe I'll make rigatoni tossed with grape tomatoes and buffalo mozzarella, and maybe I'll make . . .*

Wait, maybe I'll make Billy write the menu.

She generally doesn't feel comfortable regularly giving Billy too much responsibility. (Knowing what you know about him, would you?) It's fine for him to come up with specials once in a while – sometimes he even concocts something quite good – and she's okay leaving him in charge of the kitchen for one night a week – she definitely doesn't like giving it to him two nights in a row, because, well, it's Billy and you never know – but she doesn't particularly want him writing Tart's menus. He's a talented cook, but to Anna's mind, he simply doesn't have the chops to handle it – at least not right now. The potential is there. She just hasn't figured out how to tap into it.

Back when he first started at Tart, back in his pre-scumbag fart face days, Billy wrote menus just for the fun of it. To Anna, they were perfectly fine, if a tad pedestrian and pretentious, with lots of pointless foams[28] and need-

---

[28] Foam: Molecular gastronomy-speak for a bubbly version of things that normally aren't bubbly, e.g., banana or red bean.

lessly complicated reductions[29] and too little substance; not what Tart was about. She tried to be gentle with him whenever she told him she couldn't use any of his work – which happened every time he presented her with his latest list of concoctions – so he quit showing her his stuff. Neither of them ever discuss it, but it was around the time Billy stopped writing menus that he started dropping mangos on the floor, and winging crème brûlée at one or both of the Annas.

Coincidence? Probably not.

But now, with the FoodTube invasion looming, it's time to delegate, because for the next four weeks, her time will be better spent coming up with dishes that'll blow away Jordan DeWitt and Eric McLanahan than it would figuring out how to please the suburbanites who'll come to the restaurant on these Sundays just to get a glimpse of the TV star.

The following morning, Anna calls Billy into her office in the basement of the restaurant and gives him his to-do list. The sous chef is less than thrilled. 'An all-you-can-eat menu?' he groans.

'Think of it as a challenge. It's a puzzle. Really, it'll probably be fun,' she says, hoping her tone of voice doesn't betray her unbelievable lack of enthusiasm.

'You don't sound particularly enthusiastic about the whole thing,' Billy says. Sure enough, Anna's tone of voice betrays her unbelievable lack of enthusiasm. 'If it'll be fun,

[29] Reduction: Boiling the hell out of something until it's, um, reduced.

why don't you do it? It's your kitchen. You do everything that's fun around here anyhow.'

'Billy, don't be such a whiner. It's unbecoming.' She takes a different tack. 'Didn't you like being on TV? Didn't it help you hook up with that girl in that band you like?'

Billy tries unsuccessfully to quash a grin. 'I guess.' Is he blushing?

Anna pinches Billy's cheek and says in a baby voice, 'Awwww, wook at wittle Billy-Willy smiling. Billy-Willy *wuvs* being on television.' He slaps her hand away. She continues, 'If there wasn't television involved, you wouldn't have to do this, so think of it as a trade-off. Write a buffet menu, be on TV. Good deal, I'd say.' She puts her arm around his shoulder, no easy task, as he's six-plus inches taller than she is. 'Are we okay?'

'Yeah, we're okay.'

'Okay. Please get me the first menu by next Wednesday so we can order everything. And have some fun with it. And try and keep the costs down. And I promise I won't edit.'

Billy again attempts to hide a smile, again to no avail. 'Yes, Chef. Thank you, Chef.' Then he gives her a tiny kiss on the cheek and practically scampers off.

Anna thinks, *He called me Chef, and he kissed me. Weird.*

But that's just the beginning of the weird.

'Yo, Anna, you see what's going on out front, or have you been down here all day?'

Anna spins around and is greeted by the sight of Keith bundled up in the puffiest of puffy jackets, his hood covering his faux-hawk, as well as seventy-five per cent of his face. 'Hey, Keith. I have indeed been down here all day. What's up?' Even after his note, Anna has done her best to keep things with Keith on a professional level. Sometimes it's easy, but sometimes – like now, when he's looking all cute, and pink, and wintery, and when Byron is being a less-than-ideal mate – not so much. She still feels guilty about thinking of Keith in That Way, but the mind, and the heart and the libido will go where the mind, and heart and libido go. Anna can't help it. For that matter, *nobody* can help it, so can you blame her?

'The Channel 5 news van is right out front,' Keith says. 'The Channel 7 news van is down the block. And the Channel 2 news van is, I think, trying to find a parking spot. What happened, did Miguel get busted for growing bud in his basement or something?'

Anna tries unsuccessfully not to laugh at the thought of straight-edge Miguel selling weed. (Little does she know.) 'Well, he hasn't called me and asked for bail money, so probably not.' Keith starts to take off his jacket. 'No, wait,' Anna says, 'why don't you go outside and ask one of the news people what's going on?'

He zips his coat right back up. 'Done and done.' As Anna watches him bound up the stairs, she thinks, *That boy would do everything for me. Byron gets me on TV, but only because it's good for the restaurant. Which begs the question, do I want a boy who would do anything for me? Like all of my old boyfriends.*

It's impossible to understand the verbal tone of somebody's thoughts, being that they're not verbalized, so there's no way that you, as a reader, could tell that Anna here is being sarcastic. But she most definitely is, and sarcasm is in order here, because when it comes to her old boyfriends, Anna was happy if they did *anything* for her, let alone *everything*. Most of them did *nothing*.

Like her first high school boyfriend Derek, a very hot but very dumb lacrosse player who made her feel good because, well, because he was hot, and he always told her he thought she was hot, plus he'd always do nice stuff for her like, um, hmmm, er, um, okay, he barely ever did any nice stuff for her, except ram his tongue down her throat in the hallway in between classes, which, when you get right down to it, isn't particularly nice. Not the best boy in the world to have lost her virginity to, but what did she know?

Or like her second high school boyfriend Curt, a cute-in-a-geeky-way, super-smart violin prodigy who was so wrapped up in Brahms, Tchaikovsky and Philip Glass that she was lucky if he remembered to pick her up for their standing Saturday-night date. And he wouldn't sleep with her. He said he wanted to wait. She didn't. So she shut him down.

Or like the guy she dated in culinary school, you remember him, Stuart, the breads and pastries professor who was eleven years older than she was . . . okay, he was really fifteen years older . . . no, let's be honest here, twenty years older. And married. She didn't know he was hitched, because A) he'd never mentioned it, and B) he never wore his wedding ring to class, for fear it would fall off and end up inside a rosemary and Parmesan focaccia[30] (or so he claimed). The jig was up one day when she was alone in his office, and his cell rang, and she looked at the caller ID display, which said, *The Wife*. B'bye, Stuart.

Or like Byron Smith.

Sure, Byron does stuff for her – gives her presents and flowers, takes the trash fifty per cent of the time at home, rubs her feet two or three times a month, tolerates pizza night, and, of course, gets her on FoodTube – but it seems like his heart isn't in it these days. It feels to Anna like he's going through the motions, doing what he thinks a boyfriend is supposed to.

But then again, she could be reading into it, or projecting negatives on to him because ... because ... because ...

Because she's unhappy with him? Could that possibly be it? Could it?

After putting up with chumps like Derek, Curt and Stuart, why would Anna Rowan be unhappy with Byron Smith? He's smart, sexy, polished, cute, and all those other adjectives that anybody in their right mind would want out of a live-in lover. So what's the problem? Why hasn't she been feeling those warm fuzzies lately? Why is she watching Keith's butt as he clomps up the stairs? And why is she asking herself so many damn questions?

---

[30] Focaccia: An Italian flatbread that, when given the opportunity, the author of this book has a tendency to eat far too much of.

As Anna puts together her meat and poultry order for the week, she makes a mental list of the possible causes for her seeming discontent:

Has familiarity bred contempt? Maybe. This is by far the longest she's been with one guy, and she's heard rumors to the effect that in some cases, the magic can fade a bit with time, and you have to keep working at your relationship to keep it fresh. To her thinking, she shouldn't have to work *that* hard, especially since she's so busy working at work that the last thing she wants to do when she gets home is work some more.

Have she and Byron grown apart? That one's kind of doubtful, primarily because they're both so busy at the restaurant that neither has done any growing in any direction whatsoever.

Have they simply fallen out of love? She knows that's a no, at least on her end. She still loves him. He still turns her on. She still admires him for his good qualities and tolerates his bad ones. All of which begs the question . . .

Does *he* still love *her*? If she's completely honest with herself, she can't say for sure one way or the other. He tells her he loves her at least twice a day, but is he just saying it out of habit? Or is he trying to convince himself? Or does he want to move on, but is afraid to end the relationship, because he's concerned she'll quit the restaurant? Or is he scared to move forward – i.e. get married – and is afraid to ask for fear she'll say no? Or are his heart and head so wrapped up in Tart that he has nothing left to give her? (There's also the possibility that maybe everything's fine on his end, and she's reading into . . . *something*. But if she's reading into something, she's not sure what she's reading into, because it's possible there's nothing to read into, and that she's being paranoid or something. Does that make sense? Probably not. But that's sometimes what it's like to be stuck in Anna Rowan's pretty little head.)

Her cell vibrates. It's Byron. 'Hey, could you come into the dining room? I've got all the TV news outlets here. We're going to do a press conference thing. They want to talk to you.'

'What? Me? Why?'

'Apparently this FoodTube thing is a bigger deal than we thought. They want to do a local-girl-makes-good kind of story. And slap some make-up on, okay? I don't want you looking pasty for the cameras. Oh, and take off your chef's coat and throw on a Tart T-shirt. One of the baby doll ones. Show off your cute little belly button.'

She smiles. 'You got it,' she says. Byron loves her belly button. Hell, Byron loves her. She *is* reading into one thing or another. It's all good. She supposes. 'And I'll put on one of the extra-small ones. And I'm not wearing a bra, so I'm sure the boys out in TV land will like that.'

'No bra? Hunh. Maybe don't wear the extra-small. We don't want you to look slutty.'

'Excuse me? Slutty?' Anna never looks slutty. But now that the idea is out there, maybe now's a good time to start. Maybe Byron would like slutty.

'Okay, maybe slutty wasn't the right word. We want you to look classy.'

'What, my boobs aren't classy? Can't I be classy and slutty at the same time?'

'Your boobs are very classy, my dear. But this is basic cable. Save the nipples for pay-per-view.'

Anna laughs. 'Fine. I'll wear an extra-large. Nobody'll see nothin'.'

'No, we want people to see a little something. Wear a small. Or maybe a medium. No, go with small.'

'Honey, you're a marketing genius.'

'Right. And don't forget to put on make-up.' Then he hangs up.

After she beautifies herself – and she does end up looking lovely, despite the truncated beautification session and the baggy houndstooth chef's pants – Anna goes upstairs two steps at a time and bolts through the kitchen. She's met right outside the kitchen door by three handheld cameras, a trio of field reporters with microphones, Byron and Keith. The remainder of the Tart lunch crew stand at a respectful distance, save for Eileen, who desperately wants to get on-camera, and can't figure out for the life of her how to make it happen without actually looking desperate.

The cameras fire up. The spotlights momentarily blind Anna. All three newsies stick their microphones in her face. One asks, 'Anna, how does it feel to be the first chef that Jordan DeWitt wants to compete against on consecutive weeks?'

Anna is momentarily flustered. Talking about cooking on TV is one thing. Talking about feelings is an entirely different prospect. 'Um. Um. Um.' Byron waves his index finger in a circle, as if to say, *Get a move on.* Keith gives her one of his patented ear-to-ear grins. She takes a deep breath and says, 'It feels great.' That's it. Just 'It feels great.' Her brain comes to a screeching halt. She can't think of anything else. Wait, she can think of one other thing: *I am such a dork.*

The reporters wait for a couple moments, assuming Anna will come up with something more interesting. She doesn't. So another of the reporters clears her throat and asks, 'Do you have any ideas what you're going to cook? What kind of cuisine are we looking at here?'

Ah, a food question. Much easier to handle than an emotions question, and way more fun. 'Well, the last time Chef DeWitt and I got together, I went Italian, and as we all know, I wiped the floor with him.' Everybody laughs. 'I've always thought of myself as a good sport, so I'll give him another crack at Italian, but this time I'll focus on Southern Italy, you know, more pastas and pizzas. Of course at some point we'll have to do something Asian, because I'd like to fight him on his own battlefield. I'm not a sushi chef, but if I have to make some killer maki[31] to bring home another victory for Chicago, I'll do it. And that's all I'm willing to divulge at this moment.' She sticks out her chest, cocks her head, and bats her eyelashes coquettishly. 'After all, a girl has to have some surprises.'

---

[31] Maki: A sushi roll that can be as simple as tuna and avocado, and, in extreme cases, as complex as tuna, avocado, salmon roe, crab stick, cucumber, scallions, hamburgers, French fries, apple pies and a car engine. But that's only in extreme cases.

Then she looks directly into the center camera and winks.

The reporters and cameramen chuckle again. She hears some light applause. She cranes her neck to find the source of the clapping; naturally, Keith is leading the charge. Anna also sees Eileen pump her fist in the air and yell, 'You go, girl!' One of the cameramen spins around and points his lens at Eileen, who gives the camera a wink, a far more lascivious one than Anna's. The cameraman reaches behind him, taps his partner on the shoulder, and says, 'Let's talk to her when we're done with the chef.'

The reporter nods, then turns back to Anna and asks, 'Anything you'd like to say to Jordan?'

Anna says, 'You bet there is.' She leans forward and sticks her face directly into the center camera and whispers, 'I'm right here for you, Chef DeWitt. I'm waiting. Come and get me.'

The cameramen on the right and left simultaneously say, 'Can you do that into my camera?' A burgeoning ham, Anna complies, after which all three reporters offer up their version of thanks-for-your-time-and-good-luck-against-Jordan.

As the reporters get ready to leave, Byron says, 'Hey, wait a minute, don't any of you want to ask her something about the restaurant?'

One of the newsies gestures at his fellow newsies and says, 'I don't know about them, but I'll be talking about the place during my intro.' The other two reporters nod in agreement.

Byron says, 'Do you have anything you want to ask me?'

Another one of the reporters says, 'No, thanks. But I do want to talk to that cute frizzy-haired chick. Where'd she go?'

Eileen raises her hand in the air and says, 'Right here, baby.'

As the reporter ushers her to the bar, Byron calls out, 'Don't say anything stupid, Eileen!'

Anna smacks him on the bicep and says, 'Be nice.'

Eileen calls back, 'Don't worry, Mr Smith! I won't embarrass you! Much!'

Byron mumbles, 'God, I wish Nora was here today. Or Jenna. Or anybody else but Eileen.'

Anna says, 'Byron, stop it.'

Byron says, 'At least Jeannie is late. As usual.'

'Jeez, who peed in your orange juice, Mr Sunshine? We're getting tons of free publicity here. It's like your dream come true. I'd think you'd be sipping yourself a celebratory glass of pinot by now.'

'Listen, this is the first time we've been on the news. This is a big deal. If Eileen starts ditzing out on camera, we'll look like amateurs. This kind of thing doesn't happen at Moto.' Moto is a local house of molecular gastronomy beloved by most science-minded Chicago foodies.

'Byron, the last time we went to Moto, our server had a pierced septum and purple hair.'

'Yeah, but there weren't three cameras following her around. If Eileen gets weird, they might put her on TV, and people are going to see that. We have to come off as professional.'

'Oh, like me wearing a middy T-shirt is particularly professional?'

'That's different.'

'How?'

He sighs. 'Trust me, it just is.'

'Explain to me how. Apparently I'm too unprofessional to understand.' Remember right before the news crews showed up? When Anna was thinking about how much Byron loves her, and all the problems in their relationship were relatively minor? Well, right now, what with Byron acting all superior, and distant, and attitudinal, she's having second thoughts.

'Anna, you're the face of the restaurant . . .'

'Okay.'

'. . . and you're our star . . .'

'Thanks.'

'. . . and you're pretty much the only attractive female head chef in the city . . .'

'Thank you again.'

'. . . and you're a great commodity . . .'

'Tha— Whoa, hold on a second. Did you just say I'm a commodity?'

'No. I said a *great* commodity.'

'What the hell is that supposed to mean?!'

The wait staff stare at their boss and their chef. Byron points to the cameramen, all of whom are fortunately packing up their gear, and hisses 'Lower your voice.'

She repeats, *'What the hell is that supposed to mean?!'* She doesn't lower her voice. As a matter of fact, she raises it. A lot. The line cooks gawk.

'Let's take this downstairs,' Byron says.

'No, let's not. I'd love for my crew to hear this.' She stomps into the kitchen – Byron at her heels – and asks her cookies, 'Hey, guys, Mr Smith here tells me I'm a commodity. Do you agree?'

After an uncomfortable moment of silence, Wanker asks Byron, 'Dude, did you seriously call your girlfriend a commodity? Yo, that's fucked up.'

'It's not *dude*, Wanker,' Byron says icily. 'It's Mr Smith.'

He mumbles, 'It's messed up, is what it is.'

Byron turns to Anna. 'Can we please discuss this in private?'

'No. We can't.' She walks over to Anna Two at the salad station. 'Sweetie, what would you do if some guy you were dating said you were a commodity? Oh, and what if immediately before, he told you how attractive you are? Now bear in mind he didn't say you were beautiful, or pretty, or gorgeous. He said *attractive*.'

Anna Two says to Byron, 'You called her an attractive commodity?' Byron doesn't answer. 'That's not very romantic,' Anna Two says.

'Understatement of the year,' Wanker mumbles.

Anna asks Byron, 'Is that really how you look at me? And be honest. I can take it. Am I an attractive commodity? Am I your trophy chef?'

Byron says, 'Of course I don't look at you like that.'

'Then why did you say it? You practically never say anything without thinking about it first. You had to mean it on some level.'

'Okay, truth be told, I suppose I *did* mean it on some

level. But is it so awful I want to put the best face forward for the restaurant? It doesn't mean I don't love you.'

Wanker says, 'Too late to be romantic, dude.' Byron glares at him. 'Oops, sorry. *Mr Smith*.'

And who should walk in right at that moment? You guessed it. Keith. The kitchen becomes silent. Keith clears his throat. 'Um, hey, we were all wondering what's up with the family meal?'[32]

'We're a little behind on that, dude,' Wanker says. 'But you grab a chair and park yourself.' He gestures toward Anna and Byron. 'You'll enjoy this.'

Anna reaches into her pocket, pulls out three twenty-dollar bills, hands them to Keith, and says, 'We're not cooking a family meal today. Go to Wiener Circle and get hot dogs for everybody. Thank you.' She just wants him out of the kitchen. She doesn't mind if her line cooks see the Rowan/Smith battle, but she doesn't want to subject Keith to it. It would probably end up making things weirder between her and the server.

Keith nods. 'Cool. Thanks.' He turns to go, then turns back around. 'You okay, Anna?'

Right now, she wants nothing more than to walk with Keith to Wiener Circle and vent about the Byron situation. Keith's an attentive, sympathetic listener, plus he wouldn't judge her. Sometimes when you hang out with a person who likes everything you say, and think, and do, it can be overbearing and uncomfortable – being

---

[32] Family meal: The staff lunch or dinner, which more often than not features a less-than-prime cut of random animals.

worshipped is flat-out strange – but right now, that's exactly what Anna needs: unmitigated support from somebody who unequivocally, unconditionally likes her, and doesn't think of her as an attractive commodity, but rather an accomplished, kind, funny, intelligent woman.

But she doesn't go. Curse her and her guilty conscience. 'I'll be fine, Keith,' she says. 'Don't worry. Get us lunch.'

Keith looks at Byron, but addresses Anna. 'You sure?'

'I'm sure. Get out of here.' He gets out of here. She points at Byron. 'We're done.'

Byron pales. 'Excuse me? You're breaking up with me?'

She rolls her eyes. 'No, I'm not breaking up with you. We're done here. We're not done forever. We're done for right now. This conversation is over. The *commodity* has to go to work. The *commodity* has to order meats for the restaurant. The *commodity* has to prepare for her television appearance on Sunday.'

'Christ, enough with the *commodity* shit already. You made your point. I'm sorry.'

'That is one crap apology, dude,' Wanker says.

Anna says, 'Wanker, get to work. Byron, get out of my kitchen. Matter of fact, stay out of my sight. We'll talk about this at home.' She tells her line, 'Guys, I'll be back in half an hour. I want this place looking immaculate. And send Billy downstairs when he shows up.' Then she goes down to her office without looking back.

Wanker tells Byron, 'Dude, when a chick tells you you'll talk about something when you get home, you're totally fucked.'

Byron sighs. 'That's the first thing you've ever said that I agree with, Wanker.' He trudges out the kitchen door and walks smack into Keith. 'Didn't Chef Rowan tell you to get hot dogs?' he asks.

Keith says, 'Yes. *Anna* did.'

'Right. Anna. So go.'

'I will. In a minute.' Then he bulls past Byron, through the kitchen, and down the stairs to the basement.

Anna isn't crying. She refuses to cry in public, and especially at the restaurant. If she was home alone, forget it, she'd be a waterfall-eyed disaster, but right now, she has to hold it together. She has to make it through the day without melting down, if only for her own self-respect. She's pretty sure she'll be okay, because it looks like it'll be an easy day: there are only eight dinner reservations on the books, plus it's bitter cold outside, and it's Tuesday, so it'll likely be a slow but steady dinner service. She has some lovely Chilean sea bass on the way from her fishmonger, so she doesn't need to dress it up for the special; cooking it in a lemon and thyme oil will be all that's necessary. If it's possible, maybe she'll even cut out after the early rush. Billy's been a good boy lately, so she feels relatively comfortable leaving him alone.

The door knocks. *Speak of the devil*, she thinks, *it's my devil sous chef himself*. She stands up and calls out, 'Good news, Fart Face. I'm leaving you in charge of the kitchen for most of the night.' She opens the door, and there's Keith.

'Really?' he asks. 'I've been working on this awesome toast dish. It's got butter, and jelly, and sometimes I don't even burn it.' Anna laughs despite herself. 'So are you okay?'

'Been better.'

Keith gently closes the door and gives her a look that makes it clear he's thinking about her in That Way right this very second. 'I'm sorry, Anna.'

'You have nothing to be sorry about,' she says.

'No, I'm not apologizing or anything. I'm just saying I feel bad for you. I wish there was something I could do.'

She sighs and rubs her temples. 'Me too, Keith.'

And then, out of nowhere and much to their mutual surprise, he steps forward, takes her hands, lifts her from her chair, and pulls her into an embrace. It's not a sensual hug – it's meant to comfort – although there's a bit of sensuality involved in that their chests are crushed up against one another. Both are mindful, however, to keep their legs from touching, Keith because he's afraid if he feels Anna's thighs against his, his brain will explode, and Anna because she's afraid that if she feels Keith's thighs against hers and it feels good, she'll give him a little kiss on the cheek, which he might want to turn into a big kiss on the mouth, and if he does it and it feels good, well, she doesn't even want to think about it.

A solid minute into the hug – and a one-minute hug is damn long, and if you don't believe that, grab your stopwatch and your sweetie and get hugging – the door bursts open. 'Hey, dumbass, if you're going to maul the chef, do your mauling in the walk-in like everybody else in this dump.'

Anna squirms out of Keith's arms and checks her

watch. 'Billy, can't you get here on time?' One problem: she's not wearing a watch.

'Check the clock, baby. I am *totally* on time.' He gives Keith a playful (but still relatively hard) open-handed smack on the back of his head. 'Looks like I got here *just* in time, right, dumbass?' He gives Anna's chest a good, hard stare. 'Nice T-shirt, Chef.'

Anna smacks Billy on the back of his head. 'Can you handle the late dinner rush by yourself tonight, *dumbass*?'

'I can handle early, late, and everything in between.'

She nods her head thoughtfully. 'Keith, call Corinne or somebody to come in and cover for you. You and I are playing hooky. You pick the movie, I'll pick the restaurant. Sound good?'

Keith opens his mouth, then closes it, then opens it, then closes it, then Billy again smacks him on the head. 'Chef just asked you on a date, dumbass . . .'

'It's not a date,' she tells Billy. Then she turns to Keith. 'Seriously. It's not a date.'

'. . . and if you don't say yes,' Billy continues, 'I swear to God I'll punch you in your neck.'

In what will ultimately be the easiest decision he'll ever have to make for the remainder of his life, Keith says yes.

FOUR CHEESE PIZZA WITH CARAMELIZED ONIONS AND ROASTED GARLIC

Ingredients

For the dough:

¾ cup warm water (105°F–115°F)

1 envelope active dry yeast

3 tablespoons olive oil

2 cups (or more) all-purpose flour

1 teaspoon sugar

¾ teaspoon salt

For the topping:

1 large head of garlic

Olive oil

1 large Vidalia onion, sliced

1 teaspoon sugar

½ cup of fontina cheese, shredded

½ cup of goat's cheese, crumbled

½ cup of mozzarella cheese, shredded

½ cup of sharp white cheddar cheese, shredded

Salt

Pepper

Method

1. Pour ¾ cup warm water into small bowl. Stir in yeast. Let stand till yeast dissolves, about 5 minutes.
2. Brush large bowl lightly with olive oil.
3. Mix 2 cups flour, sugar and salt in food processor.
4. Add yeast mixture and 3 tablespoons oil; process until dough forms a sticky ball.
5. Transfer to lightly floured surface.
6. Knead dough until smooth, adding more flour by tablespoonfuls if dough is very sticky, about 1 minute.
7. Transfer to prepared bowl; turn dough in bowl to coat with oil.
8. Cover bowl with plastic wrap and let dough rise in warm draft-free area until doubled in volume, about 1 hour.
9. Place dough on lightly floured surface. Punch down dough.
10. Starting from center, roll out dough to fit into greased 18 x 13 x 1 inch sheet pan.
11. Preheat oven to 425°F.
12. Chop off top of garlic, approximately ¼ inch. Coat with olive oil. Wrap with foil and place in oven for 45 minutes.
13. Coat pan with olive oil. Add onion and sugar. Sauté on low heat for 30 minutes, or until brown, stirring often.
14. Squeeze garlic into small bowl. Stir into paste. Spread on to dough.
15. Add onion on to dough, followed by cheeses, salt and pepper to taste.
16. Raise oven temperature to 450°F. Place pizza in oven and bake for 10 minutes, or till top is golden brown.

KEITH'S AWESOME TOAST DISH

Ingredients
2 pieces of bread
2 small pats of butter
1 teaspoon of grape jelly (optional)

Method
1. Place bread in toaster.
2. Toast bread until it reaches desired level of toastiness.
3. Take bread out of toaster.
4. Place butter on toast. Spread evenly.
5. Place jelly on butter. Spread evenly.
6. Cut into quarters or halves. Serve warm.

A Month of Sundays

Jordan coughs once, then says, 'I think I have pneumonia.'

Michelle rolls her eyes. 'You don't have pneumonia.'

'Seriously, there's this tickle in the back of my throat. And I had a coughing attack when I woke up. I *never* get coughing attacks.'

'In DeWitt Land, how many coughs constitute an attack?'

'I don't know. Five, maybe? We should find me a doctor, don't you think?'

'You want to know what I think? I think you're a big California pussy.'

Jordan laughs. 'Did you just call me a pussy?'

'No,' Michelle says, 'I called you a big California pussy. There's a difference.'

'And the difference is?'

Michelle claps him on his shoulder. 'If you have to ask, pussy boy, you'll never know.'

Jordan glances out the window of his overpriced, but super-cool room at the Trump International Hotel & Tower just off Michigan Avenue in Chicago, and glares at the flurries. Chicagoans would view this miniscule bit of snow as a mild annoyance; the big California pussy, however, views it as a blizzard.

'Can't we go location scouting tomorrow?' he whines. The FoodTube honchos love Michelle's idea about shooting two episodes of *DeWitt Goes DeWild* while they're in the Windy City, so much so that they asked her to both produce and direct them. Jordan, Michelle, Eric, et al are ready to roll for the first of the four installments of *Sunday Sneak Attack: Chicago*, so Michelle wants to track down locales for the *DeWilds* in their free time, of which it looks like there will be plenty. For his part, Jordan wants to grab his laptop, curl up into bed, go online, and find the finest restaurant in Chicago that will deliver to the Trump.

Michelle says, 'I'm happy to do it myself, but if you complain about the places I pick to shoot at, I'm quitting.'

'Yikes. Somebody's in a dramatic mood today.'

'*I'm* dramatic? It gets, like, two degrees below freezing, and you think we're in the Arctic Circle.'

'Okay, fine,' Jordan says. 'You've shamed me into actually leaving the room and going outside.' He takes a deep breath, then dons his hoodie, his ski cap, his parka, his mukluks, his scarf, another ski cap, another hoodie, another parka, another scarf, and a strap-on space heater. 'Okay, I'm ready. Let's boogie.'

'Boogie where?' Michelle asks.

'Lunch, then location scouting. But if my pneumonia gets worse, I'm kissing you till I load you up with germs and you get sick.'

'It won't take much of your kissing to get me sick, Jordan.'

Jordan shakes his head and sighs. 'This is going to be a long month.'

'Tell me about it.' In the elevator, Michelle asks, 'So where do you want to eat?'

'Someplace where the heating system works.'

'Pussy. Let's see the city. Let's have some pizza. When in Chicago, do like the Romans. Or something like that.'

'Works for me.' In the lobby, Jordan asks the oh-so-smooth concierge where to get the perfect Chicago thick-crust pie. The concierge writes out a list of seven places. 'Did you put these in any order?' Jordan asks.

'No, sir. They're all excellent.'

Jordan looks out the front window. Still flurrying. 'Which one's closest?' he asks.

Michelle says, 'Jordan, there are taxis waiting two yards from the door. Pick one of the places, then we'll hop a cab, and it'll be like you never even set foot outside.' She turns to the concierge, cocks a thumb at Jordan, and says, 'Isn't he a pussy?'

The concierge shrugs. 'I wouldn't know, ma'am. And even if I did, I wouldn't say, because I'm hoping that before Chef DeWitt concludes his stay with us, he'll pose for a picture with my mother.'

Jordan tightens his scarf around his neck. 'Bring her by anytime . . .' He squints at the concierge's nametag.

'. . . Fred.' He straightens his hat, takes a deep breath, and says, 'Okay, M-Class. Let's do this.'

He trudges toward the door, looking like a man taking his final walk down The Green Mile. Michelle stage whispers to Fred, 'What a pussy.'

Without turning around, Jordan says, 'I heard that.'

Thirty minutes later, Jordan and Michelle are seated at a four-top[33] in the window of a joint in the Lakeview area of the city called Art of Pizza. (And with its mismatched tables and chairs, its cruddy TV mounted on the back wall, and the Chicago sports memorabilia hanging on the walls, it's a total 'joint.' Not a 'place.' Not a 'restaurant.' A *joint.*) It's one of those joints where the kitchen is situated so that it's viewable by the general public, a major selling point for curious pizza freaks like Jordan and Michelle.

Jordan peers at a sign above the front counter. 'It says it takes forty-five minutes for a stuffed pizza. Are they serious with that? Frigging Mario Batali isn't even that slow.' He grabs a menu from the front counter. 'I'm ordering a Caesar to tide me over.'

'Maybe they'll have those herbed flatbread croutons you made that time on *DeWild*. Love those.'

'You're kidding, right?'

She gestures at the line cooks twirling the pizza dough. 'You never know. Those guys look stellar. They might watch FoodTube.'

'Yeah, right. Place like this, the croutons come straight

[33] Four-top: A table that seats four people. An eight-top would seat eight people. A zillion-top would seat a zillion people. You get the picture.

out of the box. But I've got to get something in my stomach, or . . .'

Michelle says, 'Jesus, will you stop kvetching already? I know you're out of your comfort zone here, but relax.' She reaches across the table and takes both his hands in both of hers. 'Listen, I know you miss LA, but this month will be really fun if you want it to be.'

As he squeezes her hands, it dawns on Jordan that he is indeed homesick. *Really* homesick. He misses his house, his restaurant, his co-workers, the FoodTube studio crew, and, of course, the sun. 'Maybe I should just focus on the fact that I'm about seven hundred miles away from Nadia.'

'Which means that *I'm* also seven hundred miles away from Nadia. Awesome.' Michelle leans forward and gives Jordan a comforting kiss on his cheek. 'Don't worry, J-Money. You'll be fine. I'll take care of you.'

Jordan hears a female voice call from across the empty restaurant, 'Kissing in public, Chef DeWitt? You can't afford a hotel?'

He drops Michelle's hands and tells her, 'I thought Chicagoans were supposed to be polite.' He half turns around and yells, 'Mind your own damn business over there!' Michelle then bursts out laughing. 'What's so funny?'

Michelle points over his shoulder. 'Check it out.'

Jordan checks it out. 'Well. Fancy meeting you here, Chef Rowan.'

Anna sidles over to their table, leans down, and gives Jordan a polite peck on the forehead. 'Welcome back to

Chicago, Chef DeWitt. Hey, Michelle. Nice to see you.' She gestures at Michelle's black-and-gray V-neck Calvin Klein men's long sleeve T-shirt and says, 'Cute top.'

Michelle smiles. 'Hey, Anna. Nice to see you, too.' She stands up, gives Anna a hug, and fingers the collar of her black, fur-trimmed Michael Kors winter coat. 'Your jacket is off the hook.' She motions at the tall young man standing behind Anna. 'Who's your friend?'

Anna removes her wool cap, shakes off the snow, and says, 'You don't remember Keith Cole? From our *Attack*? The guy that called the show *Sunday Cookoff*?'

Michelle sticks out her hand. 'Right. I knew you looked kind of familiar. Michelle Fields.' She gives him a less-than-subtle once-over, smiles, and says, 'Cute fauxhawk.'

Keith instinctively touches his hair and blushes a bit. 'Thanks.'

Michelle asks him, 'You remember Chef DeWitt, yes?'

Keith nods and proffers Jordan his hand. Anna says to Jordan, 'Oh, yeah, I forgot, you guys met the day I kicked your butt all over my kitchen.'

Keith laughs. 'You're getting to be a pretty good smack talker, Anna.'

'We'll see who's smacking on Sunday.' Jordan chuckles. 'Why don't you two join us? Lunch is on FoodTube.'

'I don't know,' Anna says. 'Dining with the enemy? You think that's a good idea?'

Keith parks himself at the table and says, 'If FoodTube's paying, I think it's a *great* idea.'

Anna nods. 'I guess I can't argue with that one.' She

sits. 'You guys order yet? I'd recommend the thin crust with double cheese and sausage. Oh, Chef DeWitt, I forgot, you're scared of cheese.'

Jordan asks, 'Thin crust, shmin crust – we're getting a stuffed pie. And hey, can we talk to each other normally? You know, not banter. Actual conversation.'

Anna looks surprised. 'Oh. Um. Sure.' After an awkward pause, she asks, 'Sooooo, are you having a nice trip so far?'

'Honestly, not really.'

'Why not?'

Michelle pipes up, 'Because he's a pussy.'

Jordan glares at his assistant, chuckles ruefully, then says, 'Because I miss home. You ever been to Los Angeles, Chef Rowan?'

'No. I was in San Francisco when I interned with Chef Keller, but I never made it down to LA.'

'Did you like San Francisco?'

'Loved it.'

Jordan nods. 'Me too. I bet you'd also love LA.'

Keith says, 'I grew up there. It's cool, but I like Chicago better.'

Jordan asks, 'Why?' He's shocked. *Shocked*. Nobody should like Illinois more than they do California. It's . . . it's . . . it's *wrong*.

'Well, I mean the weather out there is great,' Keith says, 'and there's always tons of stuff to do, but it doesn't feel very homey, you know? There's no sense of community.'

'Say *what*? There's a *total* sense of community.'

'You think so?'

'Yeah, man.' He pulls out his cell phone. 'My contacts list in here is ridiculous. Very communal.'

Keith says, 'Yeah, but how many of the numbers are people you don't work with?'

Jordan thinks for a few seconds. 'One. My divorce lawyer.' Everybody laughs.

Keith says, 'I have to get in a good LA mindset, though. I'm going out there for a few weeks at the end of March to see my family.'

Michelle reaches into her purse, grabs a business card, hands it to Keith, and says, 'Give me a call when you get to town. I'll take you on a tour of our studios.'

Keith pockets the card. 'I totally will. I'm sure I'll need to get the hell away from my parents at some point.'

Anna asks Keith, 'Don't you have friends out there you could hang with?'

'I *had* tons of friends. But in retrospect, they were more like acquaintances. Out here, there are at least five people who would let me stay at their apartment indefinitely, or lend me money when I'm broke and not hassle me if I can't pay it back right away. I'm sure there are people like that in Los Angeles. I just didn't know any of them.'

Jordan nods. 'Okay, I can kind of see where you're coming from. I'm sure there are millions of people who'd agree with you, and I suppose I couldn't argue with them. All I know is that when I'm at home, I have a definite sense of community.'

'Is it actually a nice community?' Anna asks.

'Everybody's in show biz out there, and show biz doesn't seem very communal.'

Jordan says, 'You know, believe it or not, show biz is more communal than you'd think, but I'm not talking about the industry. I'm talking about foodie culture. I bet there are more foodies per square inch out there than practically anywhere. I mean, I could walk away from my FoodTube gigs and be happy just cooking at Rayong Eniwa or some random place – even an Italian place, Chef Rowan – as long as I got paid enough to cover my living expenses. People appreciate good food out there, and if people appreciate what I'm doing, that's basically enough for me.'

Anna says, 'I bet you'd miss FoodTube. It seems like so much fun.'

'It is. And maybe I'd miss it, maybe I wouldn't, but I know I'd be perfectly content being in a good kitchen.'

Michelle says, 'Wow, listen to you, all baring your soul.'

Jordan says, 'Hey, if you can't bare your soul during a blizzard, when can you?' He checks his watch then asks Anna, 'It's two o'clock in the afternoon on a Tuesday. Shouldn't you be, you know, working or something?'

'Yeah. But I'm playing hooky. And it's literally the first time I've ever done that. And the restaurant has been open five years.' She snorts. 'I maybe should get out more.'

Keith pipes up, 'She had a fight with her boyfriend, then she kidnapped me. You can't imagine how awful it's been, being all alone with her for two hours.' He mock cringes. 'Brutal.'

Michelle says, 'Ooh, this sounds juicy. Details, please.'

Anna glares at Keith. 'It wasn't really a fight.'

Michelle asks, 'What was it, then?'

Anna thinks about it for a few seconds, then says, 'It was a discussion. With yelling.'

'He called her a commodity,' Keith says.

'*Keith!*'

'And he called her attractive.'

Michelle says, 'Jesus. What a dick.'

Jordan asks, 'What's wrong with being called attractive? I like being called attractive. Doesn't happen that often, but when it does . . .' He leaves the thought hanging.

Michelle says, 'A guy telling a girl she's attractive is like a customer telling you that a dish you cooked is interesting.'

'Ah. Gotcha.' He turns to Anna. 'Sorry to hear that. It's got to be weird dating your owner.'

Keith says, 'It would be way less weird if she was dating a server. Actually, I think dating a server would put her on a path to total enlightenment and happiness.'

'*Keith!*'

Keith points at Jordan. 'He said it's okay to bare your soul during a blizzard.'

Anna looks out the window. 'It's stopped snowing. Quit baring.'

From her expression and tone of voice, Jordan thinks Anna is flattered big-time by Keith's obvious like/love/lust of her, but Jordan guesses that even if she weren't dating her owner, she probably still wouldn't go out with one of her servers, if only because someone from the back of the house messing around with someone from the front of the house inevitably leads to broken hearts and thrown *mise en place*. (Jordan, having dated his share of servers in his younger days, has first-hand experience with lovesick waitresses who have a normal compliment of free time getting pissed off at emotionally unavailable cookies who work eighty-plus-hour weeks.)

Now that they're sitting down and they're nowhere near her kitchen, Jordan can see how somebody could become smitten by Anna. Away from the restaurant, she's softer, lighter, funnier, chiller, more in the moment. Her face seems less severe, and her eyes are brighter, more alive. Jordan still digs the restaurant version of Anna – he wishes he could bottle her combination of pinpoint concentration, hyper-competence, and electric energy, then guzzle it down during a busy Friday night – but right now, in the cold and snow, at a little pizza joint in the middle of this strange city, he'd rather hang out with the real-world version Chef Rowan.

After the table scarfs down the Caesar, the pizzas, the mozzarella sticks, and several gallons of root beer, Anna asks Jordan what he's up to for the rest of the day. 'Location scouting,' he groans. He explains the *DeWild* situation.

Anna says, 'I could help out, if you want.'

'That'd be awesome,' Michelle says.

Looking stricken, Keith says, 'I thought we were going to the movies.'

Jordan chuckles. 'Don't let your boy here down, Chef

Rowan. Enjoy playing hooky. We'll see you guys when Sunday evening rolls around.'

Soon enough, Sunday evening rolls around – as Sunday evenings tend to do – and Tart is a zoo. Nora recruits Eileen to help her behind the bar, and the customers are raving about Billy's buffet, and Michelle drags Anna into the kitchen to shoot some promos, and Jeannie, who has nothing to do save for pointing people to the food, is all over Jordan, and Jordan is, well, he's kind of into it.

'So,' Jeannie simpers, 'is this your first time in Chicago?'

'Um, no, I was here in October. Remember? With all the cameras?' Okay, she's a bit ditzy, so maybe he's not *that* into it.

'Oh. Right.' She floats into his personal space. 'So do you have a girlfriend or anything?'

Okay, she's a total bombshell, so maybe he *is* into it. 'Why, are you applying for the position?' This is oftentimes his default mode when he gets around a beautiful woman: cheesy flirting. He sometimes flirts even if he's not trying to pick the woman up, as he likes to keep his flirting chops in tip-top shape. Plus Jordan DeWitt likes being liked.

'Maybe,' Jeannie says. 'But I'm not really interested if it's only a temp job. And we'd also have to discuss benefits.'

Jordan is impressed she's extending the metaphor; maybe she's sharper than he thinks. 'Well, if you'd still like to file an application, I'm here for the next three Sundays after today, so you know where to find me.'

Jeannie gives him a hug. Her perfume is dizzying. Or maybe it's just her own scent. Whatever it is, Jordan is entranced. She says, 'And you know where to find *me*.'

The hug would've lasted for a good long while had Michelle not snuck up behind him and tapped him rudely on the shoulder. 'Hey. Lover Boy,' she says. 'You're needed. We're shooting promos out back. Now.'

Jordan disentangles himself from Jeannie's sweet-smelling embrace and asks Michelle, 'Who's "we"?'

'You and Anna.' They walk through the kitchen, out the back door, and into the surprisingly neat and clean alley. Anna and one of the FoodTube cameramen are leaning against the wall.

Anna says, 'Nice of you to join us, Chef DeWitt.'

Jordan stares silently at her for a few seconds, then says, 'It's nice to be here, Chef Rowan. And might I say, you clean up nicely.'

That's an understatement. Michelle insisted that Anna wear a cute dress for their little pre-*Attack* shoot, and based on what Jordan's seeing, it was an excellent decision. Anna is rocking her favorite black-and-white-patterned De la Renta and her black Gucci stiletto boots, an outfit that Jordan feels should earn her a place on the reality television show *America's Hottest Chefs*. Not that that show exists, but if it did, she'd win, hands down.

Michelle says, 'Jordan was trying to make time with your hostess.'

'With Jeannie?' Anna asks, shivering cutely. 'Stand in line.'

Jordan says, 'Hey, she hit on me.'

'Yeah, right,' Anna says, clearly disbelieving him. 'Jeannie doesn't hit on anybody. She doesn't need to.'

'Actually,' Michelle says, 'she *was* hitting on him.'

Anna blinks. 'Really?'

'Jealous, Chef Rowan?' Jordan asks.

'Yeah, you wish.' But based on her childlike tone of voice and reddened cheeks, Jordan thinks there might be jealousy there. Or maybe he was just projecting.

Michelle claps three times. 'Okay, kids, let's take this cutesy antagonistic vibe you've got happening here and get it on tape.' She tells the cameraman, 'Vince, start shooting.'

For the next ten minutes, Jordan and Anna improvise a bunch of silly I'm-going-to-kick-your-ass trash talk. Near the end of the session, Anna gets right up in Jordan's face, points her finger at his nose, and says in a mock-cowboy accent, 'This is my town, Chef DeWitt, and us Chicagoans don't take too kindly to strangers from the West Coast hornin' in on our territory.'

For the second time in thirty minutes, Jordan is knocked silly by a woman's scent. To him, Anna smells sexier than Jeannie, probably because underneath her sexy perfume, he smells both a kitchen and food lust, which he finds sexier than most anything. He clears his throat and tells Anna, 'For somebody who's never spent any significant time in front of a television camera, you've got some game.'

Anna shrugs. 'No big deal. I'm just talking. With a camera in my face . . . and millions of people watching . . .

Oh my God, what have I gotten myself into?!' Then she bursts out laughing.

Jordan says, 'Heh. I bet you're a hit at parties.'

Michelle says, 'Anna, this is why the folks back at the home office wanted you to do this. The camera loves you. You're a natural. Right, Jordan?'

Jordan looks at his watch. 'Isn't it about time we got started?' He knows Michelle is right: Anna is a natural. When he first started with *Eastern Rebellion*, Jordan was as far from natural as you could get. It took him eight episodes before he stopped stammering every seven or so sentences. (He sometimes still wonders why FoodTube didn't can him after a month.) So as he watches Anna looking like she's done this for years, is he feeling jealous? Vulnerable? Nervous? Intimidated? Nah. None of the above. His disquiet is a symptom of his homesickness and the cold weather. At least that's what he's telling himself.

He gently takes Anna's elbow, leads her back into the kitchen, and says, 'You ready to rock, Chef Rowan?'

'As soon as I slip into something way more comfortable, absolutely.'

'So what cuisine are we looking at tonight?'

She shakes her head. 'You'll find out when everybody else does. Just because you're going to be camped out at my restaurant for a month doesn't mean you're getting any kind of preferential treatment.'

More trash talking. Jordan grins as he watches Anna walk down the stairs toward her office. Now that he's in the kitchen, now that he's getting ready to do what he does best – cooking, of course – he's in a better headspace,

Los Angeles and the freezing temperatures temporarily forgotten. 'I bet you're doing Italian again,' he tells her when she returns, clad in her chef's gear.

Anna turns away. 'Maybe I am. Maybe I'm not.'

Jordan puts his hand on Anna's shoulder, turns her back around, and says, 'Chef Rowan, I get the distinct feeling you're a lousy liar. Look me in the eye and tell me you're not doing Italian.'

She looks him in the eye for ten or so silent seconds – ten seconds that Jordan finds to be a bit, shall we say, toasty – then chuckles. 'I'm going to make an eggplant Parm that's going to destroy you.'

'I *knew* it,' Jordan says. 'You can't lie for shit. Remind me never to tell you any secrets.'

True to her word, Anna's eggplant Parm does destroy Jordan, as does her Caesar salad with herbed flatbread croutons – yes, she throws Jordan's recipe right back in his face, and, even he would admit, she does it better – her chunky minestrone, her osso bucco (Jordan has no clue as to how she got that finished in time; he suspects she did some pre-show prep work, but he doesn't want to say anything, for fear of coming off like a sore loser) and her tiramisu. Unlike their previous battle, Anna goes with classic dishes rather than haute Italian, and Eric says that it's always been his belief that it's as impressive to nail and personalize a classic as it is to concoct something brand spanking new.

Jordan, for his part, tries to concoct something brand spanking new.

Mind you, there's nothing wrong with Jordan's output,

nothing at all. On any other day, his fire-roasted tomato and smoked mozzarella bruschetta, his arugula stracciatella with toasted pine nut shavings, his squid ink linguine with roasted garlic, parsnips, and poppy seeds, his charred grouper with leeks and pancetta vinaigrette, and his apple cinnamon mascarpone tart would have carried the day. But Anna brought her A-game, and Anna's A-game is frightening.

Unsurprisingly to the Tart rooting section in the kitchen – i.e. Byron and Keith – Anna wins. Eric says that taken as a group, her five dishes comprised his single finest *Sunday Sneak Attack* eating experience.

Jordan says, 'Wait a sec.' He looks into the camera. 'Did you hear that, ladies and gentlemen? My pal Eric is basically dissing every meal I've ever made for this show.' He stares thoughtfully at the critic. 'You know what? I'm going to go out on a limb here and say that Mr McLanahan has a little crush on Chef Rowan.'

Anna drags a chair over to where Jordan is standing, climbs up on it, faces him, and says, 'So what you're saying, Chef DeWitt, is that the only reason I beat you is that I'm cuter than you?'

'Well, since you put it that way . . . yes. Yes. That's exactly what I'm saying.' He then yells, 'Eric, get over here!'

Eric, who hates being on-camera any more than necessary, trudges across the room. 'What do you want, Jordan?'

'Tell me, do you have a crush on Chef Rowan?'

Eric raises his left hand, points to his ring fingers, and

deadpans, 'I've been married for twelve years. I haven't even looked at another woman since I said, "I do."'

Jordan asks Eric, 'So you're saying you *don't* find Chef Rowan attractive?' Eric sticks an index finger in the air and opens his mouth, but nothing comes out. Jordan turns to Anna. 'Hear that, Chef Rowan? Eric here thinks you're goofy-looking. Guess that means you beat me fair and square.'

'And I'll beat you again next week. And I promise: no Italian.'

Jordan turns back to the camera. 'You heard it, ladies and gentlemen. The gauntlet has been thrown down. Chef Rowan is guaranteeing victory. I'm quaking in my black Crocs. She should be quaking in her red ones. Sounds exciting, right? Of course it does, which is why I'm sure we'll see you next week on *Sunday Sneak Attack: Chicago*.' He lifts Anna from the chair and puts her over his shoulder. 'Say good night to all the loyal foodies of America, Chef Rowan.'

As she beats her fists on Jordan's back, she squeals, 'Good night to all the loyal foodies of America, Chef Rowan.'

After a bit more squealing and back beating, Michelle yells from across the room, '*Cut!*' She strides over to the giggling chefs. 'Guys, that was awesome. *Awesome*. They're going to love that in Cali. I can't wait until next week.'

Anna says, 'Thanks, Michelle. I had a blast. It felt great. I was really comfortable, way more than last time.' She gently flicks Jordan's ear. 'If it's not a problem, would you mind putting me down, Chef DeWitt?'

Jordan is hesitant to do so. He finds that he enjoys having the squirming chef on his shoulder. She still smells excellent, but in a different way: the sexy scent is still there, but now he also soaks in the odors of hard work, and confidence, and home. Jordan hasn't smelled home in what seems like forever.

Anna continues, '. . . and if it's not a problem, would you also mind removing your hand from my ass?'

Jordan doesn't even realize he's touching Anna's backside, but once she points it out, he realizes that not only does she smell nice, but she has a remarkable butt. He immediately feels hugely guilty about the whole situation, even though he certainly didn't touch her there on purpose. He abruptly removes his hand as if Anna's tush was a hot stove, then gently puts her down. 'Sorry about that, Chef Rowan. Completely unintentional.'

'Sure,' she growls menacingly. 'Don't let it happen again.'

Jordan rightly considers himself to be a gentleman, and the thought that he's stepped over the line – even accidentally – and with somebody he'll be closely working with for the next three weeks – is mortifying. He blushes, then stammers, 'No, no, no, seriously, I didn't mean, I didn't mean, I didn't mean . . .'

Anna grins; the sun bursting through the storm. 'I know you didn't mean, you didn't mean, you didn't mean. No worries.' She reaches behind him and smacks his ass. 'Now we're even.'

Michelle says, 'Wow, I've never touched Jordan's ass. Is it nice?'

Anna shrugs. 'I've felt better. I've felt worse.'

Jordan sighs and says, 'I really, truly hate both of you.'

'We hate you too.' Michelle grins. 'Hey, Anna, how would you like it if FoodTube took you and your boyfriend out for a drink?' She looks around the kitchen for Byron. 'Where'd he go? He was here a second ago.'

Anna sighs. 'I don't know where the hell he went. We've been in kind of a Cold War lately. I kind of doubt he'd be into going out right now.'

Michelle leans forward and asks conspiratorially, 'Why don't you invite Keith instead?'

Jordan gives Michelle a sideways glance. 'You got a thing for that kid, don't you M-Class?'

Michelle smirks. 'Puh-leeze. He's just that: a kid.'

Anna says, 'Yeah, but he's a cute kid.'

'Do *you* have a thing for him, Chef Rowan?' Jordan asks.

'I have a boyfriend, Chef DeWitt. And don't you forget it.' Anna checks her watch. 'If we're going to hit the bars, we should get going. I have to be here early tomorrow, and I'd like to get at least two hours of sleep.' She swallows hard. 'I know Byron's not going to want to come out with us. Is it really cool with you guys if I bring Keith along?'

Michelle grins. 'Absolutely.'

Jordan simultaneously grunts, 'I guess.'

'Are you even going to tell Byron you're leaving?' Michelle asks.

Anna again checks her watch. 'If I can find him.'

After Anna leaves the kitchen, Jordan asks Michelle,

'You think she's going to hook up with that kid?'

'I doubt it. She doesn't seem like the type of girl who'd mess around on a guy she's living with.'

'I don't know. My masculine intuition senses she's got the wanderlust.'

'Masculine intuition?'

'Absolutely. Always had it.'

'Please. You've never intuited anything in your life.'

'Yeah? Well, I'm intuiting that you want to jump Keith's bones.'

Michelle reddens. 'I'll take the fifth on that one.'

Anna pokes her head back into the kitchen. 'Okay, go out the front door, cross the street, and go two blocks to the left. The bar's called Ziggy's. We'll be there in ten minutes.' Then she disappears.

Jordan says, 'If I'm Keith, I'm getting me some breath mints, you know what I'm saying?'

Michelle shakes her head exasperatedly. 'Yes, Jordan, I know what you're saying. Anybody with more than three brain cells would know what you're saying.'

Half an hour later, as Jordan and Michelle are huddled in a back booth at Ziggy's, working on their respective second bottles of Blue Moon ale, Anna hustles in, out of breath, flushed, sans Keith, sans Byron. 'I'm so sorry, guys. I can't hang out. I have to go. I'll see you next Sunday, okay?' Then she bolts.

Jordan takes a swig from his bottle. 'Hunh. That was interesting.'

Michelle says, 'I'm sure we'll find out what happened next week.'

They don't find out what happened next week. Nor do they find out the week after, nor the week after that. But Jordan thinks Anna's demeanor is different. None of his FoodTube compatriots agree, primarily because Anna's her usual bubbly self on-camera, and what goes on on-camera is what's really important to Michelle, Eric, and the cameramen. In spite of the fact she (in Jordan's mind) is bumming out, Anna cooks some beautiful food for the three remaining episodes of *Sneak Attack: Chicago* – she just barely loses in a Japanese contest on week two, she beats him on week three with some stellar Mexican fare, then loses the final week in a very close Italian rematch. (Deep down, Jordan thinks her Italian dishes that last episode were still better than his, so he's happy to have gotten away with a two-to-two tie.)

While the camera crew packs up their gear after the Italian battle, Anna, Billy and a couple of the other cookies wash, and scrub, and mop, and scrape, everything that can be washed, and scrubbed, and mopped, and scraped. From the back of the kitchen, Jordan watches his counterpart with a wistful smile, surprised that he's somewhat sad about leaving cold, snowy Chicago. 'Yo, Chef Rowan,' he calls, 'get over here.'

Anna looks up from the sink. 'Can it wait? I want to finish up and get the hell out of here.'

'No, it can't wait.'

She sighs, drops the stock pot she's been mauling with a Brillo pad, removes her rubber gloves, rinses off her hands, and trudges to the back of the kitchen. 'What's up, Chef DeWitt?'

'Okay, first thing, let's cut out all this Chef crap. I'm Jordan. You're Anna.'

Anna lets out a single, quiet chuckle. 'No. Afraid not. I'm Chef Rowan. You're Chef DeWitt. It's a respect thing. Deal with it.'

Jordan chuckles back. 'A respect thing. Fine. Even though everybody else at the restaurant calls you Anna. Whatever. Anyhow, moving ahead to the second thing, I have to tell you that it was an honor cooking with you. You're a brilliant chef, and I think you have the potential to be one of the greatest in the country. If you don't win a James Beard[34] Award within the next five years, I'll be shocked.'

Anna blushes and takes a step back. 'Wow, wow, *wow*. Thank you, Chef. Coming from you, that means a lot.' She fans her face with her hand. 'I'm tearing up here. Wow.'

Jordan looks at her eyes. She *is* tearing up. Wow, wow, *wow*, indeed. The last girl he made tear up was Nadia. Actually, he didn't make her tear up. She teared up on her own. On purpose. Just to mess with Jordan. Nadia sucks. 'I mean it,' he tells Anna. 'Sincerely.' He takes a deep breath. 'Finally, the third thing.' He pauses. And pauses. And pauses.

Anna snaps her fingers in front of his face and says, 'Chef DeWitt? Hello?'

---

[34] James Beard (1903–1985): A legendary American chef/cookbook author with a cooking foundation named in his honor. They give lots of awards to lots of stud chefs – or, in Anna's case, studette chefs. Think the Oscars, except with food.

Jordan takes another deep breath, then says in one breath, 'If my divorce was finalized, and you didn't have a boyfriend, and we lived in the same city, I would be all over your shit. I'd put on a full-court press so hard that you wouldn't even know what hit you.'

Anna's jaw drops. She's silent for a little bit – but a *very* little bit. 'Jesus Christ, Jordan, that's one of the crassest things that anybody's ever said to me . . .'

'Hey, you called me Jordan!'

'. . . but it's pretty cool. No, it's really cool. It's really sweet. And frankly, I needed it. Again, thank you.' She steps into his arms and gives him the best hug he's had in months. No, *years*. Nadia was a lousy hugger. He wonders why he married somebody who couldn't properly hold him. You'd think that would've been another one of those omnipresent red flags.

A good forty-five seconds into the hug – and a forty-five-second hug is a long one, and if you don't believe it, grab your sweetie and your stopwatch and get squeezing – Michelle taps Anna on the shoulder. 'Hey, can I speak with both of you for a sec?'

Much to Jordan's disappointment, Anna pulls away. 'Sure,' she says, clearing her throat. 'What's up?'

Michelle says, 'Okay, I've got some news, and I've known about it for, like, two weeks now, but I waited till now to tell you, because I wanted it to be, like, a goodbye present or something.'

Jordan says, 'A goodbye present? I'm intrigued.'

'It's pretty goddamn intriguing, J-Money,' Michelle says. She turns to Anna. 'FoodTube is offering you a show.'

Anna gulps. Then she gulps again. Then she gulps yet again. 'You're kidding.' She asks Jordan, 'Did you know about this? Is that why you said what you said?'

Michelle asks, 'What did he say?'

He tells Michelle, 'Nothing. I said *nothing*.' Then he says to Anna, 'And no, I didn't know about it.' He sure as hell wishes he'd known, though, because there's no way Jordan would have told Anna that he'd be all over her shit if he knew there was actually an opportunity for him to be all over her shit, no way whatsoever. He told her how he felt – crassly, granted – because he knew there'd be no chance of anything happening with them: his divorce, Byron, and the distance between Chicago and Los Angeles making a Jordan/Anna meeting of the minds (and meeting of some other stuff) impossible. But nonetheless, he means what he said, and she knows that he means it, and he knows that she knows that he means it, and all of a sudden, Jordan has a major problem on his hands, because when you tell somebody that, given the opportunity, you'd be all over their shit, well, that's not the sort of thing you can take back.

Anna says to Michelle, 'I don't know about this. Would I have to move to California?'

'No, not full time, but we'd need you out there for about six months of the year to start.'

She looks at Jordan, but speaks to his producer. 'I don't know, Michelle. I'm not sure I can just up and go. I can't leave the restaurant just like that.' She pauses, then adds, 'But I'm not going to lie. It's something I've kind of dreamed about. When would it start?'

'In April, but we'd need you out there in March. We need a month to hone the show's concept, and to get you comfortable working in a studio. That gives you a month, which should give you enough time to get your kitchen here in order.'

Jordan, feeling Anna's eyes boring into the side of his head, asks Michelle, 'What's the concept?'

Michelle says, 'Well, it's funny you ask, Jordan. If Anna accepts the offer, they're cancelling *DeWitt Goes DeWild*, which they think is starting to cost too much—'

'Say *what*?!'

'—and they're going to replace it with a yet-to-be-titled show co-hosted by Chef Anna Rowan and Chef Jordan DeWitt.'

Jordan blinks. 'So we'd be working together.'

Michelle says, 'Yep.'

Jordan stares at Anna. 'Well, this is certainly an interesting development, isn't it?'

Anna stares right back. She says nothing. Then she walks out the back door, into the alley. She doesn't turn around.

Michelle takes a long, deep breath, blows it out, and says to Jordan, 'Looks like we're off to a good start.'

Jordan says, 'Or a good finish.'

CAESAR SALAD WITH GRILLED HERBED FLATBREAD CROUTONS

Ingredients

For croutons:

1½ cups of warm water (105°F–110°F)

½ teaspoon of active dry yeast

4 cups of all-purpose flour

1 teaspoon of salt

¼ teaspoon of finely chopped parsley

¼ teaspoon of finely chopped thyme

¼ teaspoon of finely chopped rosemary

2 tablespoons of olive or canola oil, plus more for bowl

For salad:

1 egg yolk

3 tablespoons of fresh lemon juice

1 tablespoon minced garlic

½ teaspoon of Worcestershire sauce

¼ teaspoon of red pepper flakes

1 tablespoon of Dijon mustard

2 anchovy fillets, mashed

1 cup of vegetable oil

⅓ cup of extra-virgin olive oil

Salt

Pepper

1 large head of romaine lettuce, cleaned and cut into 1–2 inch pieces

Freshly grated Parmesan cheese
Black pepper

Method

1. Mix water and yeast in a large bowl and let stand 5 minutes to proof.
2. Gradually pour in 2 cups of the flour and stir to incorporate. Mix for about 1 minute to form a sponge.
3. Let stand, covered, for at least 1 hour.
4. Put sponge in the bowl of a stand mixer. Using the dough hook, add the salt, herbs, and oil, then add the remaining flour, ½ cup at a time, to form a dough. Remove from bowl and knead.
5. Place in a clean oiled bowl and let rise, slowly, about 2½ hours.
6. Divide dough into 4 balls, if desired, let rise again for ½ hour, and then roll out as desired.
7. Flatten flatbread dough, gently press into a large rectangle, brush liberally with olive oil, season with salt and pepper and put on grill. Grill on both sides till golden brown.
8. Let cool, then cut into strips about 2–3 inches long and ¼ inch wide.
9. In a medium bowl, whisk together the egg yolk, lemon juice, garlic, Worcestershire sauce, pepper flakes, mustard and anchovies. Slowly whisk in the oils to emulsify. Season to taste with salt and pepper.
10. Place the lettuce in a large bowl. Sprinkle with Parmesan and black pepper. Drizzle with desired amount of dressing and toss well. Sprinkle top with croutons.

California Dreaming

Six weeks later, seated at a sushi joint on an exceptionally smoggy day in a less-than-ideal neighborhood in Los Angeles:

'What were his exact words?'

' "I think we should take a break." '

'That was it?'

'Oh, God, no, that wasn't it. That was the upshot. It started okay. We were having a quiet little discussion, kind of tense, but quiet, but it moved into yelling territory in about five minutes. He was like "How could you leave the restaurant," and, "Your priorities are completely fucked," and "What am I supposed to do after you're gone?" Then he started making it all about him. He kept saying "What about me, what about me, what about me?" And I asked him, What about me, and told him that he knew this was something I'd wanted. I mean, I may not have made it clear enough. I didn't harp on about it every day, or every month, or even every year. But, I don't know, maybe I should have. The thing that pissed me off, though, was that he never once said, "What about us?" It was all, "me, me, me," and "restaurant, restaurant, restaurant." Then I couldn't think of anything to say, so I clammed up, and that's when he said, "If you're going out there, I think we should take a break." '

'A break. Hunh, I've never been in a relationship that's lasted long enough to take a break from. I mean, what exactly is a break?'

And that right there is the sixty-four-thousand-dollar question, the question that Anna hasn't been able to answer. 'Honestly, Keith, I don't know. He stormed out of the apartment right then, and whenever I tried to bring it up after that night, he shut me off.' She sniffles, and her lower lip quivers. 'He slept on the sofa the whole month until I left. He didn't talk to me unless we were at the restaurant, and even then he sent me messages through Billy, and how childish and lame is that?' Then a tear or three spills over her eyelid. 'I don't think we're broken up.'

'You *think* you're not broken up, or you *know* you're not broken up?'

'I think I know.'

'You think you know what?'

'I don't know.' Anna shrugs, wipes her eyes, blows her bangs out of her face, and takes an inordinately large swig of her saki. 'I really don't know.' One thing she *does* know is that right now, right this second, she probably shouldn't be where she is with who she's with. How smart is it to be lunching with a guy who, for the past several months, has made it more than obvious that he's way into you, only four weeks after you and your boyfriend have temporarily split up? But when it's your second day in a strange city, and you're feeling lonely and abandoned, you grab on to whoever you can grab on to, and she grabs on to Keith Cole.

But her grabbing Keith makes sense, because, in many ways, Keith is the perfect person to grab. He puts her on a pedestal like nobody ever has – Byron included – and even though getting gratification from being worshipped by a cute boy isn't the healthiest way to soothe a broken heart, it still feels good, and Anna rightly believes she deserves to feel good. And here's another mark in Keith's plus column: he always pays attention to what she says, and generally responds with something insightful, or funny, or distracting – and it must be noted that right now, right this second, distraction is a good thing, because Anna has a lot on her plate, and if somebody in Los Angeles is in need of distraction, it's FoodTube's newest on-air-personality-in-training.

Yes, that's right, after hours and hours of painful and difficult option-weighing and hand-wringing – *Will I be able to handle being away from Byron, Stinks, and Tart? Will I? Will I? Will I? Ah, what the hell, it's not permanent, I'll give it a shot* – Chef Anna Rowan accepted FoodTube's offer to share the small screen with her comrade-in-aprons, Chef Jordan DeWitt, which is why she's here in Los Angeles, wearing baggy black cargo shorts and a white-with-red-trim capped-sleeve baby-doll T-shirt, sitting in a strip-mall sushi restaurant called Chiba, eating a most excellent dragon roll with Keith.

Anna keeps stealing peeks at her watch, because she has to be at Jordan's apartment at three. It's two-ish. After only thirty-six or so hours, she's well aware that LA traffic is a nightmare, so she figures she has, at most, thirty minutes before she has to take her leave of Chiba. Anna hates being late for anything, especially when it comes to business, and despite the fact that Jordan is a goofball, her upcoming visit to his house is still a business meeting. But aside from the fact that she now feels like she could cry if somebody looked at her cross-eyed, she's thoroughly enjoying herself with Keith, and doesn't want to leave. But she has to. But she doesn't want to. But she has to. *Why can't anything ever be easy?* she wonders.

Keith says, 'Personally, I think even talking about Byron is counterproductive. And silly.'

'Why silly?' Anna asks, while at the same time wondering if there's a way she can make a dragon roll that she could serve at Tart. Sushi doesn't fit with her menu, obviously, but maybe she can Americanize it (or Anna-ize it) and serve it as a starter.

Keith says, 'Well, let me put it this way: are you going to call him while you're out here?'

'Probably not.'

'Do you care if he calls you or not?'

'No.' She pauses. 'Maybe a little.' She pauses again. 'Okay, I care. I don't want to talk to him right this second, but I hope he calls.'

Keith scratches his head, careful not to muss his perfectly triangulated 'do. 'Please explain.'

'So I can blow him off.'

'Ah. You want the last word.'

Anna deftly spears a piece of pickled ginger with her chopsticks. 'I think so. Maybe. I don't know.'

'Now do you see why it's silly to talk about him? You're making no sense. I don't know, I feel like I should be taking notes here. This is like a college course. Women 101.'

Anna chuckles, the first time she's laughed all afternoon, then, suddenly agreeing with Keith, suddenly wanting to stop discussing the Byron situation, she changes the subject. 'I like your shirt. The stripes are fun. Looks like Charlie Brown gone mad.'

He glances down at himself. 'This? I've had this since high school.'

'It's still cute. What're you going to do while you're home?'

He grimaces. 'Bond with my parents, I suppose.'

'Are they that bad?'

'No, they're okay. Thing is, I don't have too many social options out here, so unless I find some way to amuse myself by myself, the 'rents are basically it. The only friends of mine who still live around here are kind of lame. All the cool ones moved to New York, or London, or wherever.' He steals a huge piece of maki from Anna's plate, shovels it into his pie-hole, then, mouth overflowing with rice, seaweed, avocado and a bunch of other dragon roll detritus, says, 'Guess I'll have to hang out with you, like, all the time.'

Anna would be perfectly happy hanging out with Keith a few times a week for the reasons listed earlier, plus having a cute younger boy on your arm never hurts the old ego. But the fact of the matter is she can't. 'Keith, I start my how-to-be-on-television lessons tomorrow, and we start shooting in three weeks. Maybe I'll have free time on the weekends, but that'll be it.'

Keith steals another piece of sushi from her plate. 'We can get together after you're done with class. I'll take you on a dinner picnic. I'll rub your shoulders. I'll rub your feet.'

Anna perks up. 'Foot rubs? For realsies?'

'For realsies.'

Anna likes foot rubs. 'Fine,' she tells Keith. 'You can take me on a picnic Friday. But don't go crazy with the food. Make peanut butter and jelly, for all I care.'

'Are you crazy? I'm doing up some fancy food for the fancy chef.'

Anna sighs. This is something she's been dealing with since culinary school: most everybody who prepares food for her wants to wow her, to put together something that they think will be good enough for her supposed refined palate. The thing is, as we know from her love for huge midnight bowls of Cap'n Crunch, Anna's palate isn't particularly refined. 'Seriously, Keith, don't go nuts. Don't spend a lot of money. Don't take a lot of time. The fact that you're being sweet to me is enough.'

Keith beams. 'Yeah, I am a sweetie.' Then he leans over the table and kisses her lightly on the right corner of her mouth. It's a quick kiss – maybe two seconds, three tops – but for Anna, it's seismic. The boy has electric lips. There's a possibility it's the wasabi, but there's also the possibility it's him.

Anna's initial reaction to Keith's kiss is a combination of anger and fear; she feels she should somehow chastise him, tell him he has no right to kiss her – and certainly not in public – because, despite the on-a-break edict, she's still spoken for . . . or at least she is on paper. It crosses her mind to call Byron and check their status, but then Keith kisses her again, and she forgets all about Mr Smith. She kind of wants to kiss him again. Then she kind of feels like a heel for thinking of Keith in That Way. Her stomach rumbles uncomfortably. Turns out guilt and sushi don't go well together.

Keith gulps. 'I'm sorry. That totally wasn't cool. But I couldn't help it. I mean . . . you're so fucking pretty.'

Anna blushes. 'Don't apologize,' she says throatily. 'I didn't exactly pull away.' She rubs his cheek with her knuckles. 'It was nice. Really nice.'

He takes her other hand and kisses the tip of her index finger. 'Can I do it again?'

The saki must have hit her like a bomb, because suddenly Anna very badly wants to say yes. She wants to grab him by the back of his neck, pull him across the table, and run her tongue along the back of his teeth. She wants to put her hand on his cute little tummy – yes, Keith's tummy is big, but saying (or thinking) 'cute little tummy' is way more appealing to Anna than saying (or thinking) 'cute big tummy' – and rub it, and rub it, and rub it, all the way up to his chest, and all the way down to his thighs. She wants to kiss his eyes, his nose, his ears, his neck. But the more she thinks about it, the more she's overcome by guilt. Then she's overcome by lust. Then guilt. Then lust.

Then more guilt. Then more lust. Then *lots* more lust. Then she grabs him by the back of his neck, pulls him across the table, and runs her tongue along the back of his teeth.

Keith, clearly shocked, doesn't know what to do with his hands. First he puts them in Anna's hair, then on her neck, then on the small of her back, then on her knees, then he accidentally brushes her right breast, which makes both of them gasp.

Anna pulls away. 'Okay, big guy, let's slow down here.'

Keith is blushing. 'I didn't mean to, I swear, seriously, it was a total accident, I'm so sorry . . .'

From what Anna has learned over the past few months, Keith Cole is one of those guys who has zero ability to lie, so if he says it's an accident, it's an accident. 'Okay, fine, let's just slow down a bit.'

'Hey, I wasn't the one who pulled me across the table.'

Anna blushes yet again. 'No, you weren't.' She sighs. 'I don't know if this picnic is such a good idea.'

'Why not? It'll be awesome. Foot rubs. *Foot rubs!*' He catches their server's eye and motions for the check.

'No, I've got it,' Anna says, reaching into her bottomless purse and searching for her wallet. 'I can expense it.'

Keith quickly reaches in his back pocket, yanks out his wallet, and frisbees his credit card at the server. 'Too late. I want to take you to lunch.'

Still digging for her wallet, Anna says, 'Keith, FoodTube will pay for lunch. Michelle told me she wants me to taste Los Angeles.' This is the one thing about her new gig that she's most excited about. She read up on LA's restaurant scene before she left Chicago, and made a long list of eateries she wants to check out. She still doesn't know her way around – thank goodness for her GPS – but she figures that doing an eating tour of the city will help her get comfortable with the lay of both the culinary and geographical landscape. Then again, Los Angeles is the definition of sprawling, and many longtime residents don't even know where the hell they're going half of the time.

Keith repeats, 'And I want to take you to lunch.' He pauses. 'Taste Los Angeles. That's funny. Michelle's a cool chick.'

'Agreed. Chef DeWitt would be lost without her. He's pretty lost *with* her, for that matter.' Being that she can't find her wallet, she relents about the lunch tab. 'Fine, you can buy. But I'm taking you out next time.'

'That means there's going to be a next time. Right?' She shrugs, then nods. 'Sweet.'

Anna looks at her watch. 'It's getting late. I have to go.'

The server returns. Keith signs the credit-card slip with a flourish. 'Where?' he asks.

She actually doesn't have to go just yet – another ten or fifteen minutes would be okay, probably – but she's starting to have thoughts about Keith she's probably better off not having, thoughts that involve some PG-13 nudity. (Her brain is too guilt-ridden for rated R.) 'Back to my hotel,' she lies. She doesn't want to tell Keith that she's seeing Jordan, irrationally (and mistakenly) believing that he'll be jealous. 'FoodTube gave me piles and piles of reading.' That part is true. Michelle compiled a collection of *stuff* for her: an in-depth description of her and Jordan's show – which, much to Anna's chagrin, is called *One Boy, One Girl, One Meal* – a list of dos and don'ts for all FoodTube employees, the company retirement and insurance plans, a dossier on Jordan's career, and a few zillion other pieces of paper that required the destruction of some poor defenseless forest. Anna has already read all of Michelle's pile of crap twice, no small task but, Anna being Anna, she wants to make certain she knows everything up, down and sideways, so she plans to give it one more pass before she goes to sleep tonight.

Keith smiles, but Anna thinks it looks forced. They both stand up. 'No problem. If you got to work, you got to work. I'll call you tomorrow?'

'Yeah. You can call me tomorrow.' Then her hands, operating independently of her brain, find themselves alighting on the back of Keith's neck. Her lips, also moving of their own accord, give him a semi-chaste kiss on his mouth. She involuntarily presses her entire body against his. She likes the way his tummy feels against hers. She also likes the way her breasts feel against his chest. She wants to kiss him again, longer, harder, wetter, but the guilt again kicks in, and she regains control of her body, then gently pulls away.

They slowly saunter toward the parking lot, their arms accidentally-on-purpose brushing against each other. Their hands are particularly close, and Anna can tell that he wants to take hers, and she almost lets him, because she really really really likes holding hands, and Byron is, at best, ambivalent about even the smallest public display of affection, so she hasn't gotten enough quality hand time over the past few years. But she thinks right at this moment, hand-holding would be too intimate and would send a wrong signal. Okay, not a *wrong* signal, per se, but too *much* of a signal.

She pulls her keys from her bottomless purse – feeling inordinately proud that it only took her a few seconds to find them – and unlocks the door to the royal blue Toyota Prius that FoodTube has graciously provided for her. She opens the door, and, without turning around, gives Keith a little wave and says, 'Tell your parents I say hey.'

Keith chuckles. 'You can always drop by and tell them yourself.'

She slides into the car and smiles sweetly. 'Talk to you soon. Be good.'

As she closes the door, she thinks she hears him say, 'I can't be good around you, Anna.' But he might've said, 'I'll make good food for you, Anna.' Or maybe 'Your car is nice and blue, Anna.' She can't decide which one she wants it to be.

Anna jams her Bluetooth earpiece – another fun toy, courtesy of FoodTube – into her ear and turns on her cell. Three messages, all from Jordan, all asking where the hell she is. She looks at her watch and says, '*Shit.*' It's three-fifteen. Where did the time go? How long were she and Keith kissing for? Five seconds? A minute? Two? No way it could've been ten full minutes. But maybe it was, who knows? Things apparently got away from her. But maybe it wasn't just Keith who made the time disappear; the sushi was yummy, too. So the food had something to do with her losing time. At least that's what she keeps telling herself. And it's also what she plans to tell Jordan.

She starts the car, pulls out of the parking lot, and calls her new co-host. He answers after half a ring, and before he can even say hello, Anna launches into an apology. 'I'm so sorry, Chef DeWitt. So so so so so so sorry. Seriously, I'm never late. Okay, I was late to work once, this one time when Stinks got sick . . .'

'Stinks?'

'My cat.'

'Great name.'

'I sense sarcasm.'

'You sense correctly,' he says icily. 'Seriously, Chef Rowan, you're a chef, and chefs should never be late. *Never*. To *anything*. You know better than that. So what's your excuse? Are you stuck on the 110?'

'No, I got stuck at Chiba.'

Jordan's previously icy voice melts. 'The sushi place? That place is the *bomb*. All right, I forgive you. You did the omakase, right?'

'I don't think so. Maybe. I'm not sure. What's omakase?' Anna can whip up some more-than-competent Japanese food, sushi included, but she knows little of Japanese food culture.

'That's when you sit at the sushi bar, and the chef makes you whatever the hell he wants, and keeps giving you maki and nigri[35] until you beg for mercy. If that's why

[35] Nigiri: A single piece of sushi that's inevitably overpriced to the nth degree, but nobody ever complains about it, which is why it will continue to be overpriced forever and ever, world without end, amen.

you're running late, then I forgive you.'

'Yeah, that's exactly what happened. *Exactly*.' Anna accidentally cuts off a convertible that's trying to switch lanes. The driver honks and flips her the bird. So much for California mellowness. 'It was the shit,' she says, unconsciously adopting Jordan's poopy-oriented descriptive style. 'Yeah, I had the oompah-loompah . . .'

'Omakase.'

'Right, omakase.' She punches Jordan's address into Nicole (that's what she named her Global Positioning System after it started speaking to her in a Nicole Kidman-like Australian accent) and peers at the readout. 'According to my fancy GPS here, I'll be at your place in thirteen minutes.'

Jordan sighs. 'Fine. Call if you get lost. But get here as soon as you can. We have a lot of stuff to go over, and I have to leave for my restaurant no later than six.'

Anna so associates Jordan with his television shows that she forgets he actually runs a kitchen. 'Okay, but if I get a speeding ticket, you're paying for it.'

'Agreed.'

Anna arrives at Jordan's just after three-forty-five. Jordan, clad in a baggy blue T-shirt, baggier gray shorts, and some seriously worn Birkenstocks, gives her a dry peck on the cheek, points at his watch, and asks, 'You said thirteen minutes. What happened?'

She kicks off her dark green Converse low-tops. 'Remember when you said you'd pay for a ticket? Guess what.' She reaches into the back pocket of her khaki shorts, pulls out a rectangular piece of orange paper.

Jordan plucks the ticket from her hand and gives it a quick read. 'You were doing eighty-five in a sixty-five zone?' Anna nods. 'Now *that's* driving. I'm *totally* covering this. Hold on to it for the time being, though.' He reaches behind her and tries to stick the ticket back into her pocket. She swats his hand away, snatches back the ticket, and throws it into her purse, where it likely won't be rediscovered until the late twenty-fourth century.

Anna drops her purse on the floor beside the door, then walks across the living room and plops herself down on to the plush maroon sofa. 'So what exactly are we going to do today?' she asks.

Jordan takes his place on the matching loveseat facing Anna. 'You're getting together with Michelle and Rory tomorrow for your, um, personality lessons, right?'

'Yeah. And the next day. And the next day. And the next day. And so on, and so on.'

'Okay, good. So what I'd like to do now is go over what this show's about.' He gives her a thoughtful look. 'Actually, what do *you* think this show is about?'

Anna leans back and runs her hand through her hair. 'Well, the stuff that Michelle gave me says—'

'I don't care what Michelle's stuff says. I want to know what you think.'

'You want me to be honest, Chef DeWitt?'

'Yes, Chef Rowan. Please. I most definitely would.'

'Okay, well, first of all, the name sucks.'

Jordan nods. 'I agree. It's horrible.'

'You think so too?' she asks. He makes a sour face and nods. 'Then why didn't you do something about it?'

'I tried. I had a meeting with the suits a couple Thursdays back, and they gave me twenty-four hours to come up with a better one, and we got slammed at the restaurant that night, and I slept through my alarm the next morning, and I had to go to work immediately or else I would've been late – remember, I'm never late, Chef Rowan, *never* – and by the time I thought about the name thing, it was Saturday. Too late. Sorry. My bad.'

'Well, at least people won't be wondering what it's about. I mean, *One Boy, One Girl, One Meal* is about as self-explanatory as you can get.'

'Yeah, FoodTube is all about underestimating the intelligence of their viewers.'

Anna grins evilly. 'Is that why they've given you so many shows?'

Jordan tries to glare at her, but fails miserably. 'Ha, ha, ha,' he says, smiling. 'So then, Ms Brainiac, tell me how you envision our little show.'

The concept of *One Boy, One Girl, One Meal* is simple: each week, Anna and Jordan will teach their viewers how to construct a four-course meal, which will consist of a soup or salad, a starter, an entrée and a dessert. They'll work together on every aspect of every dish. According to Michelle's packet, there's supposed to be banter. Lots and lots of banter. That's why FoodTube brought Anna aboard in the first place.

She leans forward. 'From what I can gather, Michelle wants us to share the cooking from top to bottom. But personally, I think it would be better if we split up the courses. Like one week, I'll take the lead on the salad and the entrée and you'll do the appetizer and the dessert, then we'll switch, or mix it up, or whatever.'

'Why?' Jordan asks.

'Because most of the people who'll be watching are probably going to be cooking these dishes by themselves. So wouldn't it make more sense to show them how one person could make it?'

Jordan nods, clearly impressed. 'That's a fine idea, Chef Rowan. I can't believe none of us thought of that.' He stares at her hard.

After ten uncomfortable minutes – okay, it's not really ten minutes, but to Anna, those fifteen seconds sure feel like ten minutes – she snaps, '*What?!* Stop staring at me. Jeez.'

'You look great, Chef Rowan,' Jordan says. 'Did you do something different with your hair?'

'I got it cut right before I came out here. But only like half an inch.' She's flattered he has noticed. Byron hadn't noticed. But she and Byron are on a break, and apparently in Smithland, one of the rules of being on a break is, *Do not, under any circumstances, acknowledge that your partner got a haircut.* But now that she thinks about it, Byron hardly ever notices her haircuts anyhow, break or no break. 'Do you like it, Chef DeWitt?' she softly coos. *Whoa, that came out kind of sexy. Am I flirting?* she wonders. *Flirting with two guys in one day. Your boyfriend decrees a break, and next thing you know, you're a total slut.*

'Yeah,' he answers, equally softly. 'I do like it.' Then he reddens a bit . . . or at least that's the way Anna sees it.

Maybe it's the setting California sun peeking in through the blinds. Maybe not.

'So that means you won't be embarrassed being seen next to me on television?' she asks.

'Chef Rowan, I'd never be embarrassed being seen next to you anywhere on this entire planet.' He clears his throat, then says, 'And speaking of being next to you on television, let's get back to work.'

For the next ninety-or-so minutes, the two chefs bounce ideas off one another: cuisine themes, recipes, running jokes and a bunch of other dull logistical stuff that would put even the most obsessive FoodTube junkie into a deep, deep coma.

Eventually, Jordan checks his watch. 'Shit, I've got to get to work. Do you want to come to the restaurant for dinner? I won't be able to sit with you or anything – you can eat at the bar – but at least you'll be able to check out some of my food that wasn't cooked for the television cameras. Plus there're almost always some good celebs hanging out. Kanye West was there last week. Tom Hanks is a total regular. Nicole Kidman came by last night ... .'

Anna laughs. 'Nicole's in my car.'

'What?'

'Nothing. Forget it.' She does want to go to Rayong Eniwa, but the thought of eating alone in a crowded restaurant in a strange town depresses her. Plus she's still full from lunch, which makes for a perfect excuse. 'I don't even want to look at food till tomorrow. That omoosoomoo ... .'

'Omakase.'

'Right. That. It wore me out.'

'So come and have a drink. You got something else going on?'

He's giving her a sweet, inviting look that almost makes her change her mind. But only almost. 'I can't, Chef DeWitt. I'm meeting Michelle at eight tomorrow morning, and I want to be all rested. I'm just going to go back to the hotel, watch some TV . . .'

'FoodTube, I hope. There's a pretty good *DeWild* rerun on. I was in New Orleans for the Jazz and Heritage Festival. I learned how to make amazing beignets that cost, like, a dollar for two dozen.'

'Sounds cool. I'm in.'

Jordan nods. 'Well, at least you're blowing me off for a good cause.' He motions to the front door. 'Now take a hike. Go get some rest. Give me a ring on my cell tomorrow after you finish class with Michelle and Rory. Maybe I'll take you out for a milkshake.'

'Yeah, maybe.' On her way to the door, she blows him a kiss. 'I'll call you.'

He says, 'Great. Great. Great. Hey, I've got a question for you. Remember after our last *Attack* when I gave you that whole I'd-like-to-be-all-over-your-shit speech?'

Anna snorts. 'How could I forget?'

'Actually, I was kind of hoping you *would* forget.'

'What do you mean?'

He takes a deep breath, then says, 'You've never done television before.'

'Yeah. So?'

'So it's really intense. There's a ton of pressure. A lot of people are depending on you. You have to be fast, and accurate, and awake, and aware, and totally focused at all times.'

She gives him a tiny smile. 'Sounds like what I have to do in my kitchen.'

Jordan nods. 'Yeah, it's like that. But it's *not* like that.'

'What do you mean?'

'I can't explain. You'll get it after, like, three or four weeks. But here's the thing: there'll so much shit you have to keep straight that when you're on the set, you can't have any distractions.'

'What kind of distractions are you talking about?'

'Distractions like my ex-wife.'

'Why would your ex-wife distract me?' Anna screws up her face. 'Wait, she's going to be working on the show?'

Jordan emphatically shakes his head. 'No, what I'm saying is, when she was working on *Rebellion*, it was a distraction. First it was a good distraction, then a bad one. Point being, it was a distraction. When she was around, I was off my game.'

'Okay,' Anna says. 'No distractions. Got it, coach.'

'Let me finish here.'

'Okay. Go.'

'So I can't let you distract me. You're a co-worker. A colleague. My co-host. And hopefully also my friend.'

She grins. 'Of course, I'm your friend, Chef DeWitt.'

'Awesome. But what you can't be is a distraction. I can't let myself be attracted to you. I can't be crushing on you. I can't want to be all over your shit. Get it?'

Anna nods. 'Got it.' It saddened her a little bit that he

wouldn't be crushing on her – who wouldn't want a cute, smart, talented TV star wanting to be all over your shit – but she knows that he knows what he was talking about. Plus Keith is crushing on her, and Byron is, well, who knows what the hell Byron's doing, but whatever it was, it was *something*, so between Byron's *something* and Keith's *something*, the best thing she could get from Jordan DeWitt is *nothing*.

Jordan says, 'Good. Now get prepared to make television history.'

'Will do. Talk tomorrow.'

She feels him watching her walk to the car.

And she likes it.

But she wishes she doesn't.

FRUIT & VEGGIE MONSTER MAKI

Ingredients
For sushi rice:
3⅓ cups Japanese short-grain rice
4 cups water
3 inch square giant kelp

For sushi rice dressing:
5 tablespoons plus 1 teaspoon rice vinegar
5 tablespoons sugar
4 tablespoons sea salt

To assemble roll:
2 sheets toasted nori seaweed, lightly toasted
4 cups sushi rice
1 teaspoon toasted sesame seeds, half black and half white, divided
1 cucumber, peeled, seeded and cut into 4 inch strips
1 small asparagus stalk, par-boiled, trimmed and cut into sections
1 avocado, peeled and thinly sliced
1 mango, finely diced
1 shitake mushroom, finely diced
2 chives, cut into ½ inch strips
½ teaspoon orange zest

Method

1. Put rice in colander and rinse gently under cold water till water runs clear. Drain for 1 hour.
2. Put rice in saucepan with water and kelp, and bring to boil over high heat. Cover, reduce to medium heat, and simmer for 15 minutes, or until rice is cooked and water has been absorbed. Discard kelp.
3. Turn off heat. Remove lid and cover top of pan with towel to absorb any condensation. Put lid back on and set for 20–25 minutes, till rice reaches desired consistency.
4. Transfer to a wide and shallow container.
5. Mix ingredients for the sushi dressing in small saucepan. Bring to boil, then lower heat and simmer for 5 minutes, stirring regularly. Cool to room temperature.
6. Slowly and gently mix dressing into hot rice, using a rice paddle or flat wooden spoon. Add dressing to taste.
7. Keep at room temperature until ready to use. *Do not refrigerate*.
8. Cut nori sheets in half crosswise.
9. Cover a bamboo sushi rolling mat with plastic wrap. Lay down ½ sheet of nori.
10. Moisten hands and spread the sushi rice evenly, pressing gently with fingertips, layered about ¼ inch thick.
11. Sprinkle with half of the black and white sesame seeds.
12. Turn the rice-spread nori sheet over, on top of the bamboo mat, with the nori facing up.
13. Evenly arrange cucumber, asparagus sections, ⅔ of both avocado and mango in the center.
14. Roll the ingredients in the bamboo mat to make a firmly packed cylinder, then remove the plastic wrap.

15. Use mushroom, chives, zest, mango, remaining avocado and sesame seeds to make roll look like a monster.
16. Cut into 6 or 8 equal-sized pieces. Wipe knife clean in between cuts. Serve immediately.

One Boy, One Girl, One Crappy TV Show

'Cut! Can we go again, please?'

Jordan disgustedly slams down a double handful of bread dough on to the countertop. Fortunately, the work area was properly floured, so the dough doesn't stick to the granite. Unfortunately, the work area was properly floured, so Jordan's black apron is now twenty-four per cent white. 'What the hell was wrong with that, Rory?'

'You can do better,' the director calls from his position just to the right of the cameras.

'It was fine.'

Anna tries unsuccessfully to wipe the flour from Jordan's apron; all she does is get white powder all over her red Crocs. 'He's right. We can do better.'

'We can? So what do you think we need to do in order to improve it, Chef Rowan?'

Giving up the flour removal mission, Anna raises her

eyebrows and rubs her chin. 'Hmm. Actually, I *don't* know.' She asks Rory, 'What the hell *was* wrong with that?'

Rory removes his headphones and wanders into the elaborate kitchen that doubles as their set. 'Anna, you're being far too perky. We're not looking for you to be Rachel Ray, here – we're looking for Anna Rowan. But what's even more problematic is that you're *way* perkier now than you were in the first segment, and if we edit it together as is, it'll look like you snorted crystal meth during the commercial break.' He turns to Jordan. 'And you, JD, how about some smiles, pal? Some energy? Some love? You're acting like somebody pooped in your coffee.'

The thing is, Jordan's not feeling very smiley this afternoon, in part because he was stuck in the weeds at the restaurant last night until well after midnight, and he didn't get out of there until two a.m., and he had to get up at seven to be at the studio at eight, and he doesn't operate well on four hours of sleep. (He could tough it out on five, but four, not so much.) But the primary reason he's smile-free is because he's pretty sure that this new show of theirs bites the big finocchiona.[36]

Jordan and Anna are shooting the third episode of *One Boy, One Girl, One Meal*, and even though neither of the two shows they have in the can have been edited in full, everybody at FoodTube – Michelle, Rory, the suits, the interns, *everybody* – says they like what they've seen thus

---

[36] Finocchiona: A fennel-tinged salami that, in addition to being quite tasty, is useful when creating a metaphor that involves biting something big and phallic.

far, and it's off to a great start, and it'll be even greater in five or six more episodes, and people will watch it in droves, and blah blah blah blah blah. But Jordan thinks everybody's blowing smoke up his ass, because he's two hundred per cent certain that the new program is going badly. And he feels confident in his assessment, because he knows what it's like when a new program is going well.

Save for his first month or so on the air, he'd hit the ground running on all three of his other shows – *DeWild* was especially good coming out of the gate – but he hasn't been able to get his bearings on this one. Maybe it's due to the fact that he didn't have a hand in the project's creation or creative direction. Maybe it's because he didn't mentally prepare himself for the challenge, figuring that a no-frills show about no-frills cooking wouldn't really *be* much of a challenge. But those are the maybes. What he *definitely* knows is that the damn show stinks to high heaven because he hasn't brought his 'A' game to any of their three tapings.

Even though he knows he's screwing the pooch, he's also placing some of the blame on Anna. His new partner isn't doing anything wrong – as a matter of fact, considering it's her first time being a regular on network television, she's performing quite well, aside from those periodic attacks of Rachel Ray-ian perkiness – but it's her mere existence that's messing him up. The fact is, on a certain level, *anybody's* mere existence would mess him up.

Jordan has never had a television partner before, and he's finding it difficult to work in tandem, which is odd, because at Rayong Eniwa, he's all about kitchen staff unity. Away from the cameras, he's an expert teamworker, but right here, right now, right in the FoodTube studios, he's finding it virtually impossible to delegate any responsibility or logistically (or creatively) mesh with Anna. He craves autonomy in his life, and his inclination is to take control of the show . . . no, his inclination is to *be* the show. This isn't coming from a place of maliciousness or selfishness – despite his blustery public persona, Jordan DeWitt doesn't give a damn about being in the spotlight. It's just that on FoodTube, he's always done everything himself, and it's all he knows.

Another reason he's screwing up: he's distracted. Very very distracted.

He's knows it's not fair to blame Anna for distracting him. After all, is it her fault that she's a cute, and funny, and enthusiastic, and warm, and smart, and talented distraction of a woman? No. Is it Anna's fault that Jordan is finally starting to put Crazy Nadia behind him and is thus sorta kinda ready to maybe possibly jump back into the dating pool, and she's the coolest woman he's met in years, the first woman he's truly, truly wanted to ravish since that first adrenaline-and-hormone-fueled year with Nadia? No. Is it Anna's fault that she lives in ice-cold Chicago and has an ice-cold boyfriend? Okay, yeah, that part is her fault, but it still shouldn't bother him to the point that he's turning *One Boy, One Girl, One Meal* into his own personal garbage heap.

Jordan rubs his eyes hard and tries to focus, tries to get in a zone. He takes three deep, lingering breaths, dips his hands into a bowl of flour, picks up the dough, and tells Rory,

'Go back to your lair. Let's do this. Focaccia fest, take two.'

Anna points at Jordan and says, 'You. Hold up a second. I need you to explain to me again why we're not putting cheese on the focaccia. Is it your cheese phobia? You've got to get over that, because we're screwed whenever we do Italian. Or Mexican. Or Greek. Or French. Or—'

'This has nothing to do with my cheese issues, which I will admit to having. I happen to dig this focaccia recipe without cheese. I want to taste the tomatoes. I want to taste the rosemary. Personally, I think cheese dulls it . . .'

'Personally, I think cheese *enhances* it.'

'Okay, fine, you're entitled to your opinion . . . even if it is so very, very wrong.'

'Funny guy.' She turns to the director. 'Rory, has he always been this funny?'

Rory says, 'Nope. He used to be remarkably unfunny. This is the funniest he's ever been.'

'This is his comedic high point?' The director nods. Anna mock shivers. 'That's frightening, Rory. Truly frightening.'

Jordan shakes his head. 'Screw both of you. Chef Rowan, the focaccia is a starter, and we don't want people to get filled up on it. It's not a pizza; it's an appetizer. Also, you're doing that caprese,[37] and I'm sure you're going to put, like, a gallon of mozzarella in there. And don't forget there's ricotta in the ravioli . . .'

---

[37] Caprese: A salad made from tomatoes, fresh mozzarella, basil, olive oil, balsamic vinegar, salt and pepper. It should be noted that it's virtually the only salad the greens-hating author of this book will eat.

'Barely,' Anna points out. 'It's three parts butternut squash, one part cheese.'

'Yeah, but the cheese is still there. And then there's the dessert, the pannacotta,[38] which is, like, two ingredients away from being cheese.'

'Okay, fine, I see your point, but—'

Jordan shushes Anna by putting his index finger on her mouth. 'Rory, I hope you were filming, because Chef Rowan said that she sees my point. I want that documented for all eternity.'

Rory says, 'I was.'

'You were what?' Jordan asks.

'Documenting. This is the best stuff I've gotten out of you guys. Keep bickering. It's gold, baby, pure gold. I'm just going to let the cameras roll.'

Jordan, immediately seeing what Rory sees, asks Anna, 'You up for some more bickering?'

'Always. What say we keep bickering about shaving Parmesan on to the focaccia? If we were talking, say, Gruyère, I could see your point about the cheese overwhelming everything. But Parmesan won't make it any heavier, and it won't dull any flavors, as you so strangely believe it will.'

Jordan fake yawns and asks, 'Can't we bicker about something else? Focaccia doesn't merit more than two or three bickers.'

---

[38] Pannacotta: Italian flan. If you're on a diet, don't even look at it, or you'll gain five pounds.

'No new bickering topics shall be broached until the cheese issue is settled.'

'You know what, Chef Rowan? I'm clearly unable to overcome my natural bias against cheese, so ask the producer what she thinks.'

Anna turns to the eternally multi-tasking, eternally overworked Michelle Fields, who, right at this moment, is offstage left, talking on her cell, and writing hurriedly on a legal pad, and scanning the show rundown, and beating on the keyboard of the laptop that's precariously balanced on her lap, and juggling three flaming Wustoffs, all while riding a unicycle. 'Hey, Michelle! You cool with me putting some Parmesan on the focaccia?'

Michelle glances up from her, well, from her *everything*, and says, 'Anna, I truly, honestly, completely do not give the least bit of a shit.'

Anna throws Jordan a loopy grin. 'You heard her, Chef DeWitt. She *loves* the cheese idea. The Parm is a go.'

Jordan thinks, *All she had to do was smile at me like that, and I would've said yes to the damn cheese in the first place.* 'Fine,' he says, 'you can shave your cheese. Live it up. Go crazy.' He points to Rory. 'Let's do this, my man.'

Rory raps his knuckles on the red light atop of the camera. 'I told you, we've *been* doing it. Don't stop. No breaks. Keep cooking. Have fun. We'll make it look all pretty in editing. But I'm totally loving this. If it feels good for you guys, this is the way we'll roll from now on.'

It most definitely feels good for those guys. Jordan, unconstrained by any structure, finds his groove, and right away, everybody is blown away. Even though most of the crew has worked on at least one of Jordan's other shows at some point in the last year, they gawk at him like the true star that he is, and it makes him feel better about the whole endeavor, so his natural charm and boyish enthusiasm kicks in and he grooves even harder. And the harder he grooves, the harder Anna grooves. The chemistry that the FoodTube execs spotted during the DeWitt/Rowan *Sneak Attacks* is in full effect.

A mere forty-five minutes later, Rory yells 'Cut! I think we're good to go. If I need any pick-ups, we'll take care of it next week. Anna and Jordan, get out of here. I'll see you next week. Excellent work.'

After cast and crew say their goodbyes, Jordan, in a considerably better mood, hops into his chocolate-brown Lexus and drives to his restaurant. In a relaxed, contemplative head space, he thinks about how the best things in his life have happened serendipitously – his whole damn career, for instance – and the chance discovery of this non-format format for *One Boy* is yet another example of luck dictating results. Still, he wishes he had more of an ability to make his own luck, and that he didn't always have to rely on events unfolding by themselves. Jordan isn't a control freak, but he wouldn't mind shaping his own destiny for once. But before he starts beating himself up for not being proactive enough, he decides that when it comes to luck, it's virtually impossible to make it; all you can really do is prepare yourself, so that when luck lands on your doorstep, you're able to both recognize it and take advantage of it. Half of the battle, he concludes, is realizing that the luck made it on to your doorstep in the first place. Then he thinks that he should stop thinking about this too much – it might be bad luck – and he starts concentrating on coming up with something cool for tonight's special.

Early the following Wednesday, the *One Boy, One Girl, One Meal* gang reconvenes at the FoodTube studio. When Jordan arrives at work, he sees Anna sitting on the edge of the countertop of their studio kitchen, happily chatting up a familiar-looking kid. He sidles up to the pair and says, 'Morning, Chef Rowan.'

'Morning, Chef DeWitt.' She puts her hand on the kid's arm. 'You remember Keith Cole, don't you?'

'Oh, right,' Jordan recalls, 'the guy we had pizza with that time.' He proffers his hand. 'Hey, Keith. What brings you to LA?'

They shake, and Keith says, 'Hanging out with the 'rents. Seeing some of my friends. Getting out of Chicago. Bonding with Anna.'

To Jordan's semi-trained eye, Anna and Keith are looking pretty damn bonded. They're both wearing big, goofy smiles, and Anna's body language speaks volumes: her legs are cheerfully swinging up and down as if she's a little girl waiting for the guy behind the counter at the ice cream parlor to bring her a hot fudge sundae; she's hovering comfortably in Keith's personal space, offering him lingering eye contact and casual forearm touches; and she has an ease with him that smacks of sex, either past, or present, or future . . . or maybe all three.

The weird thing is that during a break in filming last week, Anna, apropos of nothing, started going on and on about how she hadn't spoken with Byron Smith since she got out to California, and she was wondering if he was doing okay, and she couldn't decide if she missed him or not. Then she started going on and on about Tart, and how Billy the sous chef kept telling her that she should stay in Los Angeles, because the place was running unbelievably well without her, and she knew he was joking, but it still made her feel kind of bad. Then she started going on and on about how Miguel the line cook who was her official catsitter calls her everyday with updates about Stinks, and how cute her kitty is, and she misses him so much. And yet here she is being all flirty with Keith Cole. Jordan rightly believes that Anna is one confused woman. He hopes she'll work everything out. She's a good person, and she deserves an uncomplicated life.

Jordan feels a quick but sharp stab of jealousy – he kind of wishes Anna would give him some googly eyes, even though he is well aware that googly eyes from his co-host would be a bad thing – but not wanting to seem fazed, he claps the young server on the shoulder and says, 'I can dig where you're coming from about getting out of Chicago. I mean, it's May, and there's still a chance it could snow, right? I don't get why people stay there. If you like the cold, why not move to Alaska? At least they've got otters up there. I like otters.' Then he thinks, *Why the hell am I talking about otters?*

Anna gives him a deservedly weird look and says, 'You are such a wuss, Chef DeWitt. It's spring out there. Spring out here is like the dead of summer in Chicago. It's nice out here, but I miss spring, dude.' She looks at Keith, chuckles, and says, 'Did I just call him *dude*?' Keith nods. 'I guess I'm an official Angelino now.'

Jordan feels a hand on his shoulder. 'He's not a wuss, Anna. He's a pussy. A big California pussy. Hey there, Keith. Give me a hug, kiddo.'

Keith smiles. 'Hey, Michelle.'

Michelle steps around Jordan and favors Keith not just with a long hug, but also a half-lip-half-cheek kiss, then asks him, 'Where've you been? Anna gets to town, and you don't call me any more?'

Keith shrugs and cocks his head at Anna. 'We've been hanging out a lot.'

Michelle starts tap-tap-tapping her foot, a gesture that Jordan recognizes as a sign of utter annoyance. And why does he know this? Because since he hired her, he's utterly annoyed her several zillion times, which has added up to a whole lot of tap-tap-tapping. 'That's nice,' Michelle says. 'Hope that works out for you guys.' The untrained ear would think that she's sincerely wishing Anna and Keith eternal (or at least temporary) bliss. Jordan's ears, when it comes to Michelle, are exceedingly well trained, and he recognizes that she's seething.

He takes her by the elbow and tells Anna and Keith, 'I'll be right back, guys. We have to go over some publicity stuff. Right, Michelle?' When she says nothing, he says through gritted teeth, '*Right, Michelle?*'

Michelle says, 'Whatever,' but she lets herself be dragged through the studio, through the hallways, and all the way to Jordan's office.

Jordan sits her down on his black leather sofa, kneels

on to his haunches, puts a brotherly hand on her knee, and says, 'Please tell me you don't have a crush on that child, M-Class.'

'He's twelve years old, Jordan,' Michelle says. 'How could I have a crush on him?'

'Yeah. I see your point.'

Michelle snorts. 'No, you *don't* see my point. I'm not saying, *How* could I have a crush on him. I'm saying, How *could* I have a crush on him.'

Jordan removes his hand from her leg, scratches his shiny, shaved, cue-ball head, and, after a three-hour pause, asks, 'Um, say what?'

'I'm in my thirties, Jordan, and Keith Cole is most definitely not.'

'You just turned thirty-one. That's barely your thirties.'

'Yeah, but it's still the thirties, and I shouldn't be crushing on a teenager. Not because it's the wrong thing to do, I don't know, from a moral perspective or something, but because I should be into a guy who's closer to my own age demographic.'

'Fine. So stop crushing on him.'

'Great idea. The thing is, we kissed. It's hard to stop crushing on somebody after you've kissed.'

Jordan – who, despite being a Jordan-centric kind of guy, is also quite the nosy gossipmonger – says excitedly, 'You kissed? Ooh, details, details.'

Michelle sighs, slouches, and rests her head on the back of the couch. 'It wasn't a big deal. When he got out here a couple months back, I gave him a tour of the studio, and he kissed me goodbye. It was quick. But it was nice.'

After another good, long, silent pause, Jordan says, 'And?'

'And what? And nothing. That's it.'

'So are we talking a see-you-at-work-tomorrow goodbye kiss like *I* give you at the end of the day, or are we talking a next-time-we-kiss-it'll-be-for-real goodbye kiss, like you undoubtedly wish I'd give you at the end of the day?'

Michelle laughs, then admits, 'Probably closer to the first one. But I thought there might've been some possibilities there. He's clearly into Anna, though.'

Jordan grumbles, 'Yeah. She's clearly into him, too. No accounting for taste, I suppose. Between that guy and the tool she lives with in Chicago, I don't know what that girl is thinking. She's a catch, and I don't see how either of them could've caught her.'

Michelle's head pops up. 'You like her, don't you?'

'You couldn't tell? And I thought you knew me so well.'

'Don't know if you've noticed, Jordan, but I've been a little busy lately. A little distracted.'

'Yeah, me too.'

Michelle leans forward and puts her hand tenderly on Jordan's cheek. 'And that's why you've been sucking on the show, isn't it? Anna's distracting you. How sweet.'

Jordan smacks her hand away and stands up. 'I thought you told me I was doing fine.'

'Yes I did, J-Money. That is what us producers call *handling the talent*.'

'I don't need to be handled. Tell me the truth. It's pointless to bullshit, because I'll find out eventually.'

'Okay. At first, you sucked out loud and she was mediocre at best. But we all knew you'd both pull it together eventually. Don't worry about it, though. We already decided not to air those first two episodes we shot. No big deal. We'll call it our dress rehearsal.'

'I'm relieved.'

'You should be. If those would've made it on to television, we would've gotten axed before we made it to episode three.'

Jordan nods. 'I agree. And thank you for being honest. And in the future, don't bullshit me about this sort of thing. Seriously. Ever. If you have something to tell me, then tell me. I'm a big boy. I can take it.'

Michelle stands up. 'I have something to tell you.'

'Let me brace myself.'

'Actually, it's more of a favor.'

'Shoot.'

'Steal Anna away from Keith.'

Jordan puts his arm around Michelle's waist and guides her out the door and toward the studio. 'So you, the producer of a new TV show that's kind of sucking, are asking the male co-host to make a move on his female co-host, even though A) the female co-host lives with a guy who she might or might not be two seconds away from breaking up with, B) the female co-host might or might not be messing around with *another guy*, and C) the female co-host has made it clear that she's not interested in the male co-host. Is that what you're saying?'

'That's exactly what I'm saying. And what do you mean, she's made it clear she's not into you? What did she say?'

Concerned that Anna might overhear them, Jordan stops walking a good twenty yards away from the studio door. 'She hasn't said anything. But I know.'

'How?'

'I've never been able to tell if a girl likes me, but I've always been able to tell when they *don't*.'

Michelle gives him a sympathetic pout. 'Wow. That kind of blows.'

'It kind of does. But it's also saved me a whole lot of embarrassment.' He peers into the studio. 'So you really want me to steal her away from Keith, eh?'

'Damn straight.'

'You really think I can do it? You think she'll go for it?'

Michelle nods. 'Personally, I think she likes you. I can tell by the way she looks at you.'

'Does she look at me the same way she looks at Keith? Because she's giving that kid some serious googly eyes.'

'Okay, maybe she's not looking at you the exact way she's looking at him, but she's still giving you some nice looks.' She gives Jordan a humorless chuckle. 'Ahh, what the hell do I know? Maybe she's not into you. But at least give it a shot. At least we'll both find out one way or the other.'

'Fine. But only if you say please,' Jordan says.

'*Pleeeeease.*'

'Say pretty please.'

'*Preeeeetty pleeeease.*'

Chef Jordan DeWitt takes and holds a deep breath. He lets it out. 'Okay,' he whispers, 'here goes nothing.'

ROSEMARY AND HEIRLOOM TOMATO FOCACCIA WITH SHAVED PARMESAN

Ingredients

2 teaspoons rapid-rising dry yeast
3½–4 cups flour
1 pinch of sugar
1 tablespoon coarse salt
1 cup warm water
¼ cup olive oil
Cornmeal, for dusting
2 tablespoons olive oil
1 onion, diced
2 garlic cloves, minced
1 small yellow Heirloom tomato, sliced
1 small red Heirloom tomato, sliced
1 small green Heirloom tomato, sliced
¼ cup shredded Parmesan
Freshly ground black pepper
2 tablespoons fresh rosemary

Method

1. Preheat oven to 400°F.
2. In the bowl of a standing mixer fitted with a dough hook, proof the yeast by combining it with the water and sugar. Stir gently to dissolve. Let stand 3 minutes till foam appears.

3. Turn mixer on low and slowly add the flour to the bowl. Dissolve salt in 2 tablespoons of water and add it to the mixture, then add ¼ cup olive oil.

4. When the dough starts to come together, increase the mixer speed to medium. (Stop the machine periodically to scrape the dough off the hook.) Mix till the dough is smooth and elastic, about 10 minutes, adding flour as necessary. Turn the dough out on to a work surface and fold over itself 5–10 times.

5. Form the dough into a ball and place in an oiled bowl, then turn to coat the entire ball with oil. Cover with plastic wrap or damp towel and put in a warm place till doubled in size, about 45 minutes.

6. Coat a sheet pan with a little olive oil and cornmeal.

7. Once the dough is doubled and domed, turn it out on to the counter. Roll and stretch the dough out to an oblong shape about ½ inch thick. Lay the flattened dough on the pan and cover with plastic wrap. Let rest for 15 minutes.

8. In the meantime, coat a small sauté pan with olive oil, then add the onion and cook over low heat for 20–25 minutes, until the onion is caramelized and light brown.

9. Uncover the dough and dimple it with your fingertips.

10. Brush the surface of the dough with more olive oil, then add caramelized onion, garlic, tomatoes, cheese, salt and pepper to taste, and rosemary.

11. Bake on the bottom rack for 15–20 minutes. Cut into squares. Serve hot.

Wednesday Sneak Attack

Despite his tender age and relative lack of experience, Keith Cole can kiss, and Anna Rowan couldn't be more thrilled.

Anna's kissing situation has been stagnant for a while now, because Byron Smith, well, let's say his game is kind of rusty. It's not like Byron is completely deficient in the smooching department – he's just become kind of passive about the whole venture. Or maybe he's always been that way. It's hard for Anna to remember. Their first kisses were such a long time ago.

This isn't to say that Byron's *all* bad; he'd always parted his lips the exact perfect amount, and he's quite good with his tongue – not too little, not too much. The main problem is that the guy barely ever moves his mouth. Anna still can't figure out whether that's simply his natural technique, or whether he's too tired and/or lazy to mix things up. His seeming tiredness (or laziness) is also a problem in that he all but ignores the rest of the area above her shoulders. He doesn't attack her neck (Anna loves having her neck attacked), or blow into her ears (ditto), or gently kiss her eyelids (ditto ditto) nearly often enough for her taste. For Byron Smith, it's all mouth, all the time, and she's never been able to bring herself to discuss it with him, because she never wanted to hurt his feelings.

Keith, on the other hand, is enthusiastic, passionate, and he seems to have a neck and ear fetish, which Anna heartily encourages. He doesn't mess around with her eyelids, though, but he's such an expert with the earlobes that she lets it slide . . . at least for the time being. If they keep up their thing for a while, she might have to drop a hint or two.

Anna's not sure if she'll be able to keep up their thing for that much longer, though. She knows for certain that what they have, such as it is, won't go anywhere. It can't. It shouldn't. Or maybe it can. Who knows? It's impossible for her to make any kind of decision about her romantic life, because Byron Smith – a man who has told her he loves her more times than she can count – isn't returning her phone calls. Or her smoke signals. Or her carrier pigeons.

Okay, he finally started returning a few calls, but he generally rings her when she's filming or asleep, and doesn't have the time or wherewithal to talk for real. Since she's been in California, they've spoken for a grand total of twenty-three unsubstantial minutes.

He is, however, returning all of her emails, but gives her only essential information: Billy's nightly specials are going over well (which she knows, because Billy tells her that whenever they talk), Stinks is totally healthy and back to eating too much food (which she knows, because she gets text and email updates from Miguel at least once a day), all the Chicago food writers are calling and begging for interviews, yadda, yadda, yadda. All business. He hasn't asked her how she's feeling or how the show is going, but what's frustrating Anna the most is the uncertainty. *Are we still on a break?*

Anna Rowan and Keith Cole have been sort of seeing each other for almost four weeks now, but they haven't had sex – she's only let the poor kid get to second base. (She can't remember the last time she left a guy hanging at second base for more than a week. For that matter, she can't remember the last time she even counted bases.) But Keith – clearly ecstatic to have Anna to himself, even for the briefest of moments – is being very sweet and understanding about the whole thing. Sort of.

'Why don't you try calling Byron again?' he asks her in the midst of yet another bedsheet-mussing makeout session in her hotel room. 'Or texting him? Or emailing him? Track him down and ask him point blank.'

She sits up and pushes her hair from her face. 'Ask him what?'

'If you're still a couple.'

'And then what?'

'If he says no, you and I will ride off into the sunset.'

'And if he says yes?'

'We quietly tiptoe off into the sunset under the cover of darkness.'

She laughs. Uncomfortable discussing her boyfriend while topless, Anna pulls on the oversized white FoodTube top she's been using as a sleep shirt. 'Listen, I know Byron's being an ass, but he wouldn't break up with me over the phone.'

'How do you know he wouldn't? Would you have thought he'd stop returning most of your calls?'

'Hmm. Good point, I guess.' She lays down, slithers under the covers and pulls them over her head. 'This sucks.'

'What sucks?' Keith asks.

Anna pokes her head out from under the sheets and points at Keith's mouth. 'This.' Then she points to her cell on the nightstand. 'And that.' Then she knocks on her head with her knuckles. 'And this.' It sucks that she likes kissing Keith, because she shouldn't even be doing it in the first place. It sucks that Byron is leaving her hanging with his lame-o phone calls. And it sucks that when she's away from a kitchen or a television studio, her brain and heart turn into cotton.

Keith asks, 'Okay, but does this suck?' before leaning down and attacking her neck in his magically Keith-ian way.

After a few tingly seconds, she looks at the clock next to her cell on the nightstand and gently pushes him away. 'It's after midnight. I think you should go.'

'We could have a sleepover party like last week. We could cuddle.'

'No. We can't. I have to be at the studio at seven in the morning, and I have to wake up at six. I need sleep, and our sleepovers aren't particularly sleep-oriented.'

For the first time since they began their pseudo-dalliance,

Anna sees a flicker of frustration flash across Keith's face. But it's only a moment. A brief moment. But it was there. He quickly pulls himself together and says, 'Cool, whatever you want. I'll holler at you.'

He gives her a brief kiss on the mouth, but before he can work his way down to her neck, she squirms out of his embrace, hops off the bed, takes his hand, pulls him toward the door, and says, 'Go, go, go. Anna needs her rest. Good night.' They smooch for a minute or two, then she sends him on his way.

While Anna brushes her teeth, she remembers the last time she was in a situation like this. Actually, it was the *only* other time she was in a situation like this. For some reason, she's never been the kind of girl who attracted more than one guy at a time. And that's fine with her, because juggling boys is a pain in the ass.

It was the summer after she graduated high school, and she'd been seeing Bill, a junior at DePaul University, for almost four months. He was all Mr Joe College, and up to that point, Anna had only been with Mr Joe High School, and she was finding that the elder Joes made for better boyfriends, if only because they were far more responsible and reliable. But there was a Joe High School who was nuts about her – ironically, his name actually was Joe – and he was considered by many to be the catchiest catch in her class: smart, funny, cute, played bass in an amazing reggae band, good kisser, the whole schmeer.[39] She'd dated Joe

[39] Schmeer: 1) A Yiddish word for 'shabang.' 2) A Yiddish word for 'a dollop of cream cheese for your bagel.'

briefly during their junior year, then they'd drifted apart after three months, because sometimes that's what happens when you're sixteen years old; you drift.

She ran into Joe while she was having dinner with Bill at a killer Italian restaurant on Chicago's north side called Angelina's. (Anna ordered a spinach and mushroom lasagna, which was so memorable that she eventually more or less replicated it on the Tart menu.) Initially there were pleasantries all around, but both Joe and Bill soon kicked into a quiet alpha male mode – lots of glaring and speaking through gritted teeth – which, truth be told, gave Anna a bit of a thrill. After all, what teenage girl wouldn't want two awesome boys fighting over her? Okay, they weren't fighting – neither Joe nor Bill had it in them to actually get violent – but they were both doing their best to claim their territory.

Joe called her two days later, and told her that he'd thought about her on a regular basis since their drift-apart, and he always hoped he'd run into her at some point, because he would've felt weird calling her out of nowhere, and now that they'd connected again, they should start dating, and she should get rid of the DePaul dork. He didn't write her an I'm-declaring-my-love-to-you note like Keith did, but his speech over the phone was in the same spirit. Anna wasn't as attached to Bill as she was to Byron when Keith made his initial overture, so it was easy (or at least easy-ish) to let Bill down gently and take up with Joe, whom she dated happily till she started attending classes at Kendall, at which point she became too busy to do anything other than attend classes.

So if Anna applies her previous boy-juggling experience to her current situation, it would play out like this: she sends Keith on his way, gets back together with Byron when she finishes shooting *One Boy*, then stays with him for another year, until her reservoir of time and energy dries up and they both go their separate ways. That was a perfectly swell option when she was nineteen, but coming up on thirty, it's not nearly as appetizing.

Another problem is that she's starting to truly care for Keith. Over the last week, hanging out with him has become more than just getting kissed well and being unconditionally adored. She legitimately enjoys being with him, talking with him, laughing with him. He's not the deepest guy in the world, but he has a ton of potential, and once he starts focusing a tiny bit on his future, and once he figures out what kind of man he wants to be, and once he figures out what the hell he's going to do with his life, he'll be one of the catchiest catches in Chicago. Or Los Angeles.

Yes, that's right, Keith Cole is considering staying in LA. He bitches to Anna about his hometown's problems on a regular basis – little wonder, as Los Angeles offers him plenty to bitch about, i.e. traffic, smog, plastic people, and Botox – but he tells Anna that there's something about it that grounds him. Even though he's been in Chicago for three years, LA is his home. Always will be. (For her part, Anna can take or leave Los Angeles. On the take side, the weather is beautiful, the restaurants are solid – she's never consistently had such good fish in her life – and the people she's met thus far are super-nice. On the leave side, it's smoggy, it's too spread out, and, well, it's not Chicago.)

Anna can relate to the importance of being grounded and having a home base. Now that she and Jordan have found a groove on the show – and now that she's had a steady diet of California sun – she's pretty damn happy with her life ... but not completely. On her way to the studio, she finds herself thinking about how much she misses her city. And Tart. And Stinks. And, in spite of herself, she kind of misses Byron. Between the restaurant and their relationship, there's a lot of history with Mr Smith. It's not easy to walk away from that without a fight ... or at least without finding out what the hell happened.

For some inexplicable reason, the 110 is running smoothly, so she arrives at work some twenty minutes early. She parks in the FoodTube lot, and as she walks to the studio, makes a Herculean effort to turn her brain off and stop wondering whether she's falling in love with Keith ... and wondering if she's still in love with Byron ... and wondering whether Billy is telling the entire truth about how well he's doing ... and wondering if Stinks could tolerate LA long term ... and wondering if *she* could tolerate LA long term.

She's so lost in her wondering that when Jordan sidles up beside her and gives her a genial 'Hey,' she nearly jumps out of her skirt.

'Christ, Chef DeWitt, you scared the shit out of me.'

Jordan looks sheepish. 'Sorry,' he says quietly. Seeing his stricken expression, Anna again notes how radically different the real-life Jordan is from the TV Jordan. She remembers that night over the summer when she and Byron were cuddled up on the couch, watching FoodTube, ragging on *Sunday Sneak Attack*, calling Jordan a lame-o loser chump. (Actually, Anna was calling him a lame-o loser chump. Byron wasn't calling him anything. But Byron was being a lot nicer back then.) After working with Jordan for the past two months, she feels pretty stupid about prejudging him so harshly. She has to stop doing that in general. Being judgemental is bad for one's karma. And probably also for one's crow's feet.

Jordan stops walking, gently takes Anna's elbow, pulls her toward him, and stares deep into her eyes for so long, and with such intensity that she has to turn away. 'Are you okay, Chef Rowan?' he asks.

'I'm fine. You didn't scare me *that* badly.'

He shakes his head, and stares harder. 'No. Are . . . you . . . okay? You seem a little spaced out.'

She sees compassion and concern in his eyes, his mouth, his forehead. She feels the sudden urge to hug him. Not in a passionate way, mind you; it's just that his expression makes him seem so warm, and Anna is in serious need some warmth. She gives him a tired grin and rubs his bicep. 'I'm fine. Really. I am. I'm cool.'

'No. No way. You're not.'

She's again able to look him in the eye. 'You sound pretty definitive about that, Chef DeWitt.'

He puts the tip of his index finger in between her eyebrows. 'When you get upset, you get this little squinchy thing right there.'

Anna pushes his finger away. 'What do you mean,

squinchy thing? There's no squinchy thing.'

Jordan again examines Anna's face, and nods definitively. 'It's there. Look in the mirror. Don't worry – it doesn't look bad or anything. It's just . . . squinchy.'

Mildly exasperated, she shakes her head, begins to walk toward the studio, and says, 'Come on, let's get to work.'

He again takes her elbow. 'We're way early. It's beautiful out. Let's hang.' She allows herself to be guided to a rickety wooden picnic table under the circle of palm trees on the knoll at other side of the parking lot. They sit down companionably close to one another. Jordan kicks off his sandals and says, 'Chef Rowan, I'm starting to really love doing this show with you. I didn't think I would. Those first two episodes . . . man. I couldn't deal.'

'Yeah. I could tell.'

Jordan barks out a single snort/laugh (or laugh/snort, depending on how you're looking at it). 'Was it that obvious?'

'God, yes. I felt awful about the whole thing. I thought it was me. During the second taping, I was this close to talking with Michelle about bailing.'

'Holy shit. For real?'

'For real.'

'I had no idea.'

Anna shrugs. 'I didn't say anything to anybody. It's not the kind of thing you advertise.'

'For sure. So why didn't you bail?'

'Because I don't bail on anybody or anything unless I think the situation is totally unfixable. And I was pretty sure this show could be fixed. And I was right. You, and Rory, and Michelle, are amazing at what you do. No way it was going to suck forever.'

'I'm really glad you stayed.'

Anna nods. 'I'm glad too.' She glances at her watch. 'Fifteen minutes till call time. Want to go?'

'No.' He takes her hand. 'I want to sit here with you for the next six hours, and talk about food, and play with your hair, and rest my hand on your knee, and buy you a corndog and a soda, and make you laugh so hard that Coke comes out of your nose. You're my dreamgirl, Chef Rowan. As much as I've tried to quash it, I still want to be all over your shit.'

She slowly takes her hand back. Her brain fogs up, and she stares off into the distance, at a complete loss for words. For the sake of her professional life and her sanity, Anna has conveniently forgotten that Jordan has a crush on her. Okay, it isn't a *forgetting* kind of thing. It's more of an *I'm-not-going-to-think-about-it-but-if-for-some-reason-the-thought-enters-my-head-I'm-going-to-banish-it-to-the-nether-regions-of-my-brain* kind of thing. This is why his speech-slash-declaration, while not coming out of nowhere, catches her off guard. And here's what's further compounding the problem: Anna likes Jordan. A lot. But she doesn't like him in That Way. She likes him as Just a Friend. She doesn't want to Get Naked With Him. It has nothing to do with what kind of person he is. She even might have seriously considered Jordan a candidate for mutual nudity after his initial *Sunday Sneak Attack* speech-slash-declaration back in Chicago if A) she didn't already have a live-in boyfriend; B) Jordan didn't live halfway across the country from her; and C) they weren't about to start working together. But those were three big strikes against him, so ever since that infamous 'all over your shit' soliloquy, any thoughts of dating Jordan DeWitt were immediately banished to the nether regions of her brain.

That all being the case, the last thing in the world she wants to do is to hurt the poor guy. He has to be let down gently. She has to handle him with kid gloves. She can't break his heart – she can't even chip it. Which is why she wants to bash herself in the head with some Calphalon[40] when she blurts out, 'I'm kind of seeing Keith. I totally shouldn't be. I totally suck.'

Much to her surprise, Jordan seems utterly unfazed and not particularly upset. 'You don't suck.' He's briefly silent, then sighs again. 'For your sake, I hope the kid realizes how lucky he is.'

Anna feels herself blush. 'I think he does. I'm the bad person. I'm jerking him around. But he's fun. More fun than Byron. Why am I telling you all this?' She shakes some cobwebs from her head and continues, 'Let's be honest, Chef DeWitt. You have a restaurant that you love out here, and I have a restaurant that I love in Chicago, and I'm not the biggest Los Angeles fan in the world, and you've made it clear that you despise Illinois, so unless we move to, I don't know, Hawaii or somewhere, and open a

---

[40] Calphalon: A line of non-stick pots and pans that are excellent for bashing oneself on the head with.

restaurant together, we couldn't make it work. And then there's that whole boyfriend thing.'

'You mean boyfriends. Plural.'

'No. Singular. Byron is my boyfriend. Keith isn't.'

'You might want to mention that to Keith.'

Anna swallows hard and rubs her eyes. 'I know, I know, I know. And I will.'

'You should.'

'I will.'

'Good.' After a brief bit of semi-awkward silence, Jordan gives Anna three asexual pats on her leg. 'Well, Chef Rowan, I guess this is as close to fondling your knee as I'll ever get.'

'Trust me, Chef DeWitt, my knees really aren't that exciting.' She stands up. 'Let's go inside, and get in front of those cameras, and make some magic.'

'Yeah, let's do it. But I have to get something out of my back seat first. Walk with me.'

So she walks with him. When they get to his Lexus, he opens the rear door, grabs this something from the floor, passes it to Anna, and says, 'Check it out.' It's a leather knife bag. The fact that it's leather is odd enough – most knife bags these days are made from a virtually indestructible rayon/nylon compound called Cordura – but unlike every other knife bag Anna's ever seen, this one is red, black being the industry standard. She wouldn't have pegged Jordan as a red-leather guy, but it wasn't till relatively recently that she pegged him as a warm and compassionate guy. She then and there promises herself that she's going to stop trying to peg Jordan DeWitt. The man is unpegable.

Jordan opens the bag, and she's blinded by a set of twelve Shun[41] Classics. She whistles her appreciation. 'Damn. Shuns. Sweet.' She runs her hand across the white-ish handles. *Knife handles that aren't black?* she thinks. *Weird.* 'Always good to treat yourself to something nice.'

'Yeah, for sure. Pull one out.'

Anna removes the paring knife, looks at it carefully, and gasps. 'Are those handles pearl?'

'Yup.'

'These are gorgeous, Chef.' She notices some red flecks mixed into the pearl. 'What's the red stuff?'

'Rubies.'

She slaps him on the bicep. 'Shut *up*. You did *not* buy yourself pearl and ruby Shuns.'

'You're right. I didn't buy myself pearl and ruby Shuns. I bought *you* pearl and ruby Shuns.'

She gawks at him. 'These probably cost as much as my car.' She puts the paring knife back in its slot. 'I can't accept these, Chef DeWitt.'

'The rubies match your favorite Crocs, and I don't have any red in my wardrobe, so they won't go with anything. You have to take them.'

'No. I *don't* have to. I'm not accepting them.'

'Yes you are.'

'No I'm not.'

---

[41] Shun: Mega-expensive, bank-breaking, wallet-melting Japanese knives that, frankly, are worth the money. This footnote brought to you by Shun.

'You will.'

'I won't.'

'No way.'

'Yes way.'

She swallows hard. 'Okay, fine, for the sake of argument, let's say I keep them. What the hell am I supposed to do with them? A leather bag is totally impractical, and I'd *never* use knives like this in my restaurant. I wouldn't even *bring* them to the restaurant.' She allows herself a small smile. 'I mean, Jeannie might break them.'

'They're pearl. You have to work pretty hard to break pearl.'

'Jeannie could find a way.'

'Then use them at home, or on our show, or get a display case and hang them in your bedroom. I don't care what you do with them, as long as you do *something*.'

Anna zips the bag and hands it to Jordan. 'Take them. I don't want them.'

He raises his arms in the air and jumps away as if the bag is a bomb. 'I don't want them, either.'

She shoves them into his chest. 'Take them, DeWitt!'

Jordan takes two backwards steps, spins around, breaks into a sprint, and calls, 'Catch me before I get to the studio and I'll keep them.'

Anna hasn't run for more than a single block at a time in over two years, and then it was only to catch a bus, and she knows Jordan goes to the gym on a regular basis, so she doesn't even bother. She leans against Jordan's car, sighs, and unzips the bag. The handles are almost completely round, which makes them even more impractical; round handles make for a lousy grip, and if they get wet, they'll fly out of your hand and kill some random line cookie. She pulls the Santoku[42] knife from its slot and runs her finger along the perfectly sharpened blade. She grips it by the handle and is surprised by how comfortable it is. It's lighter than her Wusthoff, yet it still has enough heft to engage comfortably in some quality chopping. She has no idea what the handle was treated with, but she knows that the only way it would slip out of her hand is if she coated it with peanut oil. She brings the knife to her eyes. The craftsmanship is breathtaking. It would be an honor to cook with them.

As she examines each knife, she tries to figure out what Jordan's motive is. Is he using the knives to seduce her? Was he planning to give them to her if or when she reciprocated his declaration of love? Or is he just a great guy who wants to do something nice for a woman he cares about?

The longer she stares at the knives, the more she lusts after them, not just because they're awesome tools – or pieces of art, really – but because it's such a thoughtful, generous gift. But as has been made abundantly clear, Anna Rowan has a guilty conscience, and she knows that if she holds on to them, she'll feel like a heel every time she touches them. Remember, she doesn't like Jordan in That Way. She likes him as Just a Friend. She doesn't want

[42] Santoku: A miniature cleaver used for all-purpose chopping and scaring the hell out of evil ex-boyfriends.

to Get Naked With Him. Keeping a gift that probably cost him over five thousand dollars is wrong.

She hops off the Lexus and heads to the studio, determined to force those gorgeous, gorgeous Shuns on Jordan.

He's waiting for her by the door, grinning that highwatt Jordan DeWitt grin, looking as if she hadn't flat-out rejected him only five minutes before. 'You want to keep those puppies now, don't you?' he smirks.

'Of course I do. But I can't. Can I be blunt?'

'Please.'

'These knives are not going to make me leave Byron . . .'

'I thought you were seeing Keith.'

'I told you, I'm only *kind of* seeing Keith.' Once again she notes that juggling boys is a pain in the ass. (She's going to have to make some boy decisions here, and as we now know, non-kitchen decisions aren't Anna Rowan's strong point.) 'If our situations were different, maybe we could've given it a shot.'

'Really? You honestly mean that?'

Anna shrugs. 'I don't know. Maybe. I'm a little confused about things right now. Please, Chef, let's go inside and bang out a show. Okay?'

'Okay. But only if you keep the knives.'

Worn down, she says, 'I'll keep them for now. But I can't guarantee I'll keep them forever.'

Jordan opens the door, puts his hand on the small of her back, guides her inside, then whispers something she doesn't understand. But she thinks it's something along the lines of, 'Keep *me* forever, Anna.'

She doesn't ask him to repeat it. She figures she'll be better off not knowing.

Anna heads off to her miniscule dressing room, where she powders up her cheeks and forehead. (FoodTube doesn't bother spending money on make-up people, so it's every woman for herself.) She again opens the red knife bag. *Wow*, she thinks. *Wow! WOW!*

And then out of the blue, she's smacked upside her head with an urge to call Byron. Enough of this emailing, texting, and voice messaging bullshit. No more thirty-second conversations. It's time to talk for real. She checks her watch – ten minutes till she has to be on the set. She'll call his cell. If he bothers picking up, she can say a quick hello and schedule some chat time for tonight. If he doesn't answer, she's not leaving a message – she'll call, and call, and call till he talks to her.

He picks up in the fifth ring, one ring before the call would go to voicemail. 'Hey, Anna,' he says.

'Hey, Byron. Can you talk?'

'Yeah. I'd like to.'

'For more than twelve seconds?'

'Yeah.' He chuckles. 'Maybe even a full minute.'

'It's not funny. Any particular reason you've been blowing me off?'

'I haven't been blowing you off. It's been busy. Without you here, things are moving a bit slower all around. Billy's doing a good job running the kitchen, but he's having issues keeping track of inventory, and—'

Anna interrupts, 'So at no point before, during, or after regular business hours were you able to go down to your office, close the door, and give me some quality time?'

Byron sighs so long and loudly that Anna has to pull the phone away from her ear. 'It's been busy,' he repeats.

'Yeah, you mentioned that. So what's going on here?'

'What's going on where?'

'Come on, wake up, Byron. With us. What's going on with us?'

Another lengthy and ear-shattering sigh. 'This kind of thing is hard for me, Anna.'

'What, having feelings? Not being robotic?'

'Honestly, both. The robotic part, especially.'

She chuckles in spite of herself. 'That's kind of funny,' she admits. 'Come on, honey . . .' (She doesn't mean to call him 'honey.' It slips out. But that's what sometimes happens when a fighting couple has a civil conversation. You fall back into your old habits, into your old patterns, into your old life. You sometimes can't help it. It's too easy.) '. . . this is me. You can talk. I won't yell at you. Much.'

'You promise?'

'I'm at work. My dressing room is about six square feet, and the walls are made out of filo dough. Believe me, I won't yell.'

'Okay, I swear I was going to call you the day after tomorrow.'

She believes him, because he's the kind of guy who schedules everything, even vital personal phone calls. 'Why Friday?' she asks.

'Because I needed to psyche myself up.'

'Psyche yourself up? Why?'

'Because if I'm going to apologize, I want to do it right. So here goes: Anna, I miss you so much. The restaurant misses you so much. I'm so so so sorry.'

'For what?' She was happy enough that he was apologizing, but also curious about what he was apologizing for: blowing her off non-stop for the past three months? Calling her a commodity? Treating her like an employee? His obvious ambivalence re: their relationship? Being an all-around crap boyfriend?

'I'm sorry for everything. I know it pissed you off when I called you a commodity, and I'm sorry about that. I'm sorry I've been thinking of you more as a chef than as a girlfriend and lover. I'm sorry I've been absent. I'm sorry I didn't support you at all when you decided to do the show. I'm sorry I've been a total dickwad . . .'

'Dickwad? What's a dickwad?'

'For the past six months, me. I've been the ultimate dickwad. Anna, I want you to come back here. I want you in our kitchen. I want you in our apartment. I want you in our bed. I want you to get that fatass cat of yours back from Miguel. I want to be a team again. We have too much history to let us fizzle out.'

It's a halfway decent apology, but it's not enough for Anna. 'History? Not love?'

'Well, yeah. Love, too. But history's important.'

As unromantic of a sentiment as that is, Anna has to admit that he's right. Over time, their lives have become so intertwined that to cut the cords would require a sharper knife than Shun could manufacture.

The intercom in her office comes to life: '*Anna and*

Jordan to the set please. Anna and Jordan to the set.'

Balancing her tiny cell between her ear and her shoulder, Anna stands up and puts on her apron. 'I've got to go. We have to finish this later. Keep thinking of things to apologize for. You're off to a pretty good start. I'll leave my phone on. Call me as late as you want.'

'Okay.'

'If you don't call . . .'

'I'll call. Don't worry.'

'You'd better. Goodbye.' She hangs up before he can say 'goodbye' back.

Jordan's waiting for her on the set, cool, calm and ready to go, looking every bit like the star he is. He points at her black knife bag. 'Not using your new ones, I see.'

She pulls her hair back in a ponytail. 'Not now, Chef DeWitt. Please.'

Again, he gives her that sincerely concerned look that makes her want to fall into his arms, but not in That Way. Remember, she likes him as Just a Friend. She doesn't want to Get Naked With Him. He asks, 'What's wrong?'

'I really can't talk about it now.'

'Maybe later? I'll take you to lunch after we're done here, cool?'

'I don't think so.'

'Come over to my house. I'll cook you something.'

'Jordan, today is not the day.'

Jordan blinks. 'Wow, I'm shocked.'

'About what?'

'That you called me Jordan. You must really be out of it.'

'Listen, can we . . . can we . . . can we . . .'

Before Anna makes it to her fourth (and fifth) (and possibly sixth) 'can we,' Michelle and Rory wander on to the set. 'Guys,' Michelle says tensely, 'we've got to talk.'

Jordan steps behind Michelle and massages her shoulders. 'You sound stressed, M-Class. What's the scoop?'

Michelle gently pushes Jordan's hands away. 'I'm just going to cut to the chase.' She takes a deep breath, pauses, turns to Rory, and says, 'You do this,' then walks/runs away.

Obviously confused, Jordan watches his assistant sprint off, then asks his director, 'What the fuck is going on, Rory?'

Rory yells after Michelle, '*This is the producer's job, Fields!*' He shakes his head, then makes a slashing motion across his throat. 'They're shutting us down. Today's our last shoot. They say the show's getting repetitive, and they don't see it as a full-blown series. They think six episodes are enough.' He tells Jordan, 'They're offering you *DeWild* again, but no more remotes outside of the state. They'll let you go as far as, say, San Fran, but that's about it. They said they'll understand if you say no, no hard feelings, your other shows are still in play.' He turns to Anna. 'They're going to pay your entire contract, plus you'll get a month's severance. And out of the goodness of their hearts, they'll fly you back to Chicago first class.'

Anna leans against the counter, stares at the ceiling. It's crunch time. It's decision time. No more of the typical Anna Rowan on-the-fence hemming and hawing. She's an adult, and she has to learn how to be definitive. No more juggling anything: boys, careers, cities, *anything*.

Jordan gives her that uber-concerned look, then asks, 'You okay, Anna?'

After a moment, she says to Rory, 'Tell them to hold off on that plane ticket for a minute. I don't know if I'm going back to Chicago. I promise I'll decide over the weekend.'

Okay, maybe there'll still be a *little* hemming and hawing.

SIX-CHEESE SPINACH AND MUSHROOM LASAGNA

Ingredients
Kosher salt and freshly ground black pepper
12 dry lasagna noodles
¼ cup extra virgin olive oil
2 cloves garlic, minced
6 oz fresh spinach, chopped
8 oz white button mushrooms, sliced
½ lb ricotta cheese
½ lb cottage cheese
4 ounces fresh goat's cheese, softened
½ cup Parmesan cheese, finely grated
¼ cup Pecorino Romano cheese, finely grated
4 cups mozzarella cheese, finely shredded
1 tablespoon lemon zest, finely grated
½ teaspoon nutmeg, finely grated
⅛ teaspoon cayenne
1 large egg, beaten
4 cups tomato sauce with basil (see page 243)

Method
1. Preheat the oven to 350°F.
2. Bring a large pot of water to a boil over high heat and salt
   generously. Add the lasagna noodles and boil, stirring

occasionally until al dente, about 8–10 minutes. Drain.

3. Heat the olive oil and garlic in a saucepan over medium heat till the garlic begins to brown. Add the spinach and mushrooms, season with salt and pepper, and stir until the spinach reduces and the garlic is fragrant, about 3 minutes. Transfer to bowl and cool.

4. Mix the ricotta, cottage cheese, goat's cheese, Parmesan, Pecorino Romano, 2 cups of the mozzarella, lemon zest, nutmeg, cayenne, and cooled spinach and mushroom mixture in a bowl. Season with salt and pepper to taste. Stir in the egg, but do not over mix.

5. Cover the bottom of a 9 x 13 inch casserole dish with a thin layer of tomato sauce. Cover with 3 of the noodles placed side-to-side, but not overlapping. Top with a ¼ of the cheese mixture and ½ cup of tomato sauce. Season lightly with salt and pepper. Repeat to make 2 more layers. Cover lasagna layers with remaining noodles, dollop remaining cheese mixture on top. Drizzle with remaining tomato sauce, then scatter the remaining 2 cups mozzarella on top.

6. Bake, uncovered, until the lasagna is hot and bubbly, about 40–45 minutes. Let lasagna stand for 10 minutes before serving.

TOMATO SAUCE WITH BASIL

Ingredients
¼ cup extra-virgin olive oil
4 large cloves garlic, smashed
2 (28 oz) cans whole peeled tomatoes, with juices (about 7 cups)
1 teaspoon kosher salt
⅔ cup packed basil leaves
Ground black pepper

Method
1. Put olive oil and garlic in a saucepan and cook until fragrant, approximately two minutes.
2. Add tomatoes and salt. Break up the tomatoes into small chunks with a wooden spoon and bring to a boil over high heat, lower heat to a brisk simmer, and cook until thickened, about 30–40 minutes.
3. While sauce cooks, tear basil leaves into small pieces. Remove the sauce from the heat, stir in the basil. Salt and pepper to taste.

Goodbyes & Hellos & X's & O's

Chef Rowan and Chef DeWitt's farewell the following Monday in Jordan's office at FoodTube HQ is quick, unsentimental, and even a tad terse. Here's how it goes down:

'Well, Chef Rowan, it was good working with you.'

'Yeah. Ditto.'

'So, I guess, give me a shout if you're ever in LA.'

'Yeah. Ditto if you're in Chicago. But I'm sure you won't be coming to the Midwest anytime soon.'

'I would, Chef, but there are only three days during the year when Chicago isn't a horrible, horrible place to be.'

'To you. It's my home.'

'Yeah. Homes are good, I suppose. Anyhow, give my best to Byron.'

'I'll do that.'

Then there's an awkward silence, then an even more awkward embrace. The awkwardness stems from the fact that their hug is, let's just say it out loud, oddly sexy. Jordan realizes their bodies fit together quite well, and he thinks Anna realizes it too.

He wonders if she would ever consider him as a beau down the line. He guesses not. He's not as polished as Byron, or as genial as Keith; it seems like that when it comes to guys, Anna Rowan is about extremes: you have to be either James Bond or the goofy second banana in a 1980s teen comedy to win her heart. Based on those criteria, a guy somewhere in the middle like Jordan DeWitt doesn't stand a chance. But a girl wants what a girl wants, and he respects that. Actually, he respects most things about Anna Rowan. She's a pretty respectable chick.

And then she's gone. Jordan watches her walk away. *Great girl*, he thinks. Then, recalling the *Sneak Attack: Chicago* when he accidentally cupped her tush, he also marvels, *Great ass*.

Michelle materializes at his side. She puts her arm around his waist and says, 'You pig. You're checking out Anna's butt, aren't you?'

Jordan smiles halfheartedly. 'Yeah, a little bit.'

'I can't lie: she's got a good one. But you're still a pig.' She rests her head on his shoulder. 'I don't think I ever thanked you for trying to steal her away from Keith.'

'Yeah, you're welcome. But I wasn't doing it for you.'

'Not even a little bit?'

'Nope.'

'Maybe a teeny-tiny bit?'

'Okay, fine, maybe a teeny-tiny bit.'

'Thanks. I appreciate it.' She pauses. 'Keith called me last night.'

Jordan blinks. 'Really?'

'Yeah. He was a wreck. He told me that Anna took him out to dinner on Saturday, and she told him she was going back to Chicago, and moving back in with Byron, and he lost it.'

'Lost it like he started crying?'

'No. Lost it like he started yelling at her.'

'Keith yelled? I'm not seeing it.'

Michelle smirked. 'I'm sure that Keith's version of yelling and our version of yelling differ considerably. From what I gather, he was just very firm with her. He told her he liked her so much, and that he felt like she used him to make herself feel better while she was all alone in a big city.'

'Wow. Keith stepped up, I suppose. What did she say?'

'He told me she spent, like, an hour spilling her guts. She told him how she felt about the Byron situation . . .'

Jordan interrupts, 'And how did she feel about the Byron situation?'

'Confused. Scared. But determined. She wants to see if they still have it. And then she apparently spent another hour telling Keith how amazing he was, and how if their situations were different, she'd be all over his shit . . .'

Jordan again interrupts, 'Hey, she's stealing my lines.'

Michelle cocks an eyebrow. 'What?'

'Nothing. Go on.'

'That's it, I guess. He felt horrible, but he understood. She felt horrible, too, but it was the right thing to do for everybody.'

'So how did they leave it?'

'They're going to be friends.'

Jordan rolls his eyes. 'Right. Long-distance friends. That'll happen.'

'You're a cynical bastard, DeWitt. Keith's a great guy, and Anna is one of the most sincere people I've ever met. I bet you some fish tacos at El Taco Nazo that they make it work.' (Jordan and Michelle make fish taco bets on a regular basis, which means that nobody loses.)

Jordan says, 'You're on.' They shake hands.

After a thoughtful moment, Michelle whispers, 'I didn't take it very seriously.'

'Take what very seriously?'

'How you felt about her. I guess I couldn't imagine you liking anybody this soon after Nadia.'

'What do you mean, this soon? It's been well over a year.'

'That's not a long time, Jordan.' She pauses. 'You really liked Anna, didn't you? I mean, *really* liked her.'

'Yeah. I really did. Still do, frankly.' He claps his hands once and says, 'But she's history. Let's go somewhere and talk about whether or not we want to do this bullshit version of *DeWild*.'

On their way to her office, Michelle says, 'You know what, J-Money? I was just thinking.'

'About what?'

'About how cold you are.'

'Say *what*? *I'm* cold? I'm the warmest guy I know. Why am I cold?'

'Saying that Anna is *history*. You're going to forget her just like *that*? You were practically in love with that girl, weren't you?' Jordan begrudgingly nods. 'Aren't you even going to, I don't know, *mourn* her or something?'

He shrugs. 'Wasn't meant to be. Why dwell? It a waste. I have a restaurant to run and a bunch of television crap to deal with. I don't have time to dwell.'

Michelle says, 'As much as I'd like to, I can't really argue with that.'

'You're not going to argue with me about something involving my personal life? I'm shocked.'

'Yeah, well don't get too used to it. Without me, your life would be a shambles.'

'*More* of a shambles, you mean.'

Once they park themselves in Michelle's office, it takes them two minutes and nine seconds to determine that a truncated *DeWitt Goes DeWild* is a waste of FoodTube airtime. Both Jordan and Michelle rightly believe that *DeWild*'s regional bend is what separates it from other shows of that ilk. Sure, California offers them plenty of phenomenal locales – wine country, for instance, would merit eight or nine episodes alone – but a huge chunk of FoodTube viewers in the other forty-nine states would likely get bored with Cali after a month.

Michelle leans back in her chair and puts her feet up on the desk. 'Wow, so this means only two shows for you to work on. You're going to have all this spare time on your hands. What're you going to do with yourself?'

'Hmm, let's see. I'll only be working ninety hours a week instead of a hundred, which'll give me plenty of time to, I don't know, write a novel, or learn how to fly a plane, or maybe, just *maybe* I could get some sleep once in a while.'

It must be noted that Jordan is exaggerating about his work schedule. In truth, he only works about seventy hours most weeks, and one less FoodTube gig will cut that total down to sixty. And he already knows what he's going to do with his newly freed-up time: concoct some semblance of a social life.

See, over that past weekend, Jordan needed a shoulder to cry on – a show being cancelled and your dreamgirl walking off into the sunset and back to her lame-o loser chump of a boyfriend has that effect on some people – but there is nary a sympathetic shoulder to be found. None of his siblings are particularly good listeners, nobody at his restaurant is all that sensitive, and he feels badly about pestering Michelle with his problems all the time. He knows Michelle will be there for him 24/7/365, but he doesn't want to abuse the privilege.

Point being, he's lonely. Plus he's horny. So what's a friend- and sex-deprived boy to do? Simple: online dating.

The following morning, Jordan fires up his laptop and posts a profile on Match.com, one of the world's hugest online singles meeting stops. The response is immediate – and skeptical. Only fifteen minutes after he makes his Match debut, thirteen women have contacted him, ten of whom don't believe he's *the* Jordan DeWitt. The other three ask him why a big, fancy TV guy would resort to online dating. And one of those three tells him that if Mr FoodTube can't find a girl out in the real world, then Mr FoodTube must be a big, stinky loser. Yes, that's right, a random woman out in the cybersphere calls Jordan a big, stinky loser. But Jordan isn't particularly fazed, because this woman doesn't have the guts to include a photo to accompany her profile, so he imagines her to be a big, stinky loser who is merely projecting her big, stinky loserness on to him.

Bored and annoyed, he's about to remove his profile from the site entirely, when he receives a pleasant, intelligent, grammatically correct instant message from a woman who is – and there's no other way to phrase this – a stone fox, so gorgeous that *he* asks *her* what the hell she's doing online. After several dozen back-and-forth IM's, Jordan suggests to the girl – her name is Heidi – that they cut to the chase and meet for some coffee, like, *now*. She says not *now*, but four hours from *now* would be lovely.

Jordan goes to the bathroom to primp and preen, but the amount of actual primping and preening he actually does, however, is limited: he shaved his head and face last night before bed, so he's covered (or, as the case is, *un*covered) on the hair-removal front. He showered only two hours before, so he's fresh, and clean, and smelling fine, thus a repeat performance in the tub isn't necessary. There's only one thing he can fret over, and that's his outfit. But being that this is only a coffee date, he doesn't fret too long or hard: a nice pair of jeans, a white-patterned short-sleeved button-down shirt, and he's good to go.

He shows up at Starbucks ten minutes early, orders a vente honey latte, grabs a table by the window, and considers his weirdo romantic life. His teens and twenties were a seemingly neverending series of emotionally unfulfilling but sexually thrilling one-month stands: servers from his restaurants; line cookies from restaurants down the street; foodie groupies who wanted to screw the TV guy for a few weeks. (To his credit, he was always upfront with these girls about his inability to enter into a long-term relationship, and he never dated more than one person at a time . . . except for that one instance when he was seventeen, and he hooked up with an insane thirty-year-old waitress while he was still seeing his high school girlfriend, the girlfriend to whom he'd lost his virginity. But he *was* seventeen, and that sort of behavior was to be expected. That said, he still flagellates himself whenever he thinks about it.) Nadia was the only woman that Jordan was with for any significant stretch, the only woman to whom he fully gave his heart, and look what happened there.

Post-divorce dating has been, for the most part, a disaster, mainly because up till recently, he was hauling around some serious trust issues: *Nadia the Fuckington broke my heart, so all women will break my heart*, he sometimes theorizes. He pushed all those poor girls away, and he knew he was doing it, but he was powerless to stop. So he quit trying to date altogether.

Until Anna. She's a good one, that Chef Rowan. Class. Style. Brains. Talent. Sense of humor. Hot.

Spoken for.

Somebody taps him on the shoulder. It's Heidi, and she's luminous. She sticks out her hand and introduces herself. Jordan stands up and says, '. . .' That's all. Just '. . .' Yes, believe it or not, Jordan DeWitt is speechless. But, smoothie that he is, he gathers himself, pulls out her chair (he can be a gentleman, our Chef DeWitt), takes her hand, smiles, and says, 'Heidi, you're breathtaking.'

She blushes. 'You're not so bad yourself. You're taller than you look on TV. And skinnier.'

His smile widens. 'So you're saying that on the tube, I look short and fat?'

She blushes again. 'I didn't mean it that . . .'

'I'm kidding. I *do* look short and fat on TV, but that tends to work in my favor in the real world.' *What the hell am I saying?* he thinks. *Get your shit together. She's just a girl.* 'What're you drinking?'

She points at his cup. 'What're *you* drinking?'

'A honey latte.'

'Ooh, that sounds yummy. Vente, please?'

'Vente it is.' Jordan thinks, *Same coffee, same size. It's destiny. We're meant to be together.*

Jordan is curled up in bed six hours later, attempting to remember the specifics of their coffee session . . . and their dinner session . . . and their brief make-out session, but it's all a pleasant blur. All he can recall with any certainty is the taste of her lips and the smell of her perfume, both of which were lovely, but neither of which will compel him to call her. And this is a problem, because if he isn't interested in a beautiful, intelligent, successful graphic designer – that's right, she's a graphic designer, not somebody involved in the food or television industry – who is clearly interested in him, then who the hell will *ever* interest him?

This is a disaster, and he needs to talk to somebody. He knows it's past Michelle's bedtime, but he calls her anyhow. Straight to voicemail. He texts her. No response. He's totally wound up, and he knows he's not going to sleep tonight, so he drags himself out of bed, throws on some shorts and a T-shirt, and hops into his Lexus.

Michelle rents a coach house in a dicey section of LA called Griffith Park. Jordan once asked her why she lives in such a lousy area, and she explained, 'I have a lot of crap. I need space. But trust me, when I start making serious money, I'm moving into your neighborhood.' Jordan has no problem with that.

Half an hour later, Jordan pulls up in front of her house and knocks on her door quietly so as not to wake the neighbors. No answer. He knocks a little harder. He swears he hears rustling in the house. He rings the bell. If she doesn't come to the door in a minute or three, he'll hang out in his car until she shows up. Jordan isn't concerned about getting mugged or jacked. He grew up in a place far nastier than Griffith Park. He can handle himself.

Finally the door opens an inch. Michelle pokes her nose through the crack. 'It's two in the morning, Jordan,' she hisses. 'What the fuck are you doing here?'

'Can I come in?'

'No.'

So much for her being there for him 24/7/365. 'Why?'

'*Because.*'

A male voice calls, 'You okay, Michelle? You need some help out there?'

Michelle turns around and calls back, 'I'm fine. I'll be back in a minute.'

Jordan cocks an eyebrow. 'Michelle Fields, do you have a boy in your house? When did you start seeing him? Or is this some random person you picked up at a bar?'

The door opens wide. Jordan watches a tall man amble toward him. 'Listen, buddy, it's not cool to show up at people's houses after . . . oh. Hey, Chef DeWitt. How's it going?'

Jordan, taken aback by the naked, somewhat chunky body standing behind Michelle, says, 'Hey, Keith. It's going fine. And you?'

He says, 'Awesome, man. Michelle rules.'

Michelle rolls her eyes, but is clearly pleased. 'Keith, go back to bed. Jordan was just leaving. *Right, Jordan?*'

'Can we talk? Two minutes.'

Keith says, 'Cool with me.' He kisses the back of Michelle's neck. 'See you in a bit, baby.' Then he pads back toward the rear of the house.

After Keith is out of earshot, Jordan says, 'Guess he got over Anna pretty quickly.'

'Actually, Anna told him that if he didn't make a move on me, she'd never speak to him again.'

'Ah, that's our Anna, spreading love everywhere.' Jordan notices that Michelle is wearing nothing but a bedsheet. 'Nice outfit.'

'Thanks. Now back to my original question: what the fuck are you doing here?'

Jordan spills his guts right there on her front porch: how he went online, and found this unbelievable girl, and how they had a brilliant evening together, and how sweet their kissing was, and how nice she smelled, and how he didn't give a damn if he ever saw her again.

Michelle tenderly puts a hand on his cheek. 'I wish I knew what to tell you.' She stands on her tiptoes and kisses him lightly under his ear. 'I think you'll have to suss this one out yourself.'

'Yeah, I figured that's what you'd say. It's the right thing for you to say. I just needed to vent, and you're my favorite person to vent to in the world. As a matter of fact, you're probably my favorite person in the world, period.'

Michelle beams. 'That's, like, almost the nicest thing anybody's ever said to me.' She cocked a thumb over her shoulder. 'Then again, that one over there told me I was the sexiest person in the universe. That was pretty damn nice, too.'

Jordan nods. 'That *is* pretty damn nice. Go be with him. You deserve to be worshipped.'

'Thanks. Now you go home and go to bed.'

'Nah, I need a drink. Or several drinks.' He glances at his watch. 'You know any wine bars that're still open?'

'No, but I have an unopened bottle of 2001 Shafer Cabernet with your name on it.'

Now it was Jordan's turn to beam. 'That, M-Class, sounds fucking perfect.'

'One problem. It's in the wine cooler in my office.'

'You mean your office at the studio?'

'I mean my office at the studio.'

'Damn.' He checks his watch again. 'You think anybody will be there to let me into the building?'

'I don't know. Give it a shot. Worst case scenario, you stop at a Seven-Eleven and get a nice box of Boone's Farm.'

Just under an hour later, Jordan is in his FoodTube office, sprawled out on his sofa, halfway through one of the three or four best bottles of wine he's ever had. Buzzed but not *too* buzzed, he's come to the conclusion that he should stop thinking about love and/or lust for a while. Instead, he'll focus on his work. He'll ask the FoodTube suits if he can retool *Eastern Rebellion* before it gets stale, maybe even start bringing on some guest chefs. (The one good thing about the *One Boy* fiasco is that Jordan has learned he enjoys sharing the stage with a killer cook.) He'll start writing that cookbook he's been saying he'll write for the past, well, *forever*. Maybe he'll even take a few cheese courses. Anna was right: Jordan DeWitt is a cheese-o-phobe. How can you be a well-rounded chef if you're scared of Vieux Boulogne?[43]

He examines the Cabernet bottle. There's maybe half a glass left. He doesn't want to dump it, but he can't drink another drop right now, because too much of a good thing is, um, too much. After some raging internal debate, he decides it's pointless to save such a small amount, so the

[43] Vieux Boulogne: The stinkiest cheese in the history of mankind. Can kill from ten meters away. Oddly enough, it tastes pretty good.

bottle must be disposed of. The problem now is that FoodTube employees are not allowed to drink in the FoodTube offices, so he has to dispose discreetly.

He goes to the bathroom, pours the remaining wine down the sink, takes a roll of paper towels back to his office, wraps about fifty sheets around the bottle, reaches under his desk, and grabs his garbage can. Or *tries* to grab his garbage can – unfortunately, there's no can for him to grab. (He finds out the next day that one of the janitors accidently crushed it. It wouldn't be replaced for three weeks.) So where to put the bottle? He doesn't want to stick it in the bathroom garbage; somebody would almost definitely see it there. He obviously can't leave it in Michelle's office, and everybody else's offices are locked. (You may be asking, *Why doesn't he take the frigging bottle home and throw it out there?* That's a fine, logical idea, but Jordan has five glasses of wine in his system, and fine ideas for him right now are few and far between.) After several minutes, he decides to stick the bottle in the bottom drawer of his file cabinet, a drawer he hasn't opened in approximately . . . um, truth be told, he's never opened it. He's a TV chef, and TV chefs don't do a whole lot of filing.

Anna Rowan didn't know that Jordan has no need for files, because if she had, she probably would have put the red-leather knife bag with all those wonderful pearl-and-ruby-handled Shuns someplace where she knew he would find them right away. But here they are, waiting for Jordan in that bottom drawer. There's a yellow sticky note on the shoulder strap:

Jordan –
It has to be no. I wish it could be yes.
Please use these in good health and much happiness. You
deserve it.
xoxo,
Anna

Jordan removes the bag, places it on the floor, unzips it, then pulls out and gazes at the Santoku, again blown away by the craftsmanship. The pearl gleams. The rubies sparkle. They're beautiful.

He really wishes Anna would have kept them.

He really wishes it could be yes.

He puts the knife back into its slot, closes the bag, lays down on the floor, and stares at the ceiling.

Fifteen or so minutes later, Jordan DeWitt knows exactly what he has to do.

VENTE HONEY LATTE
Á LA STARBUCKS

Ingredients
1 car (or 2 feet)
1 Starbucks Coffee emporium
$5.21

Method
1. Use car (or feet) to drive (or walk) to your local neighborhood Starbucks. There will be one within a four block vicinity.
2. Order Vente Honey Latte. Give barista $5.21.
3. Add cinnamon to taste.
4. Drink hot.

15

Welcome to Anna's New Life

A nna falls to her knees and raises her hands to the heavens above. 'Must . . . have . . . pizza,' she gasps. 'Must . . . have . . . it . . . immediately.'

Byron says, 'I'm not really hungry. Do whatever you want.' He kicks off shoes, pads to the bathroom, then closes the door with more force than Anna finds necessary.

Stinks waddles over and rubs his head on Anna's feet. She scratches him behind the ear and says, 'Looks like it's just you and me for pizza, chunks. What do you want on your half? Tuna fish? You got it.'

Anna has been back in Chicago for three months now, and not a whole hell of a lot has changed since her California sojourn. The Tart staffers who haven't moved on to those greener (or more interesting) pastures remain their usual Tart-ian selves: Jeannie is still ditzy and beautiful; Nora is still wise and brassy; Eileen is still a sweet little drama queen; the line cookies are still efficient, skilled, and whiny; and Billy still cooks up a storm even when he's plastered.

Tart's front of the house looks pretty much the same, too, except that thanks to Anna's FoodTube appearances, the restaurant is even busier, if that's possible. Anna is now a celebrity amongst local foodies, something that's alternately fun and frustrating. The fun part comes when she runs into somebody on the street who tells her they like her cooking; like most chefs, Anna toils in obscurity deep in the bowels of her kitchen, and it's nice to get a little pat on the back once in a while. (Anna didn't go into professional cooking for the accolades, but if accolades come her way, she'll take them.) The frustrating part is the eternally overflowing crowd. Tart's reservation book is filled-to-brimming not just on weekends, but every night for the next two months, and since Byron decrees that they cram as many people into the joint as possible, Anna works non-stop each and every day. She's only had five nights off since she came home, and she is fried. But Anna has always wanted to run a successful kitchen, so she doesn't allow herself to get upset, or to complain, or to be in a bad mood. But sometimes it's tough. Really tough. Especially since her life outside of the restaurant ain't exactly a tea party.

The kitchen itself is exactly the same, except for one little thing: after Billy took over Anna's post, he put together some in-your-face iPod playlists that were the diametric opposite of Anna's lighter fare. (The cookies all like Billy's song choices, especially Miguel, who, it turns out, violently despises mellow jazz and chick singer/ songwriters.) On her second day back, in the midst of a

Minor Threat megamix, Anna drags Billy into the basement office and, as sweetly as possible, says, 'I don't want to be the strict parent here, but do you really think that obscure punk is appropriate soundtrack for this particular kitchen?'

Billy belches and says, 'Fuck no. But fuck appropriateness. We're making food here, not art.'

Anna sighs. 'Billy, I don't know what you want to do with your life, but I *want* to make art. I want every dish that leaves our kitchen to be beautiful – and not just to taste beautiful, but to look beautiful, and to smell beautiful. And that's *every* dish, Billy, even simple stuff like sautéed spinach, or frites, or plain white rice. *Everything*. And you know what else? We're expensive, and I want everybody who comes here to feel like they got their money's worth. No, I want them to feel like they got *more* than their money's worth. Make. It. Art. Get it?' This sort of passionate, heartfelt sentiment demonstrates why Anna Rowan was, is, and always will be, a fucking brilliant chef.

Billy nods appreciatively. 'Got it. That's beautiful, Anna. Really, it is.'

'You sound sincere, Bill.'

'I am sincere.'

'Well, then, thank you. Coming from you, that means a lot.'

'Uh huh.' He belches again. 'So how about we play my good music on Mondays and Thursdays, and your girlie-girl crap the rest of the week?'

'Fine,' Anna laughs. 'Now please go upstairs and cook

me some art, you scumbag fart face.'

As you might have guessed by now, the one thing that hasn't changed – at least for the better – is the one thing that Anna wanted desperately to change: Byron Smith.

She and Byron have fallen right back into their post-*Sunday Sneak Attack* pattern: wake up, go to the restaurant, go home, talk about the restaurant, maybe or maybe not have unmemorable sex, repeat. Byron isn't being overtly evil. Distant, certainly. Grouchy, for sure. Inattentive, you bet. But evil? Really, the worst you can say about him is that he's not there. No, check that: the worst you can say is that he's being a lame-o loser chump of a boyfriend. Most of the time, Anna works too hard to seriously consider how bored, frustrated and unhappy she is. But when she does think about it, she doesn't blame herself or Byron on their discontent – she blames those patterns, those damn patterns that suck you back in, and as anybody who's been sucked in knows, once you're sucked in, you have to work hard to get out.

Anna digs her cell from the bottom of her purse, but before she punches in Art of Pizza's number, she drops the phone right on back into the bag, where it will be found some 1,212 years later by an intrepid team of archeologists. She stands up, strips down to her tank top and sexy panties, falls on to the couch, huddles under a blanket, grabs the remote, fires up the television, and surfs over to Channel 70, praying that she isn't treated to the sight of her silly face and her fat ass. There's a fair to middling chance that Anna *will* see herself on TV, however, because FoodTube runs episodes of *One Boy*,

One Girl, One Meal at least four times a week – which makes her wonder why the damn show got cancelled in the first place.

But she's not the least bit bitter about it. The fact is, she wasn't particularly devastated when Rory dropped the hammer on them. Sure, she liked doing the show, and California was a nice change of pace, but she couldn't see herself being happy living in TV Land. She learned quickly that being in front of the camera isn't at all about cooking, and it definitely isn't about art. It's about teaching, and while teaching is important and fulfilling in its own right, it isn't her dream, not even close. That said, if FoodTube had stuck with *One Boy*, then offered to renew her contract for another season, then offered her another show or two to host, she probably would have stayed out West and let the whole thing play itself out. Who knows? It could've been fun.

Here's another reason Anna isn't too devastated she was launched out of Cali: the Keith situation was getting messy.

During their thing – and Anna decided she would always think of it as a 'thing' rather than an 'affair' or 'dalliance,' because they never officially dallied – Keith hadn't changed one iota. He was still the same loyal and affectionate puppy of a man (or boy) who had charmed her out of her shirt, her bra, and her pants (but not her panties!) in the first place. Eternally unable to keep a single thought to himself, Keith told her time and again how badly he wanted to be with her. He never pleaded, or begged, or whined, or wheedled; he simply stated his desires. And he stated them every time they got together, without fail. It was unbearably sweet and flattering, and she almost fell in love with him; if they'd have slept together, she probably would have. But there was always a voice in the back of her head that said it would've been wrong for everybody. The timing was wrong. Their mismatched levels of maturity were wrong. Their differing views of their respective futures were wrong.

Anna decides against pizza, so she peels herself off the sofa and makes her way to the kitchen, where a lovely box of Cap'n Crunch Peanut Butter Crunch sits atop the refrigerator. As she pours her cereal, she hears a familiar voice: 'Ladies and gentlemen, tonight, on *Eastern Rebellion*, we're proud to welcome to the program, straight from the French Laundry in Napa Valley, Chef Thomas Keller. Chef, this is your first FoodTube appearance. Why the hell did you agree to come on to my little show?'

Chef Keller says, 'Because when Jordan DeWitt calls, people listen. Sometimes.' Both men crack up.

Overflowing bowl of cereal in hand, Anna runs into the living room, spilling milk all over the throw rug, much to Stinks's delight. Right there on the screen, there's Jordan and her old mentor, side by side, laughing, demonstrating to the world how to make spring rolls. She watches Jordan humbly defer to Chef Keller, smiling a smile that makes it obvious how unabashedly happy he is working next to a master.

The funny thing is that Jordan often wore the same smile when he worked next to her. And that smile gives her the chills. It makes her stomach do three, no, four dipsy-doos. It makes her wish she was in California. It makes her feel better than she'd felt in a long, long time.

CHICKEN AND SHRIMP SPRING ROLLS

Ingredients

1 oz noodles, soaked in warm water for 20 minutes, drained and cut into 1 inch pieces

¼ lb chicken, white meat, cooked and shredded

¼ lb cooked shrimp, finely chopped

½ cup onion, chopped

1 tablespoon tree ear or cloud ear mushrooms, soaked in warm water for 30 minutes, thoroughly rinsed, drained and finely chopped

1½ teaspoons garlic, chopped

1 tablespoon shallots, chopped

¼ teaspoon black pepper

10 sheets round banh trangs (dried rice wrappers available at Vietnamese or specialty markets)

2 eggs, beaten

2 cups peanut oil

Method

1. In a bowl combine the noodles, chicken, shrimp, onion, mushrooms, garlic, shallots, and black pepper, and set aside.

2. Cut the round wrappers into quarters and place on a flat surface. With a pastry brush, paint the beaten eggs over

the entire surface of each of the pieces. Before filling, wait for the egg mixture to take effect, softening the wrappers, approximately 2 minutes.

3. When the wrapper is soft and transparent, place 1 teaspoon of the filling near the curved side, in the shape of a triangle. Fold the sides over to enclose the filling and continue to roll all the way up until all the wrappers are filled.

4. In a large frying pan add oil, spring rolls and slowly heat, frying for 20–30 minutes. Turn them occasionally until they are golden on all sides. Serve hot.

And the Winner Is . . .

'I still have no idea what I'm doing,' Nora tells Anna on a sunny Sunday late autumn morning halfway through her first month as Tart's GM. 'I still don't know why he insisted I take this job in the first place.' She shakes her head. 'Anna, I apologize to you in advance for running this place into the ground.'

Anna gets up from her seat, steps behind Nora, massages her shoulders, and says, 'Don't worry. You'll do fine. At this point, this place more or less runs itself.'

Which begs the question, *Why is Nora running Tart?* Well, because Byron ran away.

They tried to make it work, Anna and Byron. They ignored the bad stuff that had been silently eating at them for a while (e.g. no communication, stagnance, boredom, lack of passion, overall mediocrity), and chose to focus on the good. And for them, the only three good things left in their relationship were Tart, Tart and Tart.

Byron is the one who mercifully pulls the plug. 'I have

to go,' he tells Anna over brunch on one of their rare Mondays off together.

She takes a small sip of her Bloody Mary. 'You're not going into the restaurant, are you? I thought we agreed that nobody's going into work today.' She found she didn't care if he went to work or not, which saddened her. But she'd been sad for a while with Byron, so this was the status quo.

'No. I mean I have to go. I have to leave. You and I, we aren't working. And I know you know it.'

'Wait, you're leaving?' He nods. '*Leaving* leaving?' He nods again. 'Just like that?'

Byron sighs. 'It's not *just like that*. We've been on life support since you came back to Chicago. Be honest with me: have you been happy since you've gotten home?'

She takes a huge guzzle of her Bloody Mary. 'Sometimes.' And that's the truth. There were moments: a big night at the restaurant here, a big night at the restaurant there, and, um, well, frankly that's it. She repeats, 'Sometimes.'

He nods. 'That's the best I can say, too. Sometimes. You're a great girl, and you deserve better than *sometimes*, and I think *sometimes* is the best I'll be able to give you.'

After another gulp of good ol' Mary, Anna's innards dissolve into a puddle of contradictions: her heart is chipped – not broken, just chipped – because, well, she loved the guy, and he wasn't always boring, and distant, and obsessed with work to the detriment of his romantic and personal life like he is now; her brain is actually kind of relieved, because, well, the cloud of mediocrity that was hanging over their day-to-day existence will be gone; her eyes and mouth cry, because, well, they *have* to.

After shedding a few quiet tears, Anna says, 'Stinks and I will start looking for a new place next week or something.'

Byron shakes his head. 'No, you don't understand. I'm leaving.'

Anna gives him a look. 'You're *really* really *leaving* leaving?'

He nods. 'Yeah. I'm going to Europe for a month, then to Asia for six weeks, then, I don't know, I might settle in New York, or London, or who knows. Chicago's getting, I suppose, uncomfortable.'

'Uncomfortable,' Anna grunts, impressed that he chose the perfect word to describe their now-finished relationship, and kind of wondering what the hell is going to happen with Tart.

Byron says, 'You're probably kind of wondering what the hell is going to happen with Tart.'

She inwardly smiles. 'The thought did cross my mind.'

'I'm not selling. The restaurant a great commodity . . .' – Anna chuckles ruefully at what has become a verboten word – '. . . and I refuse to let it go. But you don't have to stay. If you want to move to Los Angeles and open up a place with DeWitt or something, I'd understand.'

At the mention of Jordan, Anna's stomach does a little dipsy-doodle. 'I'm not leaving. I'm not moving to California. And I'm not opening a place with DeWitt. Why would you say something like that?' Anna hadn't thought of partnering with Jordan on any level since she got back to town, but doing something with her former FoodTube foil is an interesting, albeit impossible notion. He's Cali, she's Illinois. He's intensely public, she's relatively private. He's divorced, she's not . . . oh . . . wait a sec . . . she kind of is.

All of that flashes through Anna's head in a split second, then she wonders, *What was that dipsy-doodle about?*

Byron says, 'I don't know, you two looked awfully happy on the show.'

'Yeah, but that was on television.' *But*, she thinks, *I suppose we were usually pretty happy off the show, too. But it doesn't really matter, though: Jordan's Cali, I'm Illinois, etc., so never the twain shall meet.*

Byron shrugs. 'That's how it looked to me. Anyhow, I'm going to ask Nora to be General Manager. She'll do a great job. And the two of you will probably get along better at work than you and I did.'

Byron was right. Anna and Nora make a phenomenal team, despite the fact that on a scale of one to ten, Nora's confidence level is a negative fifty-one.

'I still don't even know what my job is supposed to be,' Nora complains to Anna. 'What do I do every day? What did Mr Smith do every day?'

Anna gazes around the empty restaurant. Brunch service doesn't start for another two hours, and the two women are enjoying the calm before the storm. 'I'm not entirely sure, really. I was always too busy to see exactly what he was doing. I know he sent out a lot of emails.'

'Yeah. And?'

'Um, he paid our vendors.'

'Okay, I'm doing that. What else?'

'He called up newspapers and tried to get people to write about us.'

'The newspapers have been calling me, so no problem there.'

'Ummmmm, he also helped out during dinner service once in a while.'

'I'm totally doing that. That's the only time I ever feel like I know what's going on.'

'And I think that's pretty much it.'

Nora says, 'Sounds easy enough. I can't say I'm too bummed that he bailed.'

(For that matter, her entire Tart staff wasn't particularly bummed about Mr Smith's exit. 'You deserve so much better, Anna,' Eileen said late one night during a post-service bull session four days after Byron blew town. 'Honestly, he was a tool.'

Jenna, who had downed two quick shots of whiskey on an empty stomach, mumbled, 'Calling him a tool is an insult to tools.'

Billy chimed in, 'Sheeit, he was a bigger scumbag fart face than me.')

Nora checks her watch. 'Shit, where's Jeannie? I really don't want to hostess today. I'm calling her.' She pulls her cell from the holster clipped on to her belt. 'Anna, I've got to tell you, I kind of hate my job.'

'Hang in there, Nora. And don't quit. You'll get used to it. You'll start to love it. I promise.'

'For real?'

'For real.'

'You promise?'

'I promise. Okay, I've got to go into my kitchen and make some magic.'

Anna is in a particularly light mood today, relaxed, optimistic, and strong. She feels like she did in culinary school, when it was just her, and food, and everything else be dammed. All she needed was her knife bag and a decent test kitchen, and life was good. Boys were around, but they weren't a priority. There was little drama. The future was golden. She's so cheerful that when she traipses into the kitchen, she claps once and calls out, 'Okay, who wants to listen to some punk today?'

The cookies let loose with a loud cheer. Miguel says, 'Chef, if I wasn't already in the weeds, I'd get down on my knees and kiss your Crocs.'

'How can you already be in the weeds, Miguel? We haven't even opened yet.'

'I fucked up an entire batch of Hollandaise. Have to start from scratch.'

Wanker says, 'Dude, how do you fuck up Hollandaise?'

'This coming from a guy who destroyed an entire batch of frites last night. Could you have *possibly* used even more salt, dick breath? They tasted like a salt mine. I tasted one and I'm *still* thirsty.'

And so on.

Aside from Jeannie not showing up (she went to visit her parents in Wisconsin because she forgot she was on the schedule . . . even though she's been on the schedule every Sunday since she was hired), today is literally the smoothest Tart brunch Anna can remember. The line cooks, for reasons Anna still has yet to figure out, have become as obsessive as she is about keeping their stations spotless, so the kitchen gleams. The insults are down in number (sort of). And Billy doesn't throw any foodstuff at Anna Two. Maybe she should let the kids play their punk music more often.

Suddenly, it's five-thirty, and dinner rush hasn't started yet, but it's getting damn close. Anna is prepping her *mise en place* when Nora, red-faced and practically palpitating, bursts into the kitchen. 'Chef Rowan, you'd better get out here. Now.'

Anna puts down her Wusthoff. 'What's going on? Are you okay?'

Nora swallows hard. 'Please, Anna. Come out. Now.'

A million scenarios plow through Anna's head: *Byron's back . . . somebody's choking . . . we're being held up at gunpoint . . . somebody's vomiting . . . there's a leak in the ceiling . . . somebody threw a baseball through the front window . . .* She rips off her bandanna and trots into the dining room. When she opens the door, she's blinded by an unbearably bright light. She covers her eyes and yells, *'Jesus Christ, turn that off!'*

There's applause and cheering. There's laughter and loud conversation. She hears somebody yell, 'Go get 'em, Chef!' Eileen screams, 'Yay, Anna! We love you, Anna! Kick his ass, Anna!'

One voice cuts through the din: *'Chef Rowan, this is Jordan DeWitt, and you are being attacked!'*

Anna's knees go weak. She takes two steps back, leans

against the wall for support, and roars, 'Get that damn light out my face!'

The camera swings away from Anna, and she takes in the scene: there's Eric McLanahan, scribbling into a notepad. There's Johnny Samuels, smirking. There's Michelle Fields, grinning broadly, pointing at Anna and mouthing, *You're the woman.* There are her customers, some eating, some clapping, and some just watching.

And there's Jordan DeWitt. Wearing a gorgeous suit. Walking toward her. Carrying a red leather knife bag. 'I believe this is yours, Chef Rowan.'

She takes the bag. 'Please call me Anna.'

Jordan says, 'And please call me ... well, call me anything you damn well please. Just make sure you call me.'

Anna bends down and lays the knife bag on the floor, out of harm's way. She then stands back up, steps into Jordan's personal space, grabs the lapels of his jacket, and says, 'You clean up nicely.'

He puts his hands on top of hers and pulls them tightly to his chest. 'And you dirty up nicely.'

She laughs. 'If I'd have known you were coming, I'd have maybe washed my face or something.'

'Anna, you could've come out here covered head-to-toe in red sauce, and I'd still think you were the most gorgeous being on the planet.'

Anna gulps. 'Can we please go into my office and talk?'

'Nope.'

'The kitchen?'

'Unh unh.'

'Can you at least have them stop filming?'

'No way. I want to document this moment for all eternity.'

Jordan is giving her that devastating high-beam smile, and Anna is slayed. Unable to stop herself, she takes a deep breath, looks directly into the camera, says, 'Screw it. Everybody deserves a movie moment once in their life,' then steps up on her tiptoes and kisses him. More applause. More laughter. Billy pokes his head out of the kitchen and screams, 'Jesus, DeWitt, take her to a nice hotel, you cheap ass!'

Jordan pulls away. Anna tries to pull him back – *damn, the guy can kiss* – but he says, 'Don't forget, Chef Rowan, you're being attacked. It's time to defend your restaurant. What cuisine would you like to take into battle today?'

She can't let go of him. The cameras are still running, but she can't let go of him. Everybody's staring, but she can't let go of him. Billy's calling her a slut, but she can't let go of him. She rubs his shoulder blades and thinks, *Who says I have to let him go? Nobody.* 'Tell you what, Jordan,' she says, 'since you came all the way out here, I'll let you pick. How's that?'

'That's awesome, because I was going to pick anyway . . .'

She smacks him gently on the back of his shiny head. 'Jerk.'

'. . . but I'm not going to pick a specific cuisine. I'm going to pick a couple of specific items.'

'Ooh, changing the rules. Very exciting. What've you got?'

'Okay, my first item is chocolate-dipped strawberries, which I plan to feed to you at some point in the very near future, hopefully someplace soft and warm.'

Anna blushes. 'That sounds nice.' Her voice cracks. 'I'll feed some to you, too.'

'Awesome.' He gives her a long, sweet kiss on her forehead. 'I look forward to that, Anna.'

'Me too.' She clears her throat. 'And what's your second item?'

'Cheese.'

'Really?'

'Really. You can cook five dishes with any kind of cheese or cuisine you choose.'

'My goodness, Chef DeWitt, are you not afraid of cheese any more?'

'You are correct, Chef Rowan, I am not afraid of cheese any more.' He puts his hand on the back of her neck, pulls her close, and whispers into her ear, 'I'm not afraid of anything at all.'

CHOCOLATE DIPPED STRAWBERRIES

Ingredients
½ cup semi-sweet chocolate chips
¼ cup shaved white chocolate
4 tablespoons heavy cream
12 long-stemmed strawberries

Method
1. Melt the chocolate chips and 3 tablespoons of the cream in a glass bowl set over simmering water until just melted. Stir and remove from the heat.
2. At the same time, melt the white chocolate and remaining cream in an indentical manner.
3. Dip each strawberry in the chocolate and set aside on waxed or parchment paper to dry.
4. Drizzle white chocolate over strawberries.
5. Feed to your new boyfriend or girlfriend either before, during, or after making love.

Acknowledgments

As always, mad props to the LBD crew: Catherine Cobain, Sara Porter, Nicky Jeanes and everyone involved at Headline Publishing Group.

And, as always, I couldn't have done it without the love, support, and editing eraser of the best Natty Boo that ever Natty Booed.

You can buy any of these other
Little Black Dress titles from your
bookshop or *direct from the publisher*.

FREE P&P AND UK DELIVERY
(Overseas and Ireland £3.50 per book)

Living Next Door to Alice	Marisa Mackle	£4.99
Risky Business	Suzanne Macpherson	£4.99
The Trophy Girl	Kate Lace	£4.99
Truly Madly Yours	Rachel Gibson	£4.99
Right Before Your Eyes	Ellen Shanman	£4.99
Handbags and Homicide	Dorothy Howell	£4.99
The Rules of Gentility	Janet Mullany	£4.99
The Girlfriend Curse	Valerie Frankel	£4.99
A Romantic Getaway	Sarah Monk	£4.99
Drama Queen	Susan Conley	£4.99
Trashed	Alison Gaylin	£4.99
Not Another Bad Date	Rachel Gibson	£4.99
Everything Nice	Ellen Shanman	£4.99
Just Say Yes	Phillipa Ashley	£4.99
Hysterical Blondeness	Suzanne Macpherson	£4.99
Blue Remembered Heels	Nell Dixon	£4.99
Honey Trap	Julie Cohen	£4.99
What's Love Got to do With It?	Lucy Broadbent	£4.99
The Not-So-Perfect Man	Valerie Frankel	£4.99
Lola Carlyle Reveals All	Rachel Gibson	£4.99

TO ORDER SIMPLY CALL THIS NUMBER

01235 400 414

or visit our website: www.headline.co.uk

Prices and availability subject to change without notice.